A Wind in the Hebrides

BOOK 7 · THE MONASTERY MURDERS

Donna Fletcher Crow

Verity Press

A Wind in the Hebrides
Copyright © 2024 by Donna Fletcher Crow

All rights reserved as permitted under the U.S. Copyright Act of 1976. No part of this publication may be reproduced or transmitted in any form or by any means, electronic or mechanical, including photocopy, recording, or any information storage and retrieval system, without permission in writing from the publisher. The only exception is brief quotations in printed reviews.

Verity Press an imprint of Publications Marketing, Inc.
Box 972
Boise, Idaho
83701

Cover design and layout by Ken Raney
Edited by Sheila Deeth
This is a work of fiction. The characters and events portrayed in this book are fictitious or used fictitiously.

Published in the United States of America

Verity Press

Praise for the Monastery Murders

A Very Private Grave
Like a P.D. James novel *A Very Private Grave* occupies a learned territory. Also a beautifully described corner of England, that of the Northumbrian coast where St. Cuthbert's Christianity retains its powerful presence. Where myth and holiness, wild nature and tourism, art and prayer run in parallel, and capture the imagination still. All this with a cinematic skill. A thrilling amateur investigation follows in which the northern landscape and modern liturgical goings on play a large part. The centuries between us and the world of Lindisfarne and Whitby collapse and we are in the timeless zone of greed and goodness.
—Ronald Blythe, *The Word from Wormingford*

With a bludgeoned body in Chapter 1, and a pair of intrepid amateur sleuths, *A Very Private Grave* qualifies as a traditional mystery. But this is no mere formulaic whodunit: it is a Knickerbocker Glory of a thriller. At its centre is a sweeping, page-turning quest – in the steps of St Cuthbert – through the atmospherically-depicted North of England, served up with dollops of Church history and lashings of romance. In this novel, Donna Fletcher Crow has created her own niche within the genre of clerical mysteries.
—Kate Charles, *False Tongues*, A Callie Anson Mystery

A Darkly Hidden Truth
In *A Darkly Hidden Truth*, Donna Fletcher Crow creates a world in which the events of past centuries echo down present-day hallways— I came away from the book feeling as though I'd been someplace both ancient and new. Donna Fletcher Crow gives us, in three extremely persuasive dimensions, the world that Dan Brown merely sketches.
—Timothy Hallinan, *The Queen of Patpong*,
Edgar nominated Best Novel

With *A Darkly Hidden Truth* Crow establishes herself as the leading practitioner of modern mystery entwined with historical fiction. The historical sections are much superior to *The Da Vinci Code* because she doesn't merely recite the facts; she makes the events come alive by telling them through the eyes of participants. The contemporary story is skillfully character-driven, suspended between the deliberate and reflective life of religious orders in the UK and Felicity's "Damn the torpedoes, full steam ahead" American impetuousness.

Her descriptions of the English characters read like an updated and edgy version of Barbara Pym. *A Darkly Hidden Truth* weaves ancient puzzles and modern murder with a savvy but sometimes unwary protagonist into a seamless story. You won't need a bookmark— you'll read it in a single sitting despite other plans.

—Mike Orenduff, 2011 Lefty Award Winner, *The Pot Thief Who Studied Einstein*

An Unholy Communion
A truly great mystery that had me guessing throughout the entire book. It was full of twists and turns and I learned a great deal of new information about the occult and spiritual warfare as well. The author most definitely did a lot of research and, although this book is a work of fiction, has included much fact so that it is not only a fun read but also a learning experience.

—Alicia, "Through My I's"

Erie feelings, strange happenings, premonitions and unexpected occurrences mark the many events depicted within this well researched, documented and crafted novel. When all of the clues, the pieces and the final reveal come together you will not believe who is behind everything.

—"Fran Lewis's Book Reviews"

Ingeniously plotted by a master of contemporary suspense, *An Unholy Communion* weaves Great Britain's holy places and history with an intricate mystery that will keep readers guessing to the very end. An exciting book that will keep you engrossed in the characters as well as life in England. A wonderful series.

—"Vic's Media Room"

A Newly Crimsoned Reliquary
Skillfully builds tension from one peril to another, leading to a thrilling climax and satisfying denouement. But more than just a mystery, Crow weaves in rich and colorful details of English church and political history.

— Donn Taylor, *Lightning on a Quiet Night*

If you like Midsomer Murders, *A Newly Crimsoned Reliquary* will be a comfortable read to sink into. Especially for the reader who loves centuries of English history. Perfect to read while on your vacation flight to the UK.

— Mary E. Gallagher, Gallaghers Travels

A really enjoyable, fast paced read. It's obvious the author really knows her stuff. Great book.

—Dolores Gordon-Smith, The Jack Haldean Mysteries

An All-Consuming Fire
Watch the pageant and take a front seat as the youth prove that when someone has faith they will shine to the top. Characters that are unique, true to life and interesting as Felicity, Antony and Cynthia take charge and will once again fill your heart.

—Fran Lewis: *Just reviews/MJ magazine*

Wedding preparations, traditional Advent celebrations, threats to their lives, oh, and several murders, make for a true page-turner. The suspense lover will not be disappointed, and the history buff will come away with a greater sense of 1300s England and its spiritual climate.

—Alexis Gorin

A monastery, a documentary, romance, and multiple murders all combine to make a masterful read. Set against the backdrop of a beautiful English countryside, the story unfolds with ever mounting suspense. As with all the books in this series, church history is an added bonus, and it blends wonderfully with the narrative. One learns without lecture and is entertained at the same time. With a mystery and a marriage, what's not to love? Donna Fletcher Crow has produced a masterpiece once again.

—James West

A totally gripping read. There's a fascinating mix of medieval church history, seamlessly woven into a very modern plot of a series of murders surrounding the shooting of a film, in which Antony is the polished but somewhat reluctant narrator. Naturally, the main thing on his mind is his forthcoming wedding to the irrepressible Felicity, but Felicity herself is in danger as she becomes a target for murder. There's a great cast of characters including Cynthia, Felicity's very polished, very professional and totally captivating mother. Yorkshire in winter is excellently portrayed, as is Monastery life, with the church calendar of the Christmas season adding a fascinating framework to the action. Highly recommended!

—Dolores Gordon-Smith, The Jack Haldean Mysteries

Against All Fierce Hostility
In her signature lyrical prose, Crow crafts another tale full of contemporary mystery bound up in church history. She weaves evocative ancient poetry, fascinating academic references to early Christian fathers, and descriptions of liturgical practices exotic to this Baptist worshipper into an irresistible story. Then she makes the whole thing even richer through the setting of a cross-Canada train trip, colourful as a glossy vacation brochure, that does justice to my home and native land. A thoroughly entertaining and satisfying read!

—Deb Elkirk

A long time coming and highly anticipated, Ms. Crow does not disappoint. The Monastery Murders is my favorite all time suspense series. A plot that keeps you guessing, yet teaches you some fabulous church history in an entertaining fashion. The only downside to this book is that it ends. Hopefully, Felicity will have more adventures to come.

—James West

To my lifelong friend Evelyn Bennett,
Who shared the adventure
And
To Donald John Smith
Who lived the experience

TIMELINE

- 540 Saint Mungo (Kentigern) established monastery in Glasgow

- 562 Saint Moluag establishes religious community on the Isle of Lismore.

- 563 Saint Columba Comes to Iona

- 1949-1953 Revival sweeps the Outer Hebrides

ISLE OF LEWIS

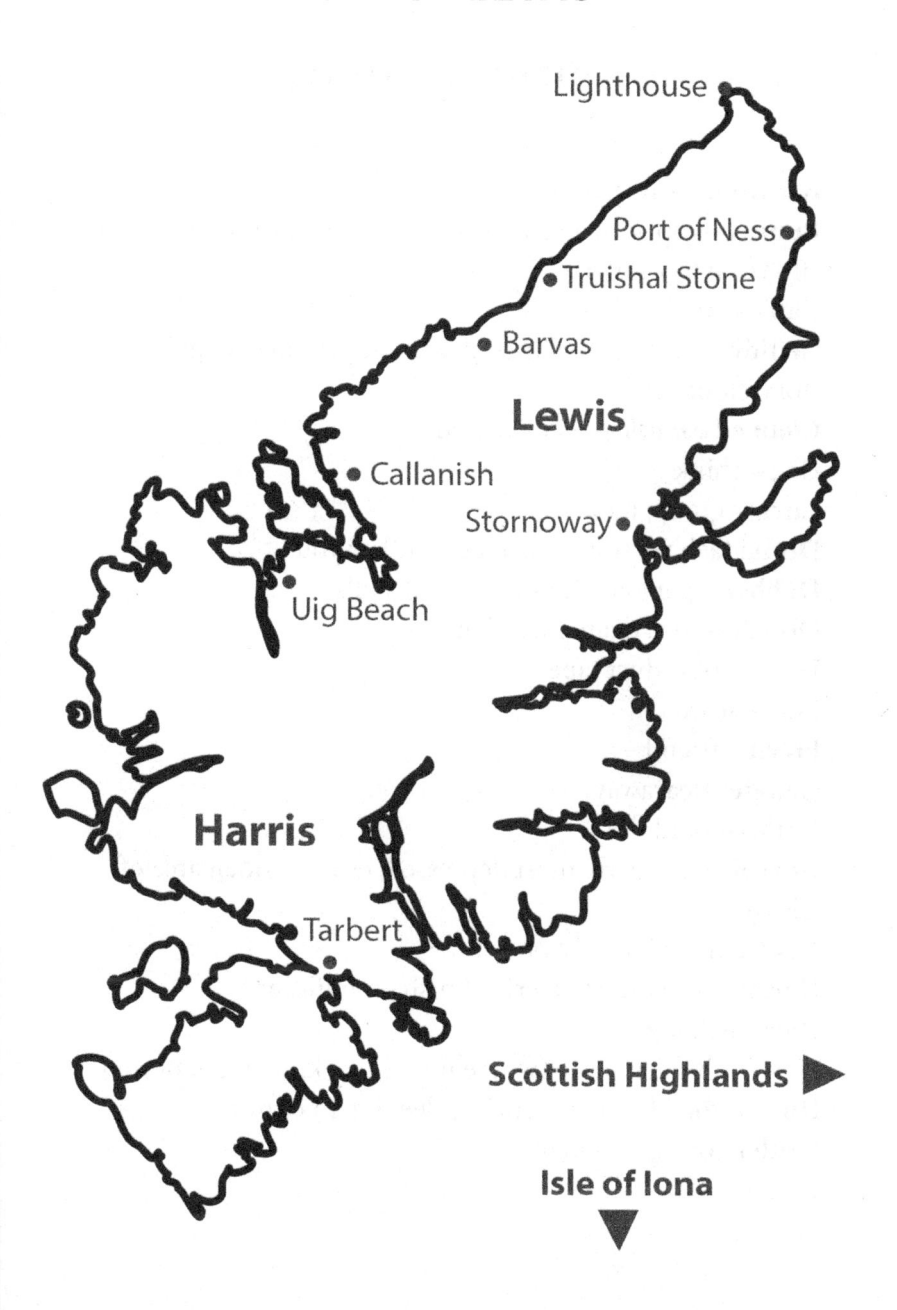

- Lighthouse
- Port of Ness
- Truishal Stone
- Barvas

Lewis

- Callanish
- Stornoway
- Uig Beach

Harris

- Tarbert

▶ Scottish Highlands

▼ Isle of Iona

SCOTTISH EXPRESSIONS

Barmpot—silly person
Bunnet—cap with a soft crown and peaked front, traditionally worn by crofters
Caff—café
Ceilidh—party with dancing, with impromptu singing, storytelling, etc.
Chan eil e math—ne'er-do-well
Cog—think
Curn—group, mob
Dinna fash yerself—don't let it bother you
Dobber—person with poor social skills
Dreich—grey, dismal weather
Duck tape—duct tape
Fleg—scare
Freen—friend
Gadgie—tearaway
Gallus—bold
Gorbals—formerly most depressed, crime-ridden area of Glasgow
Goid kent—God knows
Harled—roughcast exterior finish on buildings
Harr—sea fog
Howff—hidden place (where illegal drinking might occur)
Hurkle-durkle—lie-in (Brit.), sleeping in (Am.)
Jantleman—gentleman
Ken—know

Lewisian Gneiss—(pronounced 'nice') metamorphic rock comprising the Hebrides
Machair—Fertile, grassy plain
Menhir—standing stone
Ned—hooligan, lout or petty criminal
Numpty—a stupid of foolish person
Paddle—British word for wading in shallow water
Pensioner—person old enough to be drawing a pension, senior citizen
Poileis—Police in Gaelic
Polis—Police in Scots dialect
Richt—right
Selkie—a mythical creature: seal in the water, but a beautiful woman on land
Shieling—a hut in a remote place
Snooter—handkerchief, or the act of blowing one's nose
Stane—stone
Stoatin' doon—bucketing rain
Stooshie—loud noise, especially as in an argument
Stramash—brawl
Strathspey—a slow Scottish dance
Tairsgeir—special spade for cutting peats
Yin—Person

WHO'S WHO

Today:

Father Antony Sherwood—C of E priest, church history lecturer College of the Transfiguration
Felicity Sherwood—his wife
Francis Edward Sherwood (Teddy)—their 5-year-old son
Nigel Munro—Glasgow University lecturer, friend of Antony and Felicity
Wendy—his wife
Catriona (pronounced Katrina) Baird—Wendy's cousin in Stornoway
Cameron Baird—her husband, works on offshore oil rig
Isla Baird—their teenage daughter
Marissa—retreat house manager
Anna—B&B hostess in Stornoway
Lachlan—Volunteer Fire Department leader, Iona
George Taggart—policeman
Kenny Shea—oil rig worker
Roger Wellman—mature student of Antony, owner of *Selkie*
Owen—first mate on *Selkie*

1949:

Aileana Mackay—singer, older Mackay daughter
Skeena Mackay—Aileana's mother
Tavish Mackay—Aileana's father

Faye—Aileana's younger sister
Calum Alexander—Aileana's agent
Moira—Aileana's cousin
Struan Macaulay—childhood friend, policeman
Euan McLeod—Faye's boyfriend
Janet McLeod—his sister
Artair— young aircraftman at RAF Stornoway
Duncan Campbell—evangelist for Hebrides revival from Faith Mission in Edinburgh
The Praying Sisters:
    Peggy (also called Ida) 84, blind
    Christine 82, crippled with arthritis

THE STIRRING OF THE BREEZE

1949

Barvas, the Isle of Lewis, Outer Hebrides

The two ancient sisters sat with bowed heads before their little peat fire: Peggy, 84, her soft white hair a halo around her wrinkled face; Christine, 82, with a dark kerchief framing her face, bent forward with arthritis. Together they had they sat like this through the hours. Two nights without fail for many weeks, beseeching Heaven.

"Oh, God, send revival to Barvas."

"Reach our young people."

Here on the backside of the Isle of Lewis, the northernmost island of the Outer Hebrides, these ladies prayed without ceasing for the soul of their island. For all of Lewis to be swept by the Holy Spirit. To be filled with the Love of God. For the Light of Christ to shine forth.

And then one night Peggy—blind, but with clear-sighted spiritual vision—dreamed that Duncan Campbell, the head of the Faith Mission in Edinburgh, would come to Lewis.

She sent for the minister. The Reverend James Murray MacKay came.

"Send for Duncan Campbell," she said.

A wire was sent to Duncan Campbell who was on the Isle of Skye preparing for a convention. He replied: "It is impossible for me to come at this time but keep on praying and I will come next year."

The sisters were unmoved. "That is what man has said. God has said that he will come."

"What shall we do?" the pastor asked.

"Give yourselves to prayer."

The minister called the elders. They met in the barn of a parishioner's home and held prayer meetings for three months. One night a young man read Psalm 24: "'Who shall ascend into the hill of the Lord? or who shall stand in his holy place? He that hath clean hands, and a pure heart...'" He stopped abruptly and thrust the Bible away.

"This seems to me just so much shilly-shallying—to be waiting as we are waiting, praying as we are praying—when we ourselves are not right with God." He turned from the group and held his hands out. "Oh God, are my hands clean?" He fell to his knees in prayer.

"Donny, come here. Be hearin' this," 10-year-old Alex Smith whispered to his brother. He lay prone on the landing at the top of the stairs, peering through the railing, and beckoned to his younger brother Donald John hanging back in the darkness.

At his brother's insistence Donald crept forwards, the cold from the floorboards seeping upward through his bare feet. He knelt beside Alex, but still held back, fearful of what sight would accompany the strange noises coming from the parlor below them: an insistent murmuring, almost like the roaring of the wind off the North Atlantic that swept around their barn and house. So many voices, reverberating around the room, filling the space with intense susurrations. Then suddenly, here and there, a pleading voice. Or a groan. Were they in pain? Or was it ecstasy? Were they frightened? Or angry?

Donald hesitated at the strangeness of it all. At last curiosity made him stick his head through the opening in the stair rails beside his brother. He blinked. These strange sounds were all coming from people he knew. People from the big, beige church just down the road where he and his family attended every Sunday. The pastor was there, his parents were there...

A WIND IN THE HEBRIDES

Then, as one cried out, "Please, Lord God, do it," Donald realized—they were begging, pleading, reasoning.

The sight was like nothing he had ever seen before. He had been vaguely aware for months that there were gatherings in the little wooden barn with its corrugated aluminium roof beside their house. For months men from their church had been gathering in the barn three nights a week. He had heard his parents talking and knew his father often stayed until four or five o'clock in the morning. He hadn't given any mind to it, though, other than to shake his head at the strangeness of it all. Didn't seem Christian—out all night like that when decent folk were tucked up in their beds.

But now they had moved into the Smith house. His parents and their neighbors filled the room—not sitting comfortably on his mother's prized sofa, but rather on the floor—not sitting at all—but kneeling. Most with their arms lifted towards heaven. And they weren't talking to one another but to—Donald drew in his breath and held it, afraid even to think the word. They were talking to God.

Chapter One

"Mummy, what are the heb-radees?"

Felicity looked up from her laptop and blinked at her son Francis Edward playing with his dinosaurs on the floor behind her. Teddy looked more like his handsome father every day—and sounded more like him, too. Including his use of words far beyond the normal vocabulary for a five-year-old. Was he asking about some prehistoric animal? Maybe something from a bedtime story Antony had been telling him? Last night it had been about the dinosaur bones found on the islands of Skye and Eigg, hadn't it?

Then she realized. "Oh, Hebrides." She pronounced it carefully for him. Minimal digging through the materials on her desk produced a map of the United Kingdom—one she still had to refer to with some regularity, even though England had been her home for almost fifteen years.

She dropped to her knees beside her son and spread the map out on the floor. "Here we are," She pointed to a dot representing Kirkthorpe in Yorkshire, home to the Community of the Transfiguration where Antony taught church history to theological students in the college run by the monks. Monks that Antony had intended to join until he fell in love with a somewhat clueless and scatter-brained American student—as Felicity now realized she had been.

Felicity tousled her son's floppy, dark hair, so like his father's, then returned to the map. "And this is Scotland." She moved her finger a bit toward the top, then angled upward toward the far left of the map. "And way over here in the North Atlantic Ocean, these islands are called the Hebrides. These," she circled the ones closer to the mainland, "are the Inner Hebrides, and these," she inched on northwestward, "Are the Outer Hebrides."

She searched closer to the mainland until, triumphantly, she located Skye, then the tiny Eigg further southward, "These are where they found the Stegosaurus bones." Always keen on teaching, she reached over and picked up the plastic dino with a glorious row of plates adorning his back and planted him on the Isle of Skye.

Teddy, exhibiting his inheritance from his contemplative father rather than the rasher instincts he got from his impulsive mother, sucked his lower lip and considered. "Is that where we're going?"

Felicity, who had been kneeling, plopped to an awkward sitting position. How did the child know about that? Had he been listening to the lengthy discussions she and Antony had been having when they thought their son sound asleep in bed? Was that what the expression about little pitchers having big ears meant? The idea of pitchers having ears had never made much sense to her before. Now she smiled as she thought of her small milk jug with its large, ear-shaped handle.

"Um, well, I'm not quite sure… That is, Mummy and Daddy have been talking—we're still trying to work out our plans." The thing was, Antony was scheduled to accompany a group of students to the Isle of Iona for an advanced study on Saint Columba, and Felicity, who was scheduled to give a talk on the Hebrides Awakening to her association of spiritual directors, had suggested this would be a perfect chance for her to do some onsite research as well—never mind that she could probably mug up enough information from the internet to cobble a talk together—there really wasn't anything like actually being there. Besides, she had always wanted to go to the Hebrides. That was one location their adventures all over England, Scotland and Wales hadn't covered.

Her mind flitted momentarily to those long-ago days when the world was new, and she knew everything. Antony was a mere college lecturer to her then—one who gave long, albeit lively, lectures that left her completely confused. And yet, she had trusted him enough to flee with him to the Isle of Lindisfarne, even while wondering if he could be a murderer... That was where she first encountered the later fruits of Columba's work—and learned that Antony's lectures on church history could actually have application to modern life. Yes, it would be lovely to go to the Hebrides with Antony. She sighed.

Well, it was a great plan, but a quick telephone call home to the States had crushed the idea of her mother, doting grandmother that she was, being able to hop across the pond to take care of young Teddy. That left Felicity paling at the thought of excusing her energetic, into-everything son from infant school and taking him on a research trip. Of all the qualities he could have inherited from his mother, why did it have to be her heedlessness?

The snap of the turning latch on their front door announced Antony's return. Felicity gave a sigh of relief as she jumped to her feet and rushed into the hallway. "Antony, thank goodness you're home. Somehow Teddy seems to know about the trip to the Hebrides, and he has the idea we're all going—including him—and I don't know how to explain to him that I want to go, but Nana can't come over like she did last time, and I can't think what I would do with him if I tried to take him, and there's school, and have you looked at that map? Just getting there could take days, and—"

Antony applied his favorite trick for halting her flow of words by giving her a very thorough kiss. He then continued into the front room, pushing blocks, balls, and plastic dinosaurs aside with his foot and swept his son from the floor and into the air to shrieks of delight from Teddy.

Hours later, with Teddy finally in bed and soundly asleep, Antony closed the door on the tiny room and returned to Felicity who was still shaking her head at the map spread before her. Leaning over her shoulder, he pointed—much as she had done earlier with their son. "It isn't really so impossible when you know how to go about it—rather fun, actually. Teddy will love the trains and ferries."

Antony proceeded, tracing the route on the map: train to Manchester, change for Glasgow, ScotRail to Oban. He pointed to the very edge of the Scottish mainland and continued tracing: ferry across the sound, coach the length of the Isle of Mull, ferry to Iona. He gave a triumphant tap to the little dot on the map.

"And that will take how long?" Felicity didn't even try to keep the skepticism out of her voice.

"Oh, less than twenty hours—seventeen or so, I'd say."

"Father Antony Stuart Sherwood—have you taken leave of your senses? Seventeen hours on public transport with a five-year-old? Do you have any idea…" Words failed her. Felicity had never met an adventure she wasn't up for until she became a mother. The advent of this one, tiny human being had suddenly developed a practical side in her. The logistics of food, exercise, sleeping arrangements… the sheer fatigue of entertaining a youngster. And keeping him safe. All her protective instincts came to the fore. She had never taken a thought for herself, but this precious little one…

Antony had the grace to look sheepish. "Right. So maybe six hours on the train to Glasgow, stay overnight with friends—you remember Nigel and Wendy?"

Felicity smiled. "I would love to see them again." Nigel Munro was a lecturer from the University of Glasgow who had done some seminars on the history of Scottish Christianity for the College of the Transfiguration a few years before. His wife Wendy was an absolute darling. Some relation of hers had something to do with a faith mission of some sort in Edinburgh, and then she married her high church Nigel. Felicity was vague on the details, but she would love to see Wendy again. "I've got her email address somewhere—I'll write to her."

And so, it was settled.

Chapter Two

Even with their careful planning, however, Felicity felt as frazzled after the interminable train journey as she predicted she would have had they attempted the entire journey in one day. And, as if that weren't enough, what should have been a ten-minute taxi ride from the train station to the university area where their friends lived turned into an almost hour-long tangle as they were held up in traffic.

They had just turned onto the main road when traffic was slowed to a crawl by a large protest in the park beside the road. A band played while people shouted and waved homemade placards with slogans relating to climate change concerns. "Goodness, there must be hundreds," Felicity said.

"Aye," their driver replied. "Fine for the long-haired layabouts. A good days' work might go a right piece to coolin' them off."

At least Teddy was diverted by the sight, and, once they were past the demonstration, traffic resumed normal speed.

Until they were slowed by a broken-down lorry blocking their side of the road. Their taxi driver shook his head and slapped the steering wheel impatiently. "Can ye believe it? This's the third time this has happened to me this week. Breakdowns all over the city for no reason. It's like a plague." Felicity couldn't begin to calculate what the fare would have been if he hadn't kindly stopped the meter ticking. "Ach, it's nae yer fault. But if I could get my hands on whoever's fault it is, I wouldn't like to be responsible for the outcome. I don't know wha' they think they're playin' at."

At last Felicity and Antony were sitting comfortably on the overstuffed sofa drinking tea in the parlor of the Munro's lovely old stone house with Teddy tucked up in one of the tiny beds that had belonged their hosts' twin daughters before they outgrew them.

Felicity savored the Scottish blend tea and Wendy's delicious homemade shortbread and snuggled into the folds of the sofa, letting Antony and Nigel's conversation swirl around her head. These two historians never seemed to tire of talking shop.

After her guest had savored a few sips, Wendy turned to Felicity from her nearby chair. "I'm sae glad you're going to Iona. It's such a beautiful island. A barren sort of beauty, but the whole place seems to be infused with the holiness of its history. It's the cradle of Scottish Christianity, you know—Saint Columba and all that." Her soft Scots voice carried well under the men's conversation without disturbing it at all.

Felicity pulled herself from her near-doze. "I am looking forward to seeing it, but I'll only be there a day or two—then Teddy and I are going on to Lewis."

"Lewis? That's where my family is from. Oh, ye'll have a grand time. Teddy can spend a whole day running around the standing stanes of Callanish. And Uig Bay—where they found the chessmen—it's lovely. Just on from the stanes. Teddy can paddle in the water. Ye'll hire a car? It's nae sae easy to get around the island without one."

Felicity took a long sip of her tea, hoping the hot brew would wake her up a bit. She wasn't sure what Wendy was talking about. This trip had come up so quickly she hadn't had time to do much homework on it. "Um—you said your family was from there?" At least she understood that much.

"Oh, aye—from time out of mind. I still have cousins all over the island. Roots run deep there. I was actually born there."

"What brought you to Glasgow?"

"My da was a marine biologist—specialized in invertebrates—mollusks and such—perfect for studying in the Outer Hebrides. Then he decided to move on to lecturing. So naturally I went to uni here, met Nigel… life just goes on with a mind of its own, doesn't it?"

Felicity heartily agreed, thinking how her own life had simply swept on, driven by head, heart, and events. Then she asked, "Do you get back often?"

"To Lewis? Oh, aye. We used to go regular—every year. But now that the twins are in secondary school and Nigel doing guest lectures all over, our time isn't sae free. But why are you going?"

Felicity made a face. "For some reason SpiDir has asked me to give the annual lecture at their AGM. They're holding it at the Community this year, and somehow, they got hold of the idea I was some sort of expert." She looked meaningfully at her husband who was on the hosting committee.

"Hmm," said the man who had recommended her.

"I think they have me confused with my notorious husband." Felicity turned back to her hostess.

"Spider?" Wendy looked as dazed as Felicity felt.

"Conflated short form for Spiritual Directors association. That's what I do—spiritual direction—when I'm not chasing my hyper-active five-year-old. Anyway, in a weak moment I accepted. Then I learned that the theme this year is Spiritual Awakening and they asked if I could talk about the Lewis Awakening."

"That's amazing!" Wendy's enthusiasm surprised Felicity.

"I wish I felt as enthusiastic as you sound. I don't know anything about it but what I've managed to read on the internet. I'm hoping visiting the island can give me something worthwhile to say." Felicity sighed. "I can't just repeat what they could read in a fraction of the time on Wikipedia."

"I might be able to help you." Wendy scooted to the edge of her seat. "My
 great aunt—Aileana Mackay, as she was—was there. She experienced the whole thing." Wendy rose to her feet. "She wrote her memories of it all. I haven't read it—her handwriting's dire—but it might be of use to you. I have her notebooks somewhere…" She headed toward the door.

Felicity set her cup aside and gave into the wonderful sinking feeling that had been threatening to overtake her all evening…

"Oh, ye puir thing, ye're shattered and here I run off rummaging through yon attic, when I should be seeing you to yer bed."

Felicity blinked and forced herself to resurface. Wendy stood before her clutching a stack of thin A4 composition books with stiff black and white marbled covers. She indicated the books. "I can lend these to ye, but ye've got to be certain I get them back. Great Aunt Aileana's oldest daughter passed them on to me, but, to my shame, I haven't done anything with them."

Before Felicity could reply Wendy held her free hand out to help her guest from the depths of her cushions. "But it's bed for you first."

Antony stopped his dialogue with Nigel mid-sentence. "Yes, do go on up. I'll join you soon." He rose and gave his wife a peck on the cheek. "Are you all right?"

Felicity nodded, but it was Wendy who spoke. "Go on with your palaver, you two, I'll see the darlin' to her bed." She took Felicity's arm, then turned back to the men. "And see that ye're quiet when ye come up."

The next morning Felicity woke to bright sunshine and birdsong. For a moment she snuggled in the duvet next to her sleeping husband, then she saw the composition notebooks on her bedside table. Great Aunt Aileana's account of the Awakening. She plumped her pillows and scooted to a sitting position before picking it up. The label on the front read "1949 Glasgow."

Felicity opened the cover and blinked. Oh, my, no wonder Wendy hadn't deciphered this—she could see what her friend meant about the handwriting being dire. Still, Felicity tingled to read it. An unpublished, eyewitness account. Here was her chance to offer some worthwhile listening to her conference fellows.

She struggled through the first paragraph. Then the second, and on to the bottom of the page. This didn't seem to have anything to do with a spiritual revival in the Hebrides. It was a young woman in Glasgow bickering with her boyfriend. Something about a concert. It wasn't a journal as she had expected. It read more like a story. Could Wendy have misunderstood? Had her great aunt been attempting a novel?

Felicity started again at the top of the page. About halfway down the scrawl became clearer to her and the account began to make sense. It still didn't seem to be about a revival, but it was an interesting story.

Antony stirred beside her and the smell of frying bacon wafted from the kitchen. Then Felicity realized she hadn't heard from Teddy yet. She bounded out of bed and began scrabbling to pull on her clothes. Antony sat up. "Good morning."

"Antony, something's wrong with Teddy—he should have been in here pulling at me to get up as soon as the sun rose. I haven't heard him at all." Her voice rose as the knot in her stomach tightened.

"No, no, it's fine." Antony ran his fingers through his hair. "I didn't have a chance to tell you. Wendy said not to worry—let you 'have a hurkle-durkle' was her colorful phrase. I think it means a bit of a lie-in. Anyway, she said their girls would take care of him when he woke up. She knew you needed the sleep."

Felicity dropped to the bed with a sigh. "Oh, thank goodness." She leaned back into the pillows and allowed herself a quick snuggle with Antony. Then pushed him away, "Still, it's time to be up, you slug-a-bed. Did you and Nigel ramble on for hours?"

Happy squeals from down the hall and the sound of pattering feet on bare boards returned Felicity to her interrupted dressing process.

A few minutes later Felicity and Antony found their hosts gathered around the scrubbed pine farmhouse table in the Munro's enormous kitchen. Teddy, looked over by Fiona and Lexi, was happily alternately dipping toast soldiers in a soft-boiled egg and a plump sausage in tomato sauce. He hardly looked up when his mother kissed him on the top of his head. Felicity took her seat and Wendy set a plate filled with fried eggs, back bacon, crispy fried black pudding, mushrooms, and a grilled tomato in front of her. Felicity gasped at the sight.

"Go on—you've a journey in front of you. Ye'll be glad of it."

Felicity dabbed her black pudding in mustard and set out to follow her hostess's instructions. She was on her third or fourth cup of tea, this one accompanied with granary toast slathered with Scottish marmalade, when she started to ask about the background of the journal she had struggled with.

The youngsters at the foot of the table, however, interrupted her thoughts as Fiona wiped Teddy's hands and face with a damp cloth and the girls led him off to play. "They love an excuse to play in the old nursery." Wendy smiled as clattering footsteps sounded above their heads. "It's right at the top of the house."

Felicity sighed. "They are so good with him. I wish I could take them with me."

"I've been thinking about that." Wendy reached across to her counter and picked up a slip of paper. "I've done enough research trips with yon expert," she nodded at her historian husband, "to know how intensely you'll need to focus." She handed the paper to Felicity. This is my cousin who lives in Stornoway. I rang her this morning to be certain it would be a'right to give you her number. Her teenage daughter Isla is wonderful with wee'uns. She hasn't found a summer job yet, so she would love to help you."

Felicity looked at the name on the paper and made a stab at pronouncing it phonetically, "Cat-ri-ona?"

Wendy laughed. "Try thinking of it as spelled Katrina. Much easier to say."

"That's brilliant. All of it. And you're sure we wouldn't be interrupting them?"

"I think Catriona would welcome an interruption. Her husband works offshore—on the oil rigs—he's gone for a month or longer at a time. I think she gets really lonesome."

Felicity gave Wendy an impulsive hug. "I can't thank you enough. And your great aunt's memoir—journal, whatever it is—what a treasure trove you are."

"Just guid Scots hospitality. I'm happy to help. Could ye make heads or tails out o' the notebooks?"

"I made a start, but it's very confusing. I thought you said it was a record of the Awakening. It reads like a first-person novel about a girl who wants to be a singer in Glasgow."

"Oh, aye, Great Auntie must have been something of a firecracker in those days—in her early twenties, I think, when she went off to start her career in the big, wicked city."

"Did you know her at all?"

"Oh, aye. Saw her at plenty of family dos through the years. She lived to be 84. Died ten or fifteen years ago, just a year after her husband. The whole tribe went to her funeral in Edinburgh—three children and three grandchildren they had, and all the cousins and whatever from the island and all over. It was a grand event."

"Edinburgh?" Felicity asked.

"Aye. She and her husband ran a flourishing ministry there. It's still going strong—a spin-off of the Awakening, I suppose ye could say."

Felicity felt like she could talk to Wendy all day. She had no idea she had taken on such a wide-ranging subject. Before she could form her next question, though, Antony interrupted with a reminder that they had a long journey ahead of them: train, ferry, bus, and yet another ferry.

In a few minutes Wendy was whisking them to Glasgow's gleaming glass and golden-roofed Queen Street Station. The traffic moved freely, in spite of a few intrepid protesters holding up signs along Cowcaddens road. Felicity held her breath should they encounter the disruption of another of the unexplained traffic jams the city had been experiencing, but their drive was blessedly incident-free. Once they were on the platform Felicity felt like the adventure had really begun. She shivered—whether from anticipation or apprehension she wasn't sure.

Chapter Three

Once settled on the bright blue ScotRail train with its distinctive yellow accents, Felicity longed to dig into the notebooks she had tucked so carefully in her book bag. Nigel had provided a waterproof book protector sack to keep them securely preserved, and Felicity had solemnly vowed to keep them safe, then repeated her fervent thanks for being trusted with them. It made her think of some of the ancient documents she had translated years ago for the nuns at Oxford—and the adventure that had led to. She and Antony had been separated then, too—as they would be now—with him seeing to his uncle's funeral and then shepherding students around Oxford. And they weren't even married yet. She shook her head at the thought that she should have been warned—in retrospect it all looked like an omen of the pattern their life seemed to follow. Still, she wouldn't trade places with anyone. She gazed fondly at her husband pointing out to Teddy the shining blue waters of Gare Loch beyond the window of their carriage.

Antony turned to her just as she ran her hand over the book bag on the seat beside her. He laughed. "Go on then, I know you're dying to get stuck into those books."

"Oops, you caught me. I am rather, but I'm not sure how much I can concentrate while we're on the train."

"Well, just give it a try. I'll take care of Master Francis Edward here." Antony pulled a bag of plastic dinosaurs from the canvas toy satchel and began setting them up on the table.

Felicity took out the slim volume she had struggled to make sense of the night before and, in spite of the swaying train and difficulties of deciphering the script, she was soon caught up in the story...

"Aileana Rossalyn Mackay, ye're a true darlin'." And with that he leaned over and kissed me on the lips.

"And you, Calum Finlay Alexander, are a madman." I laughed and pushed him away with both hands. It was all very well for my newly acquired agent/manager to find my performance appealing and to have faith in my nascent career, but if he was going to expect a girl from the isles to behave like one of his city women then one of us was going to have to do some adjusting. And I most certainly had no intention of being the one to change. "My mother warned me about your Glasgow ways." I stopped, realizing how naive that must sound.

But Calum just held up both hands and took a step backwards, grinning widely. "Have no fear. My Auntie Ida—eighty years auld, if she's a day—is a woman of the Isles. I'm well-schooled in yer innocent ways. Besides, I'm not the one to be killing the goose that's sure to lay a golden egg. It's your fresh breeze of the Isles manner that's going to pack the Royal Concert Hall." He gave me a cheeky grin. "That and your angelic voice and my brilliant management."

There was no way I could hold a stern demeanor against such palaver. "Royal concert Hall! It's the back room at your local pub."

"Give a lad a chance, will ye? Tonight, the Lochnagar, next week the Royal. And, be fair, it's next door to the pub. It's not

the back room."

"Thank goodness it's not tonight. We've an awful lot more rehearsing to do." But I couldn't repress a smile as I turned to my music folder. And to give him his due, Calum had done very well by me. It was almost a miracle that an unknown singer from the far tip of the Isle of Lewis could be booked to perform a solo concert after being in Glasgow for less than five months. Meeting Calum through my cousin Moira really was the most unimaginable good fortune. It appears she knows everybody and everything, and somehow Calum seems convinced I can make a success of a singing career...

"Right, then. So, are ye going to woolgather all evening or are we going to get on with rehearsing?" Calum turned back to the old upright piano in the living room of Moira's flat. For my concert, which Calum was billing as "Blow, Bonnie Breezes", I would have a piper and a harp to accompany me, but for now, Calum was plunking the melodies out on Moira's almost-in-tune piano. "We're agreed, then—start with current hits: 'Dear Hearts and Gentle People', 'Now is the Hour', and 'Far Away Places'. Then a reprise of war songs—'Keep the Home Fires Burning', 'The White Cliffs of Dover', and 'We'll Meet again'. Then—"

I sighed and shook my head, giving my long red hair ample opportunity to swish around my shoulders. "I'm not sure, Calum. Don't you think people would just rather forget about the war? It's been four years now. You don't see nearly sae many uniforms about these days, and everyone is talking about rebuilding. Clothing isn't even rationed anymore."

"That's exactly why people will love to hear the songs. They want to remember the things that helped them hold on through all those cold, dark nights now that they can smile in the warmth of a new day. Besides, your voice has just that wonderful haunting quality that will soon be making people call you the Scottish Vera Lynn. There's no way we can pass up an opportunity like that.

"And think, there won't be a person there who hasn't lost someone they loved. We need to help them get out of mourning. Not forget their losses—that never happens—but move on to a new day. The world is beginning to glimpse that new day. We can help them."

For all my attempt to keep the rehearsal crisp and businesslike, I couldn't help catching my breath at the way he said 'we'. Did my success really mean so much to him? He had other clients, after all. Far better-established ones than myself. And he was right about coming to terms with their losses. I thought of Jamie, my dashing older brother with the irrepressible sense of humor who would never come home. "All right, I'll do as my genius manager says. As long as the whole second half can be Scots ballads." I started laying out my music: "Annie Laurie", "The Banks of the Dee", "Mist Covered Mountains of Home", "The Dark Island"...

The rattle of the onboard trolley being pushed down the aisle by an attendant brought Felicity back to the present. She had looked up only once before when Teddy had squealed loudly at the sight of the herd of shaggy, red cattle grazing in a field beyond his window. It brought back memories of Felicity's own first sight of a Highland cow. "That cow's got long hair!" She had squealed—and she still had trouble believing her eyes whenever she saw one with its alarming wide, curving horn-span.

"Time for lunch, I think," she said as the trolley approached. Both her men agreed enthusiastically.

"Orange squash and two teas, please," Antony directed the attendant and reached for his billfold while Felicity pulled out the thick beef and pickle sandwiches and packets of crisps Wendy had insisted on sending with them. Unbelievably after the breakfast they had eaten, they were already happy for lunch.

The last of Wendy's provisions had disappeared when the train pulled into the station and they were off on a quick walk to the harbor and the bustle of excitement boarding the big black and white ferry with its distinctive red funnel displaying the golden lion rampant. Felicity could easily have begun skipping and bouncing with her son had not her mothering instincts insisted she put all her effort into holding onto his hand. There was no sitting down, though, with the enticements of washing wake, shimmering water and swooping gulls that fully occupied both parents in keeping up with their son. Felicity gave thanks for the telephone number of Wendy's cousin tucked firmly in her pocket.

After an hour of the gentle rocking of the ferry and the fresh winds whipping her blond ponytail Felicity had secured so firmly with an elastic band, they debarked on the Isle of Mull and followed the queue of passengers walking to the bus station. The big red bus had wide windows that were perfect for a five-year-old to press his hands and nose against as his papa pointed out the scenes the bus trundled past: a deep, verdant green glen; the round green top of Ben More; the placid waters of Loch Scridain; and countless hillsides dotted with sheep—most especially the large rams with horns that coiled in complete circles on each side of their heads.

Felicity glanced up for each point of Antony's narrative and smiled at Teddy's appreciative squeals, but each time returned to her mental focus on the Isle of Lewis.

It must have been two hours later, although it felt more like 20 minutes, when Moira burst into the room, shaking the rain from her woolen coat. "Oh, it's dreich out there, but it's all blue skies in here. I'm so glad you're doing 'White Cliffs of Dover'. It's just grand to remind ourselves that the sun has shone through at long last."

Calum gave me an 'I told you so' look as Moira reached into her carrier bag. "And look what I bought at Woolly's!" She pulled out two pairs of silk stockings. "I got one for each of us. Can you believe we can actually buy these now? No more of that ghastly leg make-up."

"Oh, thank, you, Moira!" I gave my tall blond cousin an enthusiastic hug. "I'll save them for my concert. They'll bring me good luck."

"Darlin', the way you were singing you don't need luck." Moira returned my hug and went into the little kitchenette beyond the sitting room to put the kettle on. Above the sound of running water, she called over her shoulder, "Have ye heard from Faye recently? I rang Mam from the office, and she'd had a note from your mother. Seems the family down the island are holding prayer meetings in their barn." She laughed and shook her head. "Only in Barvas."

"Prayer meetings!" I blinked at the strength of my reaction. Why should the idea annoy me so? It wasn't likely to bother the cows, and it didn't have anything to do with me. They could pray all night for all I cared. I had left Lewis and all its doings far behind. I changed the subject back to news from my sister. "Did Faye say how Mam is?"

"She said Aunt Skeena sounded a bit down, but she didn't know why."

"I expect it's just Mam's annual end-of-autumn cold." Besides, when did my mother ever not sound down? I considered saying something about writing to them myself—whether I really intended to or not.

But Moira continued from the kitchen, "Oh, and I invited everyone from the office to your concert. Including that dreamy Lyall McIntyre from the marketing department. They're all planning to come."

"Well done, you," Calum said. "Want a job in advertising?"

"No thanks, I'm quite happy in my pokey little insurance office." She returned to the sitting room bearing a tray with a steaming brown teapot, cups, and a jug of milk.

"As long as dreamboat Lyall's there to smile at you, you mean," Calum said as I took a cup of tea, added a generous dollop of milk and handed it to him.

"Wish I could offer you sugar, but we've used up our ration."

"Greedy pigs," he teased. "Actually, I got used to sugarless tea in the army. Never could get used to toast without marmalade, though."

"What? I thought that's why we were all doing without—so our brave fighting boys could have all the sugar," Moira said.

"I think we all went without so the black-marketers could get rich. But that's just me being cynical." He took a sip of tea.

"Now then," he turned to me. "Drink up, then it's back to work, you—and plenty of fresh air and rest. I want you lively and glowing for your big night."

"Oh, Aileana, you must be so excited!" Moira gave my arm a squeeze.

I returned my cousin's smile and nodded to my manager. I was exceedingly grateful, though, when Calum and Moira began talking between themselves. Their talk of plans for the concert, contacting the newspapers, building on this sure success for more concerts all the way to a recording contract kept the bright images whirling around my head even while I struggled to breathe. All my hopes, all the dreams I had ever had for as long as I could remember, were about to come true. All I had ever wanted to do—all I could ever remember doing, really—was sing. While my little sister Faye worried about having dates or saving enough ration coupons for a new dress to wear to a dance, I just wanted to sing at the dance or the picnic or the church dinner. To me singing was breathing.

But now I was having trouble breathing. What if I failed? Calum believed in me. He had worked so hard, as hard as I had, to organize my big chance. Moira had let me stay with her rent-

free and had invited everyone she knew to the concert. What if I let them down?

My parents hadn't wanted me to leave the island to go to the city. Mam had wept when I told her I was leaving, and Da made dire pronouncements. "Ye're abandoning yer heritage, lass. No good can come from it. These are yer roots, girl. It's a fine thing when yer ideas get too big for yer own family."

I shook my head at the memory. I had been so determined to show them all that I could succeed in the wider world. And I would. I didn't have to spend my life on a barren rock on the backside of beyond. Lewis was the dropping off spot of the world. I would never go back.

But if I didn't make a success of this opportunity I would have to.

"Yes, definitely." I jumped to my feet so fast I made Calum slosh the last of the tea in his cup. "Back to work." Recalling the grim barrenness of my island was the perfect tonic for stage fright. I would succeed. I would never go back. Ever, I added for emphasis this time.

Felicity closed the notebook with a puzzled frown furrowing her forehead. She turned back to the cover just to double-check. Yes, 1949. The date was right. And Wendy had said these were eye-witness accounts of the Awakening. Well, there was mention of prayer meetings in Barvas—that tallied with what she had read, but Aileana was firmly focused on Glasgow. Felicity was quite certain the events of the Awakening only reached Glasgow indirectly. At this moment she was experiencing the wide distance between Glasgow and Lewis. And surely, the connections would have been more difficult seventy-five years ago.

Felicity sighed. She had held such high hopes that these journals would hold the key. Some really new information for her talk. She looked at the small stack of notebooks making a bulge in her bag. Was it all for nothing? If she didn't come up with something her main worry wouldn't be boring her audience—it would be boring herself.

Chapter Four

At the moment, though, there was no time for worry or boredom as the bus arrived at the terminal and they were swept up in the bustle of gathering belongings and heading to the ferry terminal, drawn forward by the sight of a narrow strip of deep blue water and the bright green mound of the legendary Isle of Iona just beyond. A mounding loaf-shaped hillock made an impressive background for a scattering of low, white buildings, and near the shore of the sound Felicity spotted a sprawling stone structure whose tower suggested it must be the abbey.

A ten-minute crossing landed them on the pier and, much to Teddy's delight, they were met by a horse-drawn wagon. "What's his name?" Teddy asked, holding a tentative hand out toward the horse.

"Diormit—named after one of St. Columba's monks. And I'm Maire." The driver smiled at Teddy. "Go on then, ye can pet him. Gentle as a kitten, this one."

After a few tentative strokes, Teddy consented to be lifted into the back of the wagon by his father for the short ride that carried them and their very minimal luggage to the Bishop's House retreat center where Antony would be spending ten days with his students. It was a long, low, stone structure, right on the shore of the sound. Even the elongated evening shadows cast by the lowering sun seemed to reach out in welcome. Felicity took a deep breath of the fresh sea air and smiled as she stepped through the low doorway to the cozy, wood-paneled interior. Even on a June evening a low fire gave a warm glow to the leather sofas and book-lined shelves of the library just beyond the door. Tranquility engulfed her. This was going to be a wonderful holiday. Pure relaxation—even with Teddy in tow.

Then her travel-weary and over-excited son began tugging at her demanding food, activity, and a toilet all in one sentence. "Right, loo first, young man." Antony scooped his son into his arms and marched down the hallway while Felicity followed Marissa, the retreat house manager, to their room and began unpacking.

"Just time for a short stroll before they serve dinner?" Antony suggested when he and Teddy returned.

"Perfect." Felicity grabbed light jackets for herself and Teddy, and they headed out into the soft evening. A short distance back toward the pier, Antony stopped at the broken walls of the ruined nunnery.

"Oh, how lovely!" Felicity exclaimed when their stroll across the grass allowed them to see that the tumbledown walls served as a perfect shelter for a riotous garden with colorful blossoms spilling over the scattered rubble. Felicity and Antony sat, hand-in-hand, on the remains of a low wall, allowing their son full freedom to explore.

Felicity took a deep, satisfied breath of the wonderful sea air and leaned her head on her husband's shoulder. Antony smiled and dropped a kiss lightly on the top of her head.

His first words, however, were hardly the stuff of romance. "These are the most complete remains of a Medieval nunnery in Scotland."

Felicity chuckled. *Always the historian,* she thought. *But then, I knew that when I married him—no sense in fighting it.* "When was it built?"

"Early 1200s—about the same time as Raghnall mac Somhairle, younger son of the Lord of Argyll, built the monastery up the road." Antony gestured toward the abbey. "Raghnall's sister, Bethóc, was the first prioress. I find it interesting that his monastery was Benedictine, while the nunnery was Augustinian, so the two houses on the island would have followed somewhat different rules."

"What was the difference?" In those long-ago days when Felicity had visited several convents, considering her fleeting desire to become a nun, the houses had all been Benedictine, as she remembered.

"Augustine's rule is the oldest, and shortest of the rules for religious communities. Its essence is to value community life over seeking fulfillment for oneself. Members share what they have, care for one another, and take special care of the sick. It's pretty basic. Benedict spelled things out a bit more fully."

Felicity laughed. "How counter-cultural that sounds today." She paused. "Or maybe for any day." A cry from Teddy wanting his parents' attention ended her philosophical musings.

They continued their ramble toward the tiny village. A low stone wall ran along the path to their right and, some distance beyond that, a green field tumbled down to the sound whose breeze-ruffled surface reflected pink and gold rays from the setting sun behind them. Teddy alternately held a parent's hand, ran ahead of them, or lagged behind. Until they came to a tiny stone chapel beyond the wall to their right with various gravestones and monuments scattered across the lush grass. Teddy, who was racing ahead at that moment, entered a break in the wall and began a running skip dance between the markers.

Felicity shook her head. "I tell myself he'll sleep better tonight for some exercise—I hope he isn't just winding himself up."

Antony nodded. "We'll take him back in a minute. He'll probably fall asleep over his sausage and mash."

"We can only hope." Felicity grinned. "What is this place?"

"St. Oran's Chapel, probably twelfth century, but rebuilt. There's a tale that Queen Margaret built it—nice thought, but no real evidence."

"Who's buried here?"

"Kenneth MacAlpin, who united the Scots and the Picts in the mid-9th century, and, it's said, succeeding Scottish kings until Macbeth."

"Macbeth? *The* Macbeth?"

"The same. He was really a rather good king, in spite of Shakespeare's depiction. Queen Margaret's father-in-law, as it happens. Malcolm, yes—Shakespeare's Malcolm, was her husband—grand story, really. She wanted to be a nun, but their ship—on its way to Hungary from England—was blown ashore in Scotland. Because they were English royals, fleeing William the Conqueror, Malcolm came out to meet them and fell madly in love with Margaret. Malcolm was apparently too much a force of nature for her to resist. Anyway, she did a wonderful job civilizing and Christianizing the barbaric Scots."

"Here endeth the lesson," Antony grinned as Teddy came barreling back to his parents, requesting food.

Teddy wasn't the only one for whom the combination of exercise, fresh sea air, and a solid dinner produced a good night of sleep. After breakfast Felicity felt energized for a day exploring the island. This would be her only day on Iona, as Antony's students would be arriving this afternoon and she and Teddy would be going on to Lewis tomorrow.

Felicity handed Antony the child-carrier in case Teddy tired, and shouldered the rucksack herself: water bottles, sunscreen, sandwiches, and a box of plasters—which Felicity still thought of as Band-aids, but were sure to be needed whatever name one called them by. They retraced their steps from the evening before.

The village was really little more than a cluster of buildings along a single narrow road winding around the bay: hotel, café, schoolhouse, village hall, grocery store. And a great variety of arts and craft shops—jewelry, pottery, pebble and shell, Scottish gifts…

Beyond the abbey the road wound upward, curving around rocky outcroppings. Antony stopped before an impressive stone mound rising from the lush velvet carpet of grass to a flat, if uneven, top covered with tufts of grass and patches of lichen. He extended his hand to Teddy. "Want to climb?"

"I do!" Not bothering to take his father's hand, Teddy began scrambling upward. Attacking the nearest stony wall of the hillock, he scrabbled for toe and finger holds in the rough surface.

"No, Wait!" Felicity darted forward in time to grab the little monkey around the waist and pull him back under protest. "This isn't a playground climbing wall. We'll go this way."

Grasping his hand firmly, she led to the side where a grass-covered slope offered an ascending ramp. They arrived at the top breathless but exhilarated—especially when all three climbers turned as one and gazed out across the sound from almost the height of the abbey roof. Glimpses of islands and small boats dotting the glistening water pulled all eyes to the more distant scene beyond the activity of visitors moving about the abbey grounds and viewing the shops beyond.

Antony, however, drew their attention to the nearer scene. "This very spot, Torr an Aba," he pointed to the stone and turf beneath their feet, "is where Columba built his hut more than 1400 years ago."

Teddy, unimpressed by the concept of time, responded to his father's interest in the ground beneath their feet by plopping down and examining the flora. Following her son's lead Felicity saw that the entire hilltop was sprinkled with small wildflowers, red and white clovers, bright yellow silverweed, and a tiny blue blossom she had no idea what to call.

Realizing Antony was still talking about the site she turned back to him with a smile. She should have known. "Sorry, my mind wandered. You were saying about archeology?"

Antony grinned. "Don't worry about my nattering—I was just saying that the experts had always disparaged the idea of the remains of buildings found here actually dating to Columba's time, but recent work has proven the naysayers wrong. Samples of hazel charcoal recovered by researchers sixty years ago have only now been carbon dated using modern techniques."

"And?" Felicity prompted. She knew how much Antony enjoyed sharing the stories of places they visited—and he was a good storyteller.

"The results of the tests show that the wooden hut, believed to be where Saint Columba spent much of his time in isolation, was built between 540AD and 650AD."

Felicity ran her hand over the soft green moss, trying to imagine what it would all have been like in Columba's day—the peace, the solitude, the difficulties… A bell rang from the abbey tower, calling the Iona Community to prayer. Columba and his band were so long ago—and yet people still came here to pray. Little wonder Iona was considered a thin place where heaven touched earth.

She looked at their son who had moved on from his botanical studies to treating the sloping green ramp up the side of the hillock like playground equipment, running up and scooting down on his bottom. She sighed, wondering if the grass stains would ever come out of his jeans. Then she turned back to Antony. "Go on, I know you're dying to tell me story."

"A little preview of the seminar?"

"Sure, why not? As long as Teddy is happy."

Antony sat on a boulder and Felicity selected a soft patch of grass.

Columcille, or Columba as we know him, was a prince in Ireland, born a Scot in Donegal, a member of the royal family of O'Neill, descendants of the High King Niall of the Nine Hostages, who ruled in Tara. A fine man and tall, bard-taught and sword-skilled, he could have chosen to rule in Ireland, to sit on the throne of his ancestors. But he made dwelling place within himself for the Holy One, and the pleasures of kingly courts held no attractions for him.

A monk he was, a holy brother vowed, Columba the Dove—the Dove of the Church. But not always a dove of peace. For there was war in Ireland. And Columba prayed. Fiercely and mightily Columba prayed. For the slaying of his enemies Columba prayed. And mighty and fervent were his prayers, and mighty and fervent was the slaying. Until, at the end of the day, three thousand lay slain. Three thousand men that had lived and breathed with the rising of the sun that morning now bled and died in the field at the sun's setting.

And Columba was filled with remorse. He went to his king to plead succor for his soul. For Columba knew there could be no peace for him in Ireland. He must perform the penance of exile. He must leave all that he loved best in this world. He must leave Ireland. He must travel beyond the faintest sight of his native home.

"With your leave, Your Majesty," spoke Columcille, "I would take twelve men strong and bold against evil, twelve men who have taken vows of holiness, twelve men who would help me bear the light to the darkness beyond. And I would do penance with the wearing of a hair shirt and sleeping on a pillow of stone."

So, the king gave Columba leave. "Take your twelve men. Choose them well. And take a boat well equipped with all you will need."

So did Columba choose. And so did Columba and his men sail: up the Irish Sea, past the places we now have named the Isle of Man, the Mull of Galloway, the Mull of Kintyre, into the North Atlantic Ocean, past the Isle of Islay... At every island, every promontory, every speck of land, Columba went ashore and gazed longingly back at his beloved homeland. And at every site he was able to see the fair emerald isle lurking on the horizon.

Shaking his head each time, he returned to his comrades. "This is not the place. We must sail on." Until a fair wind and rolling waves landed them on the silver white sands of the southmost tip of the island that then was simply called I. And there, at last, Columba knew he had found his new home.

Antony paused and drew a deep breath, but before he could go on Felicity jumped to her feet. "Teddy!" She whirled and strode to the incline where he had been playing so contentedly a few minutes before. No sign of him. "Teddy!" she descended the torr at breakneck speed, calling her son's name. Where could he have gone? How could he have disappeared that fast? "Teddy!" Did he go up or down? Maybe back along the road toward the village? Or away from it?

Then she glanced beyond the road toward the abbey. And there was Teddy. Standing stock-still, staring up at the high cross that stood before the abbey. Relief propelled her to his side in a flash. She was torn between hugging him or chastising him.

"Look, Mummy—snakes." He pointed to the writhing figures entwined around the bosses carved into the stone cross.

Antony arrived at Felicity's side and put his arm comfortingly around her shoulders. As soon as her trembling steadied, Antony knelt by Teddy and joined his scrutiny of the cross towering over them. "Mmm, lots of snakes, aren't there?"

"Why would they put snakes on a cross?"

"Well, we don't know for sure. The Celts—the people who carved this cross—loved curvy designs and animals. They probably chose to use snakes on this cross because the first monks here came from Ireland—and you remember the story about St. Patrick chasing all the snakes out of Ireland."

Teddy frowned. "You said he didn't really."

Antony grinned and tousled his son's hair. "Good boy. Quite right. There were no snakes in Ireland. Do you remember what I said the real snakes were?"

"Bad men."

"Right. Gold star for you, young man." Antony rose and took Teddy's hand. "Let's see the pictures on the other side." They walked around, still gazing up at the cross against the blue sky. "See, these pictures are different. There's Mary and Jesus," he pointed to the circle in the crossbar. "And Daniel in the Lion's den, and David and Goliath..."

"Who's ready for lunch?" Felicity asked.

Both of her men responded enthusiastically, and Antony suggested they walk toward the back of the island to find a picnic spot. Felicity was considering whether she should suggest Teddy ride in the child carrier Antony held slung over his shoulder, but at that moment a clop of horses' hooves and a jangle of harness announced the approach of the horse and cart taxi that had met them at the pier on their arrival.

Teddy had spotted it first and already darted to the road, waving at Maire and Diormit. Antony laughed. "That's decided, then. We'll ride as far as it goes."

The decision proved to be a good one because, although a road led from the village toward the back of the island, the way was steep and curving. The view from the wagon seat was wonderful as the sun warmed their heads and breeze whipped their hair. Felicity was glad she had chosen to wear her long blond hair in a plait down the center of her back today for better control.

"Hold on," the driver called and jiggled the reins guiding Diormit. The horse immediately broke into a rhythmic gallop that made Teddy shout with delight and clap his hands. Felicity was glad Antony had a good grip on their son because she felt she needed both hands to clutch her seat and the railing behind her. The brown rump and black tail of the horse rose and fell, and the green turf sped past them on each side. And then, with a firm call of "Whoa" from the driver, they stopped. "End of the road," Maire told her passengers.

Felicity looked at the land spreading below them to a thin strip of silver beach and the open Atlantic Ocean beyond. "Is this a golf course?" Her voice carried the surprise she felt. Her only clue was the poles bearing small red and yellow flags waving in the wind to mark holes.

"Aye, ye're in Scotland, Lass. Of course we'd have a golf course. All this natural turf and a God-given sand trap. No Scot worth the name could stand to let that go to waste."

"But there are sheep and cows all over it." Felicity's mind filled with memories of the meticulously groomed golf courses at home in the States.

"Ooh, aye. The wee balls nay bother the beasties."

Felicity was still chuckling and shaking her head as Teddy waved Diormit away on his return journey.

Antony suggested they follow the path down the island to Loch Staonaig—Iona's only lake and only source of fresh water—to find a picnic spot. The tarmacked path shortly dwindled to little more than a sheep trail—and there were plenty of sheep grazing contentedly on the sturdy turf among the outcropped boulders. The fresh air and exercise ensured that the hikers arrived at the shore of the long, narrow, loch ravenous for the lunch the retreat house kitchen had provided. A hillside covered with long grasses and clumps of purple heather offered the perfect spot for eating and admiring the wind-ruffled, slate blue waters below them.

The provisions disappeared quickly, leaving Felicity's pack considerably lighter, and only a few minutes more walking brought them to the silver-white crescent of Saint Columba's Bay. Felicity stood gazing out as Teddy ran ahead onto the beckoning sands. "Amazing, isn't it? It can't have changed that much since Columba and his monks arrived here in—whenever it was."

"The year of Our Lord 563," Antony supplied. "Yes, that's one of the charms of Iona—it truly is unspoiled."

Felicity thought for a moment. "So remote, and yet Columba's work spread through the isles and across the mainland, you said."

"That was the Celtic way—which became known as Columban Christianity—first, establish a monastery, then go out from there to spread the Gospel. And always from the top down. It was necessary to get the king or overlord's permission—then reach out from there."

He paused and turned to see that Teddy was still happily engaged in playing in the sand. The gentle lapping of the waves accompanied his continued words, like the strumming of a bard's harp, just as an occasional piper's trill was provided by seabirds soaring and swooping overhead.

So was Columba's pattern. He went first to the King who was Columba's kinsman. Conall ruled Dalriada—the Kingdom of the northern parts of Ireland and Scotland and the Isles. Columba sought permission from Conall to establish his monastery on Iona and to preach the Gospel. Conall granted leave for this undertaking and land to build on this island.

Conall was easy. Not so, the fierce King Bude of the Picti who ruled the Kingdom of Alba—most of Scotland that wasn't Dalriada—from the royal dun on Craig Phadrig at Inverness. The pagan king was a man of great power. Columba, a mere missionary monk. But Columba served a God of greater power than any earthly ruler. Power faced power as Columba preached the Word of God. And King Brude maqq Maelchu, ruler of the Picti, converted to Christianity, and all his kingdom with him.

Then did Coumba journey southward to the Scottish Lowlands, the Kingdom of Strathclyde, where taught the saintly Mungo of Glasgu. It was a meeting of mind and heart, but even more a meeting of spirit as the kindred saints embraced, held converse, and exchanged pastoral staves.

And so did Columba, the energetic, and his devoted band of monks travel, preach, and minister throughout most of pagan Scotland and northern England. Not the smallest or remotest islands—Hebrides, Shetlands, Orkneys—none were beyond their reach until the entire land was converted to the Christian faith.

Tales of wonder abound. And who is there to say that the prayers of the sainted Columba, so close to the heart of God, didn't save his monks from an attack of the waterhorse we now call the Loch Ness monster?

Nor would one gainsay the chronicler's accounts of the maiden rescued from sacrifice. She of great beauty, just come on her womanhood—such as 'twas said the spirits most favored. She to be sacrificed at the full of the moon. But for Columba's intervention she would have been slain by the silver sickle in the sacred grove on Craig Phadrig, her blood caught in a basin and returned to the loch for its spirit to empower the archdruid.

And Columba's healing of King Brude's chief druid by sending him a stone of Iona Marble…"

"I found a stone." The fluting five-year-old voice returned both parents to the present to see their son holding out a smooth pebble of white marble veined with streaks of light green.

Antony took the rock from Teddy's palm and held it up so the sun could make it shimmer. "Well done, you. This is Iona marble—just what it is said Columba sent to the druid. Columba's old enemy Broichan, King Brude's Archdruid, was struck down by fever. He sent his assistant from Craig Phadraig to Iona to fetch Columba. He was to come immediately. He was to save the druid leader from death.

"Columba searched the ground beneath his feet, selected a pebble—just like this one—drew the knife he wore at his belt and carefully incised a cross on the stone.

"'Let him who has ears heed the Spirit's word. To him that

over-cometh I will give a white stone, and on the stone a new name written, to be known by him who receives.'

"'Take this.' He handed the newly marked pebble to the druid messenger. 'The white stone was ever a symbol of victory. And on it, the cross of Christ. Tell Broichan to meditate on it day and night. Therein is healing for all the world. And the high druid must pray to the living Christ who died on the cross for his sins. Pray and meditate and believe. Of such is all healing.'

"And so, the assistant druid did as Columba said. And likewise the archdruid did pray and meditate. And he was healed." Antony dropped the stone back into the hands of his son who was still staring at his father open-mouthed at the strange story his pretty pebble had evoked.

"And now, after hearing that, we really must visit the marble quarry before we return." Antony studied his map for a moment. "Yes, just around the corner, so to speak." He pointed to the east, catercorner across the tip of the island. "But it's a pretty faint trail. How about a ride, young man?"

Teddy readily agreed to take a seat in the carrier and Antony settled it on his shoulders. They retraced their steps up the island a short distance, then turned down a gentle ravine to their right. "Bear to the right," Antony called to Felicity who was leading. "A note on the map says the gully to the left is treacherous."

Felicity obeyed readily; the trail was faint enough as it was. But it was well worth the trek when she arrived at the mouth of the quarry. Steep marble walls rose on each side, before her a tumble of white marble chunks plunged to the water's edge where waves lapped a rectangular slab extending into the sound. Most surprisingly, enormous structures of abandoned equipment punctuated the scene: tanks, wheels, some sort of engine shaft, perhaps? And the centerpiece, a vast, rusting metal structure like the skeleton of a giant's table.

"What is it?" She pointed as Antony came alongside her.

"Frame for a saw to cut the marble blocks. Old pictures show some sort of triangular frame supporting a pulley to raise the marble chunks up to the bed. Amazing, isn't it? The only quarry in Scotland with its original equipment in situ. It's been designated a SAM—Scheduled Ancient Monument."

Felicity shook her head. "How do you know all this?"

Antony gave his characteristic lopsided grin. "I swotted it up. Have to keep ahead of my students and they're a pretty sharp group."

"Daddy, can I get down?" Teddy began swinging his feet impatiently.

"Ouch! Wait." Antony grasped the feet kicking his thighs. "You can get down and look for a stone to match the other one you found. But don't run off. This can be a dangerous place."

The child's freedom was an obvious relief to both him and his father, but Felicity kept one eye on her son as she continued to marvel at the very existence of a working quarry in such a place. "This must have been, what? A hundred years ago?" The machinery bits certainly looked Victorian. "How did they get it here? Where did the workers come from?"

"The Duke of Argyll sponsored the operation, but it closed after World War I. The seam had run out by then. Still, they shipped marble to build churches all around the world. It does boggle the mind, though, doesn't it? There were houses up top," he pointed above the sheer marble walls, "for the quarrymen. Workers from the island joined them on a daily basis. Except for supplies the locals provided, everything had to come in by the sea."

Felicity considered the waves washing white foam against the disordered marble blocks. "They actually landed boats here?"

Antony shook his head. "Too treacherous. I've read there was some sort of derrick or winch to swing the stone out to boats waiting offshore, or to bring supplies in, I suppose."

Felicity considered. "It sounds as daunting as building the pyramids." Seeing that Teddy was happily engaged in his treasure hunt on the edge of the left-behind marble chunks, she added. "I'd like to get down to the water."

"Pretty rough walking for anything but a mountain goat, but you might get a bit closer. That big stone over there should give you a good view."

Felicity found footing on the nearest block and proceeded cautiously, testing each foothold. The huge white lumps were solid. They had lain here for a century, after all. From atop her stony perch, she was able to view the shoreline more clearly as she tried to imagine loading or unloading a boat in such a location. Then she spotted the iron bars sticking up from the large, flat slab that extended into the water. That must be the remains of the winch they used. Now she could picture it—the whole arrangement still looked sturdy enough. A boat rocking in the surf, men on shore somehow operating the hoist. Did the boat sink lower with each load? Did they swing the derrick manually or have a motor attached? How…

"Felicity!"

She spun at Antony's sharp cry, then began leaping from rock to rock to return to smooth ground. She had understood at once. "Where is he, now?"

"Must have gone back up the trail." Antony started up the steep green slope, but Felicity, with longer legs, outdistanced him.

At the top she stood panting after her sprint. "Teddy!" She took a deep breath and increased her volume. "Francis Edward!" A note of command rang in her voice.

"Mummy, help me." The child's light voice carried from above in the direction of the neighboring ravine.

A few strides upward and she spotted the soles of his trainers at the ends of legs extended across the turf as he hung face downward peering into the deep crevice. "I dropped my stone."

Felicity grabbed her son's legs and pulled him back from the brink. "What are you doing?" She managed not to yell at him. Just.

"I was throwing it and catching it, and I missed."

"But what were you doing up here?"

"Walking. I had enough stones."

She rose, pulling Teddy to his feet in the same motion. "It's time we went back."

"But my stone," he wailed and pointed to the gully.

"Hold him." Felicity thrust the small hand into his father's. "Don't cry." She submitted with a sigh. "I'll look."

She knelt at the edge and peered over. It was odd that Antony's map would have bothered warning people not to take that route. Surely no one would choose it, warning or no warning. "That does look treacherous," she commented to Antony standing behind her. "But I doubt many people would even see it. It's so nearly hidden by that bend of the ridge." She looked closer. "And the whole gully is so overgrown with bracken and full of junk." Scrap metal, it looked like—undoubtedly left over from the quarrying operation. Yet, some must go this way—or attempt to—because a faint trail descended from the top into the depths.

She scanned the closer ground and saw it. The prized pebble that had so nearly led Teddy into disaster. Lying flat, as he had, she stretched toward the small round lump of marble, but it was just out of reach even for her long arms. "Antony, come hold my feet."

"Felicity don't be silly. It's just a rock. The island is covered with them. Come on."

But another howl from Teddy countered his father's good sense. "Sit there. Don't move." Felicity heard Antony order their son, then felt him grasp her firmly around the ankles.

She only needed another few inches and the wayward rock was hers. "Hold on," she called to Antony and felt his grip tighten. She stretched to her full capacity and her fingers closed around the pebble. "I've—" Her triumphant cry ended in a gasp. "Wait!"

But it was too late, Antony was already scooting her back.

Still, it was enough. She knew what she had seen. She dropped the small white stone into her son's outstretched hand and opened her mouth to blurt out the scene she had just glimpsed, filling her mind in vivid detail. Then she stopped.

Teddy clutched his recovered treasure with such a heart-melting smile at all being set right in his world that she couldn't shatter such serenity. Besides, as she looked more closely at the snapshot her mind had taken, she realized there was no hurry.

Teddy obediently straddled the carrier his father had lowered for him to step into. Antony raised the warm, heavy bundle to his back, snapped the buckles, and they headed across the scrubby turf toward the main path back to the village. Head against his father's neck, Teddy's eyes drooped, and he dozed.

"Listen, Antony, I—" She stopped when another a hiker came round the bend toward them. It had been so long since they met other tourists, she had begun to think they had this whole end of the island to themselves. The man appeared to be heading toward the left-hand ravine. "Not that way!" Felicity didn't mean to sound so urgent. "Trail to the right goes to the Quarry," she called. He nodded, his curly red hair and bright yellow tee shirt glinting in the sun as he waved a wordless acknowledgement and veered to the right.

Felicity checked that Teddy was still sleeping soundly and tried again. "Antony, there was more in that gully than discarded trash. There's a body. I saw it just before you pulled me back."

"What?" Antony stopped mid-stride.

The abrupt interruption to the gentle rocking of Antony's tread made Teddy stir, and Antony resumed walking, but at a much-reduced pace. "A body?" he asked quietly.

"Well, a leg, at least. I assume—" An involuntary shudder shook her. "He must have taken the wrong turn. One misstep would do it, hit his head on a rock and rolled. He would have gone to the bottom of the gully if that gorse bush hadn't stopped him."

Antony whirled. "Then we must go back. He must be badly hurt. We can call that other hiker to help…"

Felicity grabbed his arm. "No." She gulped as she examined the image in her head more closely. "No. There's nothing we can do."

"But—"

"It's too late. Probably several days too late."

"How can you be sure?"

She forced herself to overcome her squeamishness. Putting words to what she had seen made it more real. Something she couldn't just pass off as vivid imagination. "The leg was swollen. There were flies. Open sores." Again, she couldn't suppress the shiver. "He's probably been pecked by those seagulls." She sighed before delivering the final clue. "And there was no blood from the wounds. Dead bodies don't bleed."

Back on the main trail the walking smoothed out and Antony picked up their pace. "I don't know who we should tell. I don't even know if there are emergency services on the island." He strode on at a clip that Felicity, even with her long legs, had trouble keeping up with.

She could see her husband was thinking deeply. She usually loved it when she could see his wheels turning, but now it would have been more comforting if he had tried some meaningless reassurance like: I'm sure it's a simple accident, poor guy. Or, no need for police anyway.

Instead, after a few paces Antony said abruptly, "What was that about trash in the gully?"

"I don't know. It was really just more of an impression—I was concentrating on that pesky stone and my sobbing son, and then I was interrupted by—" She struggled to focus her internal vision further down the ravine toward the ocean. What had she seen? "Stuff from the quarrying, I thought. You know—like the old machinery."

"Metal, then?"

"Mmm, yes. But now that I think about it—it couldn't have been from the quarry work because it wasn't rusty. I don't think it was—it was just a glancing look, but I'm pretty sure I saw shiny spots through the gorse and all."

Antony went back to his deep-thinking mode, and they returned to the Bishop's House in record time.

Felicity lifted her son from his carrier and took a well-rested Teddy to the kitchen for a snack, leaving Antony free to locate Marissa and report to the authorities—whoever they might be on this tiny, quiet island. At a time like this it was wonderful to have a small, lively person to care for. There couldn't possibly be a better antidote to the grisly scene in the gully her imagination kept replaying in her mind.

By the time Antony joined his wife and son, they were sitting at a comfortable table in the kitchen with a freshly filled teapot in the center. Teddy was happily nibbling on oatcakes and cheese and drinking milk. Antony slid into a chair and Felicity filled a sturdy mug for him.

"Help is on its way," he said after he had swallowed his first sip. "Marissa said the Volunteer Fire Department is the sum of their emergency services here, but she assured me their leader is very efficient although he's only been here a year. He should be here soon. The fire station is just five minutes away—near Martyr's Bay." He cocked his head in the direction they had walked the night before. "Ten volunteer firemen on call twenty-four hours a day. I got right through to the leader." He took another drink of his tea, then added, "He's coming here first to hear your story. Said it might be helpful in locating the casualty."

Antony had hardly finished one more gulp when they heard the doorbell ring. "I'll take Teddy to our room. The rescue leader'll want to talk to you."

A minute later the retreat house manager ushered in a middle-aged man with sun-bleached hair, weather-tanned skin, and startling, pale blue eyes. He held out his hand, "I'm Lachlan."

Felicity at once felt they were in capable hands. She offered him a chair, but he said, no, he just wanted to get her statement, then they would be about their business. "I've already called the team. They're assembling at the station. Now, your husband reported an incident near the Old Quarry." He took out a notebook and pencil. "What can you tell me about it?"

Felicity closed her eyes to concentrate more fully on the picture in her head. She gave as detailed a description of everything her mind had recorded as she could. Lachlan frowned as he wrote. "A body? A human body. Ye're certain? Couldna been an animal?" He seemed disturbed by the report—which was understandable. It was disturbing. But Felicity repeated her assurance of what she had seen. The more she thought about it, the sharper the image in her head became.

"And this was where? Exactly?"

Again, Felicity struggled to remember the details: coming up from the quarry, rushing toward the gully following Teddy's cry. How far had they gone? So hard to estimate. Then the incident with the pebble. How far along the lip of the ravine? She struggled to estimate. One thing she could be more precise about—she knew she had stretched to the full length of her reach. "I was lying flat and stretched this far." She demonstrated standing up. Even in her tennis shoes, she managed an *en pointe* from her ballet days and gave her best *bras en avant* to her arm's full extension.

Lachlan smiled. "Got the picture. Any other landmarks?"

"Oh, yes, the gorse bush. A big one. It stopped the body from rolling to the bottom—that's why I only saw his leg—the bush hid the rest of, er—the body."

"That should be helpful in finding him. You're sure it's a him? Although you only saw the leg?" For the first time he seemed skeptical.

Felicity thought. What made the limb seem masculine? She

closed her eyes again. "The leg looked heavily muscled—but then it was bloated so it's hard to tell. The boot was large and sturdy. But then, most hiking boots are." She sighed. "Sorry—that's the best I can do."

"Nae. Ye've done a brilliant job." Lachlan snapped his notebook shut and turned to his task. "I'll get the team right out there." Felicity felt the weight lift. It was out of their hands.

Back in their room Teddy was playing happily with the shells and pebbles he had collected—perfect accompaniments for his dinosaurs, while Antony sat at the small table that served as a desk, going over his notes for the seminar. She could see that her husband's focus had shifted into lecturer/director mode. She needed to do the same thing.

What a day it had been—exploring the peace and beauty of Iona, then encountering what must have been a sudden death. Her mind played the scenario: a lone hiker on a beautiful day, striding along, probably looking at the sky—maybe distracted by the seagulls—starting down the wrong way… She brought herself up short. No. She wasn't going on with that. She needed to follow Antony's example and shift into work mode.

She had almost forgotten her commission to prepare for her conference: keynote address followed by a workshop. The full morning of the first day of the conference. She sighed. Why did she ever accept? It sounded so easy—and so far in the future—when she said yes last autumn.

And it was still far away in distance. Iona seemed such a world apart, so magical—which made concentrating on her task all the harder. Even in such a short time Iona had cast its spell over her— yet even here calamity could intrude, she reminded herself. And so must work.

Antony would be busy with his group tonight. Six students

from the College of the Transfiguration who had chosen to major in Church History and elected to fit this onsite seminar into their schedule. There was no better place to do a deep emersion into the Celtic Christianity which had played such an important role in the early formation of British faith—as Antony had explained to her more than once.

All had arrived by the time the welcome tea was finished. All except the one eccentric—Roger Wellman—a mature student with no plans to become a priest, or even a deacon, but simply studying to learn more about British Christianity. Older and rich—a student who would be arriving in his own boat the next morning. Antony grinned and shook his head when he told Felicity about Roger. "Interesting chap. Not many in his tax bracket take up Christian history as a hobby."

As the group assembled in the cozy retreat house lounge for their orientation session that evening after supper, Felicity felt her husband's focus deepen on the task before him and she knew it was time for her to get back to work, too. She would be on her way in the morning, and the better she was prepared for the task ahead, the better job she could make of it.

Chapter Five

Pajama-clad, Felicity snuggled under her duvet with a sigh and leaned back on the extra pillows she had piled against her headboard. She had thought Teddy would never get to sleep. Just that twenty-minute nap on his father's back had set him up for the evening. As had all the extra attention he received at dinner from Antony's newly arrived charges. She smiled at her son sleeping so soundly on the narrow cot beside their bed. Peace at last.

Antony's introductory lecture would go on for at least an hour yet. This was the perfect opportunity for her to work on her own orientation and get her head together for the task ahead. Shifting gears between the various roles of her life was never easy. Sometimes she used simple tricks like donning an apron when she returned to her mothering role after hours of conducting classes, or lighting a candle when she needed to focus on her own spiritual growth after a lengthy counseling session.

She supposed returning to the notebooks Wendy's great aunt had written would have to serve to as a means of shifting her thoughts now. Reading this firsthand account of events could be something like a time-travel portal. She reached for the notebook she had dug out of her luggage. Needing a refresher to get into the story, Felicity turned back a couple of pages from her bookmark. Oh, yes—Aileana from the Isle of Lewis, making her singing debut in Glasgow, determined to succeed. *I'll never go back...*

 I took a deep breath and peeked around the corner of the stage, then drew back with a gasp, my heart lurching to my throat. Even accounting for the fact that the Lochnagar was a small hall, the room was bursting with people. There must be more than a hundred out there. All smiling and chatting and waiting to hear me sing. My head felt light, my body cold. I was going to throw up.
 And then the piper was playing, the audience was clapping, and I was on the stage, the folds of my long white gown swirling around my ankles, and I was lilting, "I love those dear hearts and gentle people who live and love in my home town..." It was several hours later that the irony of those words, and especially the ones that followed, "They read the Good Book from Fri' till Monday, that's how the weekend goes..." struck me. For that moment—that one glorious moment—the reality, or really, the unreality of it all held me in an enchanted bubble.
 Then, with a simple glissando of the harp, the mood changed from stirring to dreamlike and, with a flip of my red hair, I was singing of those "Far away places with strange-soundin' names" that "Are callin', callin' me". By the time I got to "I pray for the day when I'll find a way Those far away places to see", everyone in the hall was swaying with me, and I gestured for them to join me on the final "callin', callin' me".
 From there it was a seamless switch to my wartime repertoire: "Keep the Home fires burning While your hearts are yearning..." If I didn't see white handkerchiefs dabbing at eyes on that song, I certainly did when I moved on to:

> We'll meet again. Don't know where, don't know when,
> But I know we'll meet again some sunny day.

A WIND IN THE HEBRIDES

> Keep smiling through, just like you always do,
> Till the blue skies drive the dark clouds far away.

How many in my audience were thinking of those who wouldn't be returning? Of those they wouldn't be meeting again? The thought brought a small catch to my voice that made me end,

> Don't know where, don't know when,
> But I know we'll meet again some sunny day

with a tremolo that truly brought the house down. It was glorious. A memory I'll carry with me for the rest of my life.

I bowed and blew kisses until I was dizzy, then ran from the stage, applause still ringing in my ears, right into Calum's arms.

"Oh, Calum, you were so right. The war songs. They loved them."

"They loved you. Ah, Aileana, ye're a hit. They're wild for ye, lass."

I dropped my face into my hands, trying to seal the moment. "I loved them. What happened out there—it's a kind of magic. I had no idea it'd be like that. One minute I was so scared I was frozen stiff, the next I was, I was... I don't know, I was just there."

Calum handed me a cup of soothing tea with honey. "Here, ye must be parched."

I was, but I hadn't realized it. I drank thirstily. "Perfect. Thanks. I must get ready. How long is the interval?"

"Ye've got plenty of time. The Lochnagar does nae have a bar like a posh concert hall, so everyone will go next door to the pub."

"What if they don't come back?"

"No worries there. I'm just wondering what we'll do when they drag everyone else in the pub back with them to hear

Glasgow's new songbird sensation."

I had barely registered that Calum was referring to me when Moira rushed backstage. "Oh, darling, you were wonderful!" She engulfed me in a hug, but when she drew back I saw the worried look on her face.

"Moira, what is it? What's wrong?" A flutter of chill air made me shiver.

"Nothing." The reply was sharp, almost harsh.

And I didn't believe it for a minute. "Tell me!" My voice dropped to almost a whisper. "Did somebody die?"

Moira shook her head. "It's Faye. Well, not Faye. It's your parents. Faye rang just before I left for the concert. She was almost hysterical."

Calum stepped in front of me as if to protect me from a physical assault. "Moira, can't this wait? Aileana needs to get ready for the second half. It's important she not be distracted."

"I know. I know. I'm so sorry. But I promised Faye I'd tell you at the very first opportunity. She said it was life or death— that a few hours could make the difference."

I pushed Calum aside. "Moira, what are you talking about. The difference in what?"

"Your parents. They're desperately ill. The last train for Kyle of Lochalsh leaves in just over an hour. You can catch the first ferry in the morning..."

Anger clouded Calum's rugged features, making his black hair look even darker in the dim backstage light. "Are ye daft, woman? She can't leave now. She's in the middle of a performance. You heard her. You heard the audience— News of Aileana's singing will be all over Glasgow in the morning. You can't seriously imagine she would walk out on that."

Calum's voice rose and his countenance darkened on each sentence. His anger frightened me more than Moira's words. I had never seen him like that. "There's a phone in the pub, isn't there? I can ring from there." I forced myself to smile through the fear I felt gripping me. "You know what Faye's like, Moira. I'm sure she's exaggerating."

It was almost impossible to hear the operator over the roar of lively voices filling the pub, and it took forever to get the trunk call through. Like most on Lewis, my family weren't on the telephone, and I didn't have the number to place a call to the lone, red phone box next to the post office in Port of Ness—even if anyone would have heard the ring at this hour. But the police station in Barvas should still be manned... they could ring the post mistress, who would run across the field...

People were beginning to drift out of the pub and back to the concert hall by the time the operator came on the line to say she had made the connection. A few people saw me around the corner from the bar and waved, pantomiming clapping and blowing kisses.

"P C Macaulay," the voice came through the crackly line.

"Struan, is that you?" I nearly cried with relief at the voice of my childhood friend. I had heard he was recovered from his war wounds and back home, but I hadn't seen him. No time for any of that right now, though. "Struan, it's Aileana Mackay in Glasgow. Faye rang. She said my parents are terribly ill. Do you know anything about it?"

"Oh, aye, I'm afraid I do. Yer da's not quite sae dire. He'll recover all right, I think, but yer mam—" the line crackled.

"What? Are you saying Mam might not? Struan, what is it? Has the doctor been?"

But the line snapped, crackled and went dead. The operator came on to apologize. Did madam want her to try to reconnect? "No, never mind." With a sick heart I returned the receiver to its hook and ran for the concert hall just ahead of the last of the stragglers to leave the pub.

I caught up with Calum at the stage door. "Calum, I can't.

My mother. She's—" My voice strangled on the horror of the words. "She's dying. I have to be there."

Calum's face was grim. "Your career. My investment. Your audience." The words ground out with an intensity that seared them on my brain. "You'll throw it all over? Let everyone down." The last wasn't even a question.

"I don't have any choice." The words were barely a whisper.

"Of course ye have a choice. There's always a choice." He took a deep breath, and his expression became grimmer yet. "You realize ye're burning yer bridges. This isn't done. I thought you were a professional. Professionals don't walk out on an audience."

"Calum, she's my mother. We don't even get along, but—"

"But she's yer mother—and probably just as cantankerous as you are. Everybody on that god-forsaken island is. I know. I spent my childhood visiting my auld aunties there, ye ken." He looked at his watch. "Right. For the record, I'm furious with you and I entirely disagree with this decision. But if ye're going to be a muleheaded fool, at least do it right. You sing one last song—the piper and harper will have to finish the program without you—and I'll get you to the station."

Relief flooded over me. I hadn't realized that I had been holding my breath for what seemed like hours. I threw my arms around Calum. "Oh, thank you! Thank you."

He tore my arms from around his neck, then gripped my shoulders so hard I almost cried out. His eyes bored into me. "Just don't think you can ever do this again." He shoved me towards the stage. "Now get going."

I rushed backstage, picked up the length of bright red and blue Mackay plaid, threw it over my shoulder, and strode out onto the stage to thunderous applause. Even as my mind formed the dreadful words of what I must say, I savored the applause—knowing very well that it would be the last time I would hear it. My first and last curtain call in one glorious night. I held up my hands for silence.

"Thank you, thank you. Truly, I can't thank you enough for your generous reception tonight. You've been wonderful—beyond my wildest dreams. And I can't tell you how much I had looked forward to sharing this second half with you—my very favorite of our beloved Scots songs." Wild applause and cheering greeted my statement. I had to hold up my hands up again for silence. "It breaks my heart, but I must tell you that I learned during the interval that my mother on Lewis is dangerously ill. She may only have a few hours left."

My hand at my throat felt the deep swallow. It was a moment before I could continue. A murmur of sympathy and disbelief swept over the audience. "I'm afraid I have time to share only one song with you and then my fine accompanists will complete the evening without me." I felt the protest from the audience, but like me, what could they say in the face of this? "I'll leave you with the song that best expresses my feelings, 'The Dark Island'." I nodded to my piper. He struck in and the skirling melody filled the hall.

> When I first left my home I was young and I wanted
> The whole world to roam;
> But now... that lovely dark island Is calling to me.
> O, I've wandered away From the land of my birth,
> And been roaming around To the ends of the earth,
> Still my heart is at home In that land far away
> That lovely dark island Where memories stray.

I wasn't sure how honestly I meant the sentiment, but I sang it for all the world as if my deepest desire was to return home. And perhaps, in some remote corner of my being there was a true spark of home-feeling—or perhaps it was the audience reading in their own feelings for loved ones who had died far from home—

because I was still hearing the applause as I wrapped my plaid around my shoulders for warmth, grabbed my handbag, and ran from the theatre to Calum's waiting car.

The train was already steaming and chugging on the track when we pulled into the station. "Run for the train. I'll get yer ticket," Calum called, propelling me towards the platform. At least it was a push of haste, not anger.

"Boooard!" the stationmaster called as I leapt onto the first carriage. He closed the door behind me. I opened the window and leaned out as Calum came running out of the station. The train had begun lurching forwards as my hand closed on the small slip of pasteboard he thrust towards me.

A great white cloud of steam engulfed him, and a shrill whistle drowned his parting words. When the steam cleared, all I could see was a solitary figure in a long, tan raincoat and trilby hat standing on the platform, his hands shoved in his pockets. I could almost see his brooding scowl and feel his icy anger.

I chose a compartment with a single occupant, a fat man in a Harris tweed jacket, snoring raggedly. I threw myself into a seat. And that, my girl, is that, I told myself. The beginning and end of my brilliant career. Oh, sure, I could go back someday. Maybe. Start again. Maybe. But who knew how long I would have to stay in that house on the cliff at the tip of the island? Would I really ever get away again? It had taken me all of my twenty-three years to make the first break—even though I had known all my life that I wanted to get away. Would I now be trapped for another twenty-three?

No, surely I could rebuild, I tried to comfort myself. I had made a good start. But I had well and truly blotted my copybook. Running out on a concert—and a full-house audience— who would ever take a chance on me again? It was certain Calum wouldn't.

Calum. My heart rose to my throat, and I thought I would

cry out from the pain. Not quite five months I had known him, and yet in that short time he had come to fill all my waking hours. And all my dreams. And now I would never see him again. I would never forget the frozen silence in the car on the way to the station and the controlled ferocity in his voice as he shoved me towards the train. My last memory. Mine to carry for the rest of my life.

I saw him again, thrusting my ticket towards me through the train window—undoubtedly anxious to be rid of me by then. I would repay him for the ticket. I could never repay him for all he had done for me. In spite of the pain it brought, I couldn't stop my mind flying back to that evening when I had been in Glasgow less than a week. I was still feeling so overwhelmed and disorientated in the big city I had hardly drummed up the courage to venture out of Moira's flat. Moira insisted that I join her and some friends at a pub off Sauchiehall Street at the end of Moira's workday spent banging away at a typewriter for an insurance company.

The pub had undoubtedly been full of noise and people, but, looking back, all I could remember was the tall, dark man with the laughing eyes Moira introduced me to. Those eyes weren't laughing now. The thought brought such an ache I had to stifle a sob in order not to wake my sleeping companion.

The train swayed and I closed my eyes tightly against any more memories. Gradually my compartment mate's heavy breathing and the clack of the wheels over the tracks blended in a rhythm. I jerked awake when the train stopped. A porter came through announcing Stirling. The fat traveler across from me snorted awake, heaved himself to his feet and yanked his case from the rack over my head. As he exited, he trod heavily on my right foot—a sharp reminder that I was still clad in my concert gown and high heels. It would be the last straw if he made a ladder in the silk stockings Moira had given me.

I was about to attempt going back to sleep when I saw something on the floor. It must have fallen from my companion's satchel. A petrol ration book. Oh, the poor man, he would miss this dearly. I jumped up and ran to the window in the aisle of the carriage, but the man had disappeared into the station. I didn't dare get off the train to go after him, although I couldn't imagine how a person could get along without a whole book of ration coupons. I looked inside the book and discovered that it was completely unused.

I was about to put it in my pocket when I noticed the date on the book. These coupons didn't start for months yet. How odd that he would have a book now, before it had even been issued. He must work for the ration board, someone who received the books early to have them ready for distribution at the next quarter. That heavy briefcase he almost crowned me with must have been full of coupon books. I put the book in my handbag. I could turn it in later. There was obviously no rush.

Fortunately, none of the straggle of passengers that boarded at that late hour chose my compartment, so I was able to snuggle back into the corner of my seat and continue the journey to Kyle of Lochalsh in splendid isolation. How different it had been in the war years when every train had been crammed with uniformed servicemen. The few journeys I had made to Highland installations on the mainland, as a lowly volunteer delivering messages for the communication post at the RAF base in Stornoway, had given me a taste for travel and deepened my determination to escape from the island when the war was over.

I was almost back to sleep when the train pulled into Inverness where I had to change trains. At least I didn't have any luggage to worry about as I stumbled onto the deserted platform, but I did wish I was wearing more appropriate attire. And a warm coat. The cold was unbelievably piercing on the platform, and the tiny spark of warmth put out by the minuscule heater in the ladies' waiting room was hardly worth the bother.

I looked at my watch, then the notice board, then back at my watch. Two hours until the next train. If I wasn't dead of pneumonia by then. Funny, how one felt the cold more as an adult. I had never thought anything of it as a child. Island children must have been particularly impervious. In spite of the chill, I smiled as I recalled riding my bike over one of the rutted tracks serving as a road that led out of our tiny Port of Ness on the northeast edge of the island. We were always led by Jamie, the organizer of all our adventures, the leader far out in front of the pack. I could never keep up with him. But how hard I had pedaled to match the pace set by Hamish and Struan, the energetic Macaulay brothers who were just enough older than us younger stragglers to seem alternately Celtic gods or oppressive tyrants.

I paused in my reminiscence to mourn Jamie, the big brother so full of life and promise. All he hoped to achieve—would have achieved—all gone. And Hamish, he of the flaming red hair and blue eyes, the first of our close island circle to fall in the war. Then I pushed bravely on, as one always must, focusing on the happy times.

At least it kept my mind off the chaos I left behind me and whatever tumult my connecting train would carry me toward. I shivered on the hard wooden chair and hugged my plaid more tightly. Then almost smiled as I returned to those far-off days, remembering Faye's frantic calls that they wait for her, and our friend Janet's brother Euan teasing her when she couldn't keep up. Euan, from their farm further down the island, seemed to spend all his effort on either impressing or tormenting Faye.

Sometimes we clambered over the peat turf and rocks to the shores of a loch to share our oat cakes and cheese in an impromptu picnic, and sometimes we rode south to one of the ancient blackhouses to stare wide-eyed at the ragged children dwelling in those almost prehistoric buildings.

One day Struan's uncle had taken us in his lorry to visit the standing stones of Callanish. That was a day that would forever live in my memory as the pages of a storybook coming to life. I remember all of us struck silent—stock still and open-mouthed—as we stared wonderstruck at the giant stones marching in columns reaching high over our heads. We ran, chasing with wild abandon, hiding behind the stones, then calling to one another and laughing when the sea breeze and gulls' calls confused the direction of our voices. Until Jamie organized us into an orderly unit and we paraded, singing, up and down the long processional way erected by our ancient ancestors lost in the mists of time.

Another day—the memories all jumble in my mind but we must have been older because Struan's big brother Hamish drove us—we had a glorious picnic at Uig Bay. Too old for playing pirates or buccaneer smugglers, we chose a rather serious expedition of cave exploration, even into the next cove. Hamish, a geology enthusiast, had instructed us to bring torches for the purpose, and we learned a great deal about Lewisian gneiss, of which most of the Hebrides isles are composed, but named for our own island. Over the years I've forgotten most of Hamish's information, but what stuck was the fact that Lewisian gneiss represents the oldest rocks in Britain and dates back to around three billion years ago. Hamish would have made a fine university lecturer if he had survived the war.

My most frequent memory—it seemed almost daily, in spite of the time we must have spent working at the never-ending chores set us by our parents and studying in restless fidgets at the tiny school house—was of feeling the wind in my hair, chilling my face even in summer, as I pedaled over the barren sweep of green turf towards the edge where it met the blue sky, my view broken only by ragged outcroppings of rock or a small, harled crofter's house standing a bare sentinel against the sky. At Ballantrushal we would abandon our bikes and run, screaming, to the enormous lone standing stone where, as the mood took us, we would play red Indians, pirates, or ancient Celts—the stone serving as execution stake, ship's mast, or high altar, as required for our scenario. Or some days we would stop at the lumpy piles at Shader where a collapsed burial cairn inside the irregular remains of a stone circle invited us to play druids or Vikings as best suited our mood.

No, I reminded myself, it hadn't been a bad childhood at all. Friends, fresh air, imaginative play. And yet even then, somewhere in the back of my mind, I knew I would leave one day. Even before my brief day of freedom ended by returning to the dour, white lime render house of Skeena and Tavish Mackay. I hadn't known as a child what I longed for—I just knew there was an emptiness inside me. An emptiness that could only be filled by—what? Beauty? Joy? Exultation? I had hardly known the words as a child, but always I was subconsciously reaching for something when I sang. Something bigger. Higher.

I hadn't known until Calum told me. No, not told. Showed me. Taught me optimism. Revealed it to me by his own large-hearted enthusiasm for life. The way he embraced every opportunity. Made me believe anything was possible. Saw the good in everything. Until I abandoned him. There was no good to see in that.

"All aboard for Kyle of Lochalsh!" The stationmaster's voice broke my reverie so abruptly I almost jumped off the hard wooden chair I was huddling on. I hadn't even heard the train pull into the station. The engine released a great cloud of steam as I ran, wafting me into my carriage.

The train to Kyle stopped at every station as it made its way across the Highlands to the western shore: Garve, Achanalt, Strathcarron, Stromeferry, Plockton, Duirinish... I heard every one called, torn between wishing it weren't pitch black outside my window and being thankful for the covering dark. There would have been a sensation so bitter it was almost sweet to have watched the scene go by as I recalled those all-too-recent days last summer when I had made the forward journey, my head too full of dreams to sleep as I saw the rolling green, the highland cattle, the rushing burns welcoming me into my new life.

Now, I would dearly love to sleep only to block out the crushing sense of loss. Every time I did doze, though, I was roused by the announcement of another town.

A pale, grey dawn had broken by the time I reached Kyle of Lochalsh and suffered through the interminable wait for the seven-hour ferry ride. At least the waiting room of the Caledonian Steam Packet Company was warmer than that of the newly nationalized railway. Finally, I boarded the ferry beneath the great red, black, and white funnels of the steamer newly built to replace the one sunk whilst in use as a troop carrier during the war. Although they could never replace the crew who went down with her.

We sailed up the sound and, by the time we reached the wider waters across the North Minch, the sun broke through the morning mist, casting glimmers of silver on the grey water as sea birds called and swooped. Then the golden orb was swallowed again in the grey gloom. And that, I thought, was what the last few months of my life had amounted to. It had all been a dream—a burst of bright light swallowed by a cloud. The reality was before me, beyond Stornoway on the rock-bound coast of the island.

Felicity closed the journal with a sigh. Tomorrow she would be heading for the same destination. She could only hope her journey would be more hospitable than Aileana's. But of course, it would be. This was a different century. Her route was different, modes of transportation had improved. All would be quicker and easier.

Chapter Six

Aileana's journey to Lewis was still vivid in Felicity's mind the next morning as she stuffed items into her small rollaboard suitcase, making certain to choose only absolute necessities for herself and Teddy. She thought of the harried odyssey Wendy's great aunt had undertaken in 1949. The young woman had raced more than half the length of Scotland, then the ferry across the turbulent water of the Minch in inappropriate attire and a fraught emotional state. Thank goodness her own journey, undertaken in more modern times, would be simpler.

Certainly nothing could have been farther removed from Calum's seething anger and harsh, icy demeanor toward Aileana than was Antony's solicitous care for her and Teddy as he saw them off at the tiny ferry dock. She could still feel his ardent embrace and hear his words as his hands rested on the heads of his two dear travelers: "The Lord protect you from all evil; the Lord protect your very life. God give you strength and grace when you are weary and guide you to make your time meaningful and your efforts fruitful." One more hug followed the final Amen. Then, gripping Teddy's hand on one side and pulling her bag on the other, Felicity ascended the gangplank.

"There he is—wave to Daddy," Felicity instructed Teddy from the deck as soon as they were aboard. She held the small hand tightly as he leaned against the white railing waving and shouting.

The wide gangplank was just folding into the stern when a sleek white yacht flying an enormous red ensign slid into the harbor. The boat's elegant lines made it look as if it were racing over the water even as it idled, waiting to pull up to the pier. *Selkie* was written in large script along the sharply pointed prow. Felicity watched in fascination as the ferry chugged into the sound and the *Selkie* slipped smoothly to the dock.

To her amazement, the tall, silver-haired man who strode ashore clapped Antony on the back and they turned together to walk up the pier. Could that be the eccentric seminar student Antony had described as an "interesting chap"?

Incalculable hours later, though, it was the words of Antony's parting prayer that filled Felicity's thoughts far more than any luxury yacht. She missed Antony more than she had imagined possible and was inexpressibly grateful for his words. She had certainly needed all the grace, strength and guidance she could get. Teddy lay in a deep sleep, curled on his side, a thumb in his mouth, on his foldaway beside her bed in the B&B she had booked in Stornoway. Her son's heavy, rhythmic breathing told Felicity he was deeply asleep, for which she gave thanks. Her own exhaustion kept her tossing and turning, unable to relax, and going over and over again the day's expedition.

What had she, in her innocent ignorance, thought so many weary hours ago about her travel being easier and more modern than Aileana's would have been? Was it possible that so little could have changed in three quarters of a century? When the whole idea of Felicity going to Lewis had arisen, she and Antony had spent hours poring over maps, ferry schedules, train, bus and airline timetables. There had been absolutely no choice but to retrace their travel of two days before by ferry, bus and another ferry to Oban on the mainland. She had been confident traveling onward from Oban to Stornoway would be simpler, cheaper, and more scenic than returning all the way to Glasgow and flying to the Isle of Lewis.

Certainly, she had been right on the scenic score. And probably the price. But she had calculated without the fatigue-inducing nine-hour-plus bus journey through the rugged Highlands with a five-year-old, and then another wind-tossed, three-and-a-half-hour ferry ride across the Minch…

A violent jostling of her bed brought Felicity back from the deep darkness she had finally slipped into. What was wrong? Another storm? The ferry about to sink? She sat up with a jolt, the blazing sun dazzling her eyes. "Teddy!"

A high-pitched trill of laughter, accompanied by another vigorous bounce brought her to full consciousness. "Oh, Teddy, stop bouncing. Mummy's sleepy," she pleaded.

"I'm hungry. Bacon,"

Now she could smell it, too. She groped for the jeans and light jumper she had discarded the night before. In a few minutes they were sitting in their hostess's cheery kitchen being plied with bacon, sausage, tea, toast and far more than Felicity could take in, but it did manage to bring her back to life.

"Would ye care for anything more?"

"Oh, Anna!" Felicity laughed and grasped her stomach. "I couldn't hold another bite. That was amazing."

"Good, it'll set ye up for the day."

"I certainly feel readier to cope with the tasks at hand. Thank you."

Back in her room Felicity went over her mental list: Contact Wendy's cousin and pick up her rental—hire, she corrected herself—car. Then she would be set to dive into her research.

Felicity couldn't have been more delighted than she was with

Isla, Wendy's cousin's daughter. Thankfully, Teddy took to her immediately and readily acquiesced to being led out to the garden while Isla's mother Catriona assured Felicity of her daughter's reliability and experience with young children and went over the list of possible activities the island offered: Adventure Island, Standing Stones of Callanish, Lews Castle, soft play area at the sports centre, an endless choice of beaches and playparks around the island…

Felicity gratefully chose a visit to Adventure Island for her son, primarily because Catriona explained it was only a few minutes from their home and Felicity could be completely free to venture across the island for her explorations. After the briefest of "Bye, Mummy," the required "Give me a hug," and repeated admonitions to "Be a good boy. Be sure you obey Isla,"

and Isla and Catriona both assuring her, "The wee laddie will be just fine," Felicity was driving northwestward across what seemed to be the only road to the back of the island.

Her little silver Vauxhall, which seemed to be the only hire care on the island with an automatic transmission, behaved beautifully. In her years of living in Britain Felicity had become reasonably comfortable driving on the "wrong" side of the road, but she still found the heavy traffic and confusing roads a challenge. Thankfully, these concerns didn't apply to driving across the Isle of Lewis. The incredibly narrow road was blessedly almost deserted, and it ran essentially straight across the flat, barren island. This allowed her opportunity to observe the peat bogs, stretching on both sides of the road, striped by long ridges where the turf had been cut. Little hillocks of drying rich, mahogany brown bricks lined the furrows, testifying to the warmth they would supply that winter.

Felicity felt confused, disoriented. She had expected Stornoway, perched as it was on the edge of the world, to seem desolate. Instead, in even her short time there she had found the port city, which she was told was the largest in the Hebrides, to be charming—almost storybook-like with its Victorian castle above the harbor; the Town Hall with its turrets and cupolas, now used as an events centre; the bustling, bunting-draped shopping area with hanging baskets of flowers; and pink, white, and green painted shops lining Church Street. But here, in the middle of the island, the unbroken emptiness made her feel she could be driving across the moon—the dark side of the moon. She couldn't help wondering how it could all have happened—this amazing spiritual outpouring she had come to learn about. How did the Holy Spirit even *know* this place existed?

At the western edge of the island, the road turned to aim straight north at the town of Barvas. Felicity spotted the enormous sand-colored rectangle of the Barvas Church of Scotland building, dominating the landscape with its row of long, narrow windows and small, one-sided bell tower pointing like an arrow to heaven.

She turned off the main road at Ballantrushal and headed down the narrow lane as her directions instructed her, then pulled into the drive of a small white bungalow overlooking the wild western coast of the island. Donald John Smith, surely well over his eightieth year, she calculated, was looking out for her and gave a welcoming wave for her to enter his sitting room, at the same time shooing out the big gold cat. Donald had the wonderful clear, glowing complexion everyone on Lewis seemed to have, and eyes as blue as his jumper—worn properly over a white shirt and tie.

As soon as they were seated Felicity drew out her notebook and began asking questions. Donald simply smiled and handed her a well-worn pad of yellow paper covered with closely-written script. She saw immediately it was his handwritten memoir. "It saves me a lot of talking," he explained.

Then he went on to tell her that here, in this remote falling-off place—next stop Iceland—the world beat a path to his door to hear his story. Even as they talked, he was expecting six South Africans, he had welcomed twelve intercessors from Glasgow last Friday, people from Colorado Springs in the US were due later this week, next Thursday six from a Lanark prayer group...

He sat back in the folds of his easy chair and let Felicity get on with her work. She had scanned only a few lines when she realized this account was worth coming here to read. Donald John Smith was a poet: *I saw the beauty of God's creation in a different way. The singing of the birds was different. The grass was greener and the sea was a different blue. I saw people and my heart was full of love for them—the love of Christ and the warmth of the Gospel.* What an astute, thoughtful child he must have been to have such remarkable recollection from his childhood.

We heard of religion in other places, but now we saw it in floods. Waves of spiritual blessing—we saw it everywhere. The spirit of prayer poured down like rain. Daily living was fragrant.

Felicity's pen flew as she copied every word. Then she looked up. Her face must have registered her amazement. Her host smiled and nodded.

"Aye, that's how it was," he said. "On the road, by a cottage, beside a peat stack, behind cairns of stone—everywhere there were loud prayers. Everyone could hear them. Even singing could be heard from village to village as if it was floating on the air. After the house meetings, which followed the meetings in the church, people walked home—three or four linked arms together and walked home singing. It could be heard in the next village.

"Coming back from a service which ran late into the night, we'd see lights in a house and know someone was being transformed."

Felicity shook her head, trying to imagine. Three quarters of a century ago—and yet the memory was obviously as fresh in his mind as if it had been last week.

He smiled and nodded, and Felicity returned to copying his notes: *It was 'Every home a sanctuary, every shop a pulpit, every barn an altar.' People's faces radiated beauty, their daily living was fragrant. It was a wonderful thing, but there is a price to pay for revival: Prayer. There is prayer—prayer and tears. We still have prayer meetings every week. People still enter into joy every week."*

Felicity paused at the end of the document and shook her cramped fingers as she looked at her host questioningly. "Still?"

His brow furrowed. "Aye. Well—ye'll understand I wrote that a good many years ago now. But, aye, we still bear the hallmarks. I can tell in the singing—there was something in the singing. Ye can still hear an echo. We still have prayer meetings. Young people still attend church.

"That was the thing, you see, it was a young people's revival. The entire teenage world of the island was touched—one way or another. No one was left the same. A veritable stream of young people became full-time ministers and missionaries." He paused and nodded. "Aye a lasting legacy."

He stood, surprisingly spry for his age, took a picture from a bookshelf behind him, and held it out to Felicity. She looked at a small, grainy black and white photo of two elderly ladies. "Peggy and Christine Smith," Donald said. "It was their prayers that started it. Prayer and more prayer. That's the key."

Felicity looked closely as Donald pointed them out: Christine's white hair forming an aureole around her head, Peggy wearing a black kerchief, one on each side of Duncan Campbell, the evangelist wearing a proper black shirt with clerical collar. She felt as if she were holding a time capsule in her hand.

Donald John put the picture away and pointed out the window. "That's my father's house next door." Felicity saw the tan, harled cottage, and behind it, a long, low stone structure. "That's the byre where the people gathered to pray. There were three rooms, and Duncan Campbell would go from room to room praying with people. That's all it was. Just prayer and the most wonderful sense of the holy.

"Then they moved into the house. What is now a garden was wasteland and they put planks of wood on concrete blocks for seating for overflow from the house. We children were sent to bed upstairs, but we didn't sleep. We would creep out of the bedroom, venture down a few steps of the stairs, and sit there to listen to what was going on in the meeting. Sometimes we would hear someone praying in one room and someone else in another room at the same time. The cry of the penitent frightened us…" He continued and Felicity wrote as fast as she could.

The sense of being in another time, another world, stayed with Felicity through the half-hour drive back to Stornoway. How could she possibly encapsulate this into a single talk and workshop? How could she make this meaningful to her hearers from such a very different culture, such different circumstances? What could she find to link modern lives to such a remote past event?

Chapter Seven

Late that evening after a tasty dinner of Scottish lasagna, which included streaky bacon and sweetcorn, supplied by their hostess, Felicity was still trying to make something concrete of the unreality of what she had heard that day. Teddy was lost in the peaceful slumber of a day of satisfying, active play, but Felicity's mind was far too engaged for sleep. Work was the only remedy. She had just taken out Aileana's journal when her phone vibrated.

She grabbed it, slipped into the tiny ensuite bathroom and shut the door so she could talk without waking Teddy. "Antony! I'm so glad you rang! I've had the most amazing day. Surreal. Donald John—the ancient man I interviewed—lives in this little house in the back of beyond and he's incredible. He saw the whole thing in his own home—his father even unscrewed the door of their lounge and took it away because it was in the way of people praying. And the singing—"

"Felicity!" Antony's voice broke through her torrent of words, and she realized this was not his first attempt.

"Oh. Sorry. Running on again, I know."

"Well, that way I know I have the right person." She could see his grin. Then his voice got serious. "Actually, I'm sorry to interrupt, but I don't have long to talk, and I need to warn you."

"Warn me?" Did she hear right?

"The police were here today."

"Police at the retreat center? Do they *have* police on Iona? Oh, you mean to ask more about that poor hiker. I'm sorry, but I already told them all I saw. You know what a quick glance it was. You did explain, didn't you?"

"No. They didn't mention the body. So, I asked them. There wasn't a body. The Iona rescue team didn't find a body."

"But that's impossible! It was only a few minutes. What—"

"They say he might just have been resting."

"Resting! He had wounds all over—"

"I told them. They said maybe he fell and hurt himself, then managed to walk on after a bit."

"No! That isn't right!" But she didn't have any more arguments. "So why did they even need to talk to you?"

"That scrap metal you thought you saw—turns out it was hardly scrap. They were new barrels. One of the volunteer rescuers noticed them. Said he later realized something was wrong, so he called the police in Glasgow."

"Apparently, they contained dodgy diesel." What was Antony talking about? Felicity was too confused even to ask. But he explained. "Diesel mixed with paraffin."

"What?" Now he really lost her as her mind filled with images of chunks of white candle wax floating around in fuel. Would that even flow through a petrol pump? Then she realized. "Oh, kerosene," she said.

"It's cheap and commonly used to fuel rocket engines but is much too harsh for road vehicles. Do you remember the lorry breakdowns they were having in Glasgow?"

"Ahh—dodgy diesel?"

"That's it. Black-market fuel. The theory is it is smuggled to the Hebrides where the paraffin is added, then it makes its way to the mainland."

"But how—" she began.

Antony cut her off. "I'm so sorry, but I have to go to Compline. The point is, when I told the police what we—well really you—saw, they said we might have been seen poking around the ravine. They just warned that we should be aware. They don't know the smugglers' route, but if it's through someplace like Norway, the Outer Hebrides would be a logical conduit—and Lewis the closest stop."

"Norway? Why Norway?"

"Just guesswork, but they are Europe's largest exporter of petrol." A bell rang on Antony's end. "I'm really sorry," he repeated. "I'm leading the service, or I'd give it a miss. Just be careful."

She was left staring at a blank screen.

"Wait!" She tapped the screen, but he was gone. Her words echoed off the walls of the tiny bathroom. The police might be worried about contaminated fuel, but she wanted to know more about the body—no, person—she had seen. Had they followed up at all? Did they find an injured tourist? At a minimum he would have needed medical help. She was far from happy about this. But surely it was a good thing, wasn't it? If the police were certain it was an accident…

She turned to her phone and googled medical help on Iona. She could text Antony and he could find out about a wounded hiker tomorrow. If the police were too busy worrying about other things it was the least she could do.

The information she found wasn't comforting. "Iona doesn't have a resident G.P." the article reported. "The main surgery is back on Mull." It named some town she had never heard of. Still, that must mean the injured man had caught a ferry and gone back to Mull. All was well.

She told herself she should feel relieved, but the disturbing scene in her mind still niggled.

She moved on to questions about the adulterated diesel. After a day of hearing about the island being flooded with peace and joy, singing heard from town to town… How could anything so sordid intervene?

She turned to her favorite source of information. A few minutes of Googling revealed several somewhat unrelated facts. Around half the vehicles in Britain ran on diesel. Kerosene was far cheaper than legal additives to diesel. Fuel sold at prices too good to be true probably meant it would harm your engine. Dodgy diesel had been showing up in Ireland for some time. Normal diesel was amber-green; darker color was a sign of tampering...

She clicked off her phone in frustration and crept back into bed with far less elation than she had felt a few minutes earlier. And even less inclination to sleep. What did Antony mean *Be careful?* Don't fill your tank with bad fuel? Avoid caches of metal tanks? Don't hang out with smugglers? She sighed.

Aileana's notebook lay where she had dropped it on her duvet. She picked it up.

As the ferry sailed into the harbour I realized I was holding my breath. The pale winter sun was just touching the top of the Arnish lighthouse, then rimming the low green and brown hills behind Stornoway, catching in the December-bare branches of the trees imported to surround Lews Castle. Even that pile of Victorian stone seemed to be struggling to appear cheerful, but the calls of the seabirds swooping overhead sounded enthusiastic, if not actually welcoming. Still, it felt like anything but a homecoming. As I walked across the rocking gangplank, I couldn't begin to picture what lay ahead. Not the least of which would be somehow making my way across that wide strip of desolate peat bog, then up the back of the island to the falling-off tip of the world—my home. I supposed I would have to wait for hours for a bus. I thought I had put all that well behind me.

I was so tired and hungry I couldn't think. My stomach growled. I couldn't even begin to calculate how long it had been since I had eaten. I had been too excited to eat before the concert, and Calum had planned a grand celebration dinner for me afterwards...

My knees almost buckled at the thought. Perhaps it would be just as well if I simply collapsed and let myself fall into the icy waters of Stornoway Harbour. It would make little enough difference. My life was over anyway.

"Aileana. Aileana Mackay! Here, lass!"

A lilting male voice cut through my morass as I staggered the last few feet down the gangplank. "Struan?" I blinked, unable to believe my senses. "Struan! Is that really you?"

For an answer he engulfed me in a huge bear hug and lifted me off my feet. "And who else would it be at the crack of dawn on the wrong side of the island?"

In spite of everything, I had to laugh. "But how did you know? I didn't tell you I was coming."

He tapped his forehead. "Canny police work. I rang Moira, didn't I?"

"Oh, I'm so glad. I couldn't remember the bus schedule and I didn't want to lose more time hanging about. How are Mam and Da?"

"I don't know. Daft of me, I should have contacted Faye this morning. I didn't think."

"No, no, it was early. Best you didn't bother them." Besides, if anything—anything serious—had happened he would know. Everyone knew everything in that tiny community. The news was carried on the sea breeze that blew incessantly over the heath.

He held out a parcel wrapped in brown paper. "I thocht ye might be hungert. Or would ye rather have a proper breakfast? Maybe the hotel?"

"No, no. I don't want to take time." I tore off the brown paper and sank my teeth hungrily into the thick brown bap with a sausage stuffed inside. "Oh, heaven! It's still warm. Mmm, thank you."

"I've a flask of tea in the car, too. Like the picnics in the old days, huh?"

In spite of my fatigue, I found myself sitting forward in my seat as we wound our way across the flat, barren island. The heather, which had been blooming several shades of purple when I left, was brown now. The bogs were striped by long ridges where the peat had been cut, little hillocks of dried bricks lining the furrows. Many a fireplace and stove would glow brightly this winter.

With each mile I felt the tension mounting. After all I'd been through—all I'd given up. What if I was too late? My mind refused to take in what that nebulous phrase "too late" meant. Mam had always been strict and distant, all the more so since Jamie's death, but she had always been there. Da had been the one more likely to voice any parental thoughts or decrees. No one voiced feelings. Except Faye, my shyly ebullient, blue-eyed, blond little sister who would sometimes whisper her latest raptures to me, usually for a hero she had met in a book. Oh, it would be good to see Faye again, at least.

The two-story white house stood on a green cliff squarely facing the crashing waves of the North Atlantic. Its unadorned blank windows stared out on the road looking even more bleak in the pale morning light than I had remembered it. I suddenly felt I could have been gone five years instead of five months. I shivered with a sense of foreboding at what I would find behind that sturdy oak door.

And then the door opened and Mr. Ritchie, the doctor for the district, came out carrying his black bag. He pulled his hat well down over his forehead and made for the little black car parked around the side of the house, then turned towards us when Struan pulled up beside the low stone wall next to the verge.

I jumped out of the car. "Doctor. How—how are my parents?"

He shook his head. "Nothing for me to do."

I stifled a sob and ran into the house. I was too late. I started to dash upstairs to my parents' room when I heard voices from the kitchen, so went straight through to the back. Inside the door I stood stock still, unable to believe my eyes.

My mother sat at the kitchen table, drinking tea from a large earthenware cup. My father sat in his favorite chair by the fire, rocking gently. He spoke first. "Well, lass. So ye've come home."

"Aye," my mother said.

"Aileana!" Faye dropped the wooden spoon she had been stirring porridge with and flew to me. "You came!"

The words flooded my mind. Well, of course I came! You said our parents were dying. What did you expect me to do? I abandoned my career. I walked out on an audience. I left Calum. I thought they were dead. And here they are drinking tea and eating porridge! I wanted to scream the words. Throw something. Pull my hair.

Instead, I stood rooted to the spot. No one had ever made such a scene in the Mackay household, and I wouldn't be the first. Even in my outrage I knew I could hardly throw a temper tantrum because my parents weren't dead.

"I came. Hello, Mam. Da. I thought you were poorly." I allowed myself an icily accusing stare at Faye. Had the child lied to ruin my life or simply given in to misguided hysteria?

"Aye. We were nae sae weel." Da nodded in rhythm with his rocking chair.

"They were desperate. I thought—I truly did, Aileana. The doctor said it must have been food poisoning to come on so violent so sudden and then go away."

"Fish paste," I muttered. Ma would keep it far longer than she should. But everyone had been so hungry during the war. It was little wonder if no one threw anything out. The wonder was that anything lasted long enough to go off.

"Tea?" Mam asked, holding up the heavy brown pot.

"Why not?" I sank into the chair at the end of the table with a sigh. My life was over. I might as well drink tea.

Later in our room, the room I thought I would never have to share with my sister again, Faye came to me. "Aileana, I'm that sorry I gave you a fleg. I didn't mean to frighten you."

I shook my head. What was the use? Calum had tried to warn me. It had been my own rashness as much as anything. Or was it something more? Was it my own fears as well? Had I only been running to my parents, or had I also been running away from—what? success? Calum? Could anyone be daft enough to run away from realizing their dreams?

When I didn't respond Faye went on. "I suppose you'll be going right back now?"

Calum's harsh voice bit into my memory so sharply I all but looked around the room to see him. 'Just don't think you can ever do this again.'

"I don't know what I'll do." I wondered if my words sounded as hopeless to Faye as they did to me.

"Well, I know what will cheer you up. We're having a grand ceilidh at the hall tonight. It's all anyone has talked about for weeks."

I threw myself down on the bed. I felt as though I hadn't slept for days. Actually, I hadn't. "Oh, Faye, I couldn't think of it."

"But sure you can. You must. Euan will bring his mates. It'll be good fun. They're even having pipers. None of Angus Brody's oom-pah-pah accordion or Iain Macbride's squeaky fiddle like we usually have. And look," she flew to the tall oak wardrobe and flung open the door. She pulled out a shimmery blue dress and held it up to herself as she whirled around the room. "Isn't it a dream? Euan gave it to me especially to wear to the ceilidh when I complained about all my dresses being so worn."

In spite of my fatigue, I gasped at the dress. The fitted bodice and crossover waist emphasizing the broad shoulders was the very latest in fashion. And the fabric. It looked like silk. But that wasn't possible, surely. "Faye, where did Euan get that? Do Mam and Da know?"

Faye hung the dress away with a merry giggle. "What do you think? Of course they don't. I'll be wearing a coat over it. They'll never know."

"Yes, but where did he get it?"

Faye shrugged. "Who knows? Clothing rationing has been over for months now. And who cares? It's mine. That's what matters. And I have new leather shoes and silk stockings."

I wanted to probe more. Protest more. But I was too weary.

"You sleep now, Aileana. I'll wake you in plenty of time to get ready. Here, give me your gown. I'll sponge it and press it so you'll look fresh tonight."

Several hours later I awoke surprisingly invigorated. I heaved a sigh of submission as I realized I might as well go to the party. It would certainly be better than sitting in a silent room with the parents. Besides, once Faye got an idea in her head it was much easier just to go along with it. I pulled myself out of bed and slipped into my white gown, duly refreshed from its travel stains by Faye's efforts.

A moment later, I heard the back door bang and footsteps on the stairs as Faye came in from the outdoor loo. She took her new dress from the wardrobe and slipped it over her head. My eyes widened. "You look a dream. That icy shade of blue is perfect with your hair."

"Euan says I can always dress in silk when we're married." She gave her blond hair a final fillip with her hairbrush and turned back to me, beaming.

"Married?"

"Oh, don't tell! You won't, will you, Aileana? That just slipped out. Mam and Da would have a tizzy. They don't approve of Euan because he wasn't in the war. But he couldn't help it. It was because of the rheumatic fever he had when he was a bairn."

I was spared the need to reply by a knock on the front door. Faye flew to cover the exotic dress with her tweed coat and headed towards the hall. "Euan must have changed his mind. He said he'd just meet me there. How lovely of him to come for us." She flew down the stairs and flung the door open. I watched as she drew back with a crestfallen face. "Oh, Struan. What a surprise. Come away in."

I caught my breath from the top of the stairs as he stepped over the threshold. I had forgotten how fine Struan looked in his kilt. "I thought I'd chance my luck to see if you ladies would allow me to escort you to the ceilidh?"

He led the way to his car and held the door for us. Faye crawled in the back seat with a sulky attitude. Apparently, she preferred to be unescorted if she couldn't have Euan, but I was happy enough to have the companionship of an old friend and the luxury of going in a car rather than on a bus. "How do you have enough coupons for this after driving all the way to Stornoway for me this morning?"

He grinned at me and winked. "Ach, I'm verra careful. I only use my petrol for the most important errands."

We were nearing Barvas when the sight of a crowd of lorries, carts and bikes around the church caught my attention. "What's going on there?"

"Oh, have ye nae heard about the meetings?" Struan asked. "Well, I guess ye wouldnae in Glasgow, but it's all the talk hereabouts. Duncan Campbell, the big preacher fella from Edinburgh. The twa sisters, Miss Peggy and Miss Christine, ye ken them?"

I nodded. "Of course I remember. Miss Christine taught me

my letters. She retired the year after I went on to secondary school. She had to quit to take care of her sister because Peggy was going blind."

"That's right. Weel, seems they've been praying for years. Then a few months back a group of men from the Barvas church started meetin' in a barn—prayin', too. All of a sudden like, Miss Peggy said Duncan Campbell was supposed to come here to hold meetings, so Reverend MacKay called him. Mister Campbell said, Sure, he'd come. Next year. This year he was going to a big convention on Skye."

"So, what's he doing here?"

"Miss Peggy said, 'Nae, he'll come this year. Keep praying.' And so, the deacons and all the kirk prayed. The Tourist Board in Skye suddenly commandeered all the hotels and guest houses on the island. The convention was canceled. Duncan Campbell came to Lewis."

I laughed. "That's amazing. He came? Just like the sisters said he would? So have the meetings been guid?"

"Och, fine, I reckon. If ye like that kind of thing. Too dour for me. But guid enough as meetings go."

I nodded. That was all right then. Just so long as I didn't have to go to their long-faced meetings.

Another ten miles down the island we arrived at Carloway and long-faced was the last term one would have used to describe the crowd inside the village hall. Four busloads of young people had come to dance to the reels, jigs and strathspeys of the highland pipers. The air simply shimmered with expectation.

Faye and I found chairs along the wall to await the opening notes that would call the dancers to the floor. I was happy enough to look around for familiar faces—any distractions that would keep my mind from drifting back to Glasgow and might-have-beens. Where was Calum tonight? Did he miss me even a little bit? Or had he scrubbed me completely out of his life and mind?

Faye, however, lacked any such discipline to sit still and wait. She shifted restlessly on her chair, craning her neck to scan the crowd and jumping up every few minutes when she thought she spotted Euan, then sinking back with a sigh. "Where can he be? What can be wrong? He said he'd be here. And the pipers? Surely, it's hours past time to start? What can have happened? They've been advertised for weeks."

The incessant string of questions left me free from any obligation to answer, but I was beginning to notice similar questioning looks and comments all over the hall. The atmosphere that had fairly sizzled with excitement when we first walked in was beginning to dampen and turn irritable. Nothing could raise the spirits, get the blood up, and make the feet move like the pipes. And nothing could be more disappointing than to have such high hopes dashed. "Where are they?" was on everyone's lips.

At last Alan Ian Macarthur, the schoolmaster's son who was acting as M. C. for the event, took his place in the middle of the floor. His kilt swirled behind him as he turned with outstretched arms to encompass every side of the room. "Ah, ladies and gentlemen, lads and lassies, I'm afeard I've nae mare news of our pipers than any of ye." A wave of groans and disappointed calls filled the room. Alan Ian held up his hands for quiet. "But while we wait, I've a wee special treat for ye. I'm telt that we have in our company tonight a lovely lassie, just returned from giving a fine concert in Glasgow, and I'm thinking that if we give her a grand island welcome our own Aileana Mackay might be willing to favor us with a wee tune."

My gasp was audible. I couldn't believe my ears. How dare he without asking me first? But as the hall echoed with applause and encouraging calls, I knew I had no choice. I had seen Struan and Alan Ian talking, but I never thought of this.

"Oh, go on, Aileana, do," Faye all but shouted in my ear and *gave me a shove.*

And then Struan was standing in front of me, holding out his hand to escort me to the center of the floor. "I hope ye don't mind me putting a wee flea in his ear, but it would be sae guid to hear ye sing again. Like old times."
I shrugged. Then smiled. Struan could be mighty persuasive. Besides, what would it hurt? Everyone was restless; it would help pass the time. And surely the pipers would show up soon. I would give them a ballad.

> Flow gently, sweet Afton, among thy green braes!
> Flow gently, I'll sing thee a song in thy praise…

Even as I sang, I was aware of the irony. Only a few hours before, I had thought I would never sing again. But here I was, the songs of my childhood lilting out of me almost effortlessly. And I felt the affection of all in the room flowing back to me, warming me. Their generous applause at the end led me on to "A Red, Red Rose" which was even more enthusiastically received.

In spite of calls for more, I took my seat, and at Alan Ian Macarthur's introduction, the energetic, if scratchy, fiddling of Iain MacBride set toes to tapping. It certainly wasn't the same as the pipes, but it was something. Even Faye managed to smile at the tall redheaded fellow beside her and they joined the reel.

I danced two sets with Struan and found myself relaxing and enjoying the evening far more than I had thought possible. Struan seemed on the verge of asking for a third, but I suggested he dance with Faye so I could catch my breath. As I watched from my seat along the wall, I enjoyed the sight of my sister's fair hair bobbing up and down as she wove her way between the lines of dancers.

It must have been getting on for three hours after midnight when Alan Ian sought me out. "That was fine singing, lass. Will *ye gie us another?"*

At least he asked this time. I nodded and allowed him to lead me forwards when the reel ended. I sang "Twilight on the Tweed," then, encouraged by the warm reception, sang two Gaelic tunes from my childhood. I was just finishing "Oran Chalum Sgaire," the story of a Lewis girl who left on a ship for America in the 1850s never to return, when there was an altercation at the door.

Probably someone reeling home from the drinking-house up the road. Pity to interrupt now that the good spirits of the crowd seemed to be restored. I acknowledged the applause, hoping it would cover the interruption, but it couldn't block out the angry voice of the M. C. "What do ye mean comin' in here? Why have you come to disturb our night of amusement? Have ye got a ticket?"

"Aye. I've got a ticket that will get me in anywhere." The intruder pulled open his tweed jacket to reveal the clerical collar beneath.

I blinked when I saw the small man push his way into the room with his concerned-looking wife behind him. Surely Alan Ian wouldn't throw the minister out. A minister had the right to enter any building in the parish—even if it was completely unheard of for a minister to attend a ceilidh.

The fiddler had stopped, but the M. C. strode to the center of the floor and called for a dance, glaring at the Reverend Murdo McLellan. "'The Gay Gordons', if ye will please, Iain."

The fiddler didn't move. No one moved. No one breathed.

The minister took the floor. "Young folk, a most remarkable thing has happened up the road in Barvas. I've come to give ye a report. My guid wife and I were just there, helping out with the meetings. Happin ye've heard tell of the meetings they've been having in our neighboring parish?"

A murmur of low groans and plenty of eye-rolling acknowledged that they had heard—and demonstrated what the youth of the island thought of such goings-on. Faye leaned over and whispered in my ear. "Aye. I've heard, all right. And I don't want anything to do with it. We have little enough fun here. All we need is a ranting preacher breaking up our one ceilidh."

Ignoring their response, the minister continued, "Well, it's been a fine thing to have the Reverend Mister Duncan Campbell here all the way from Edinburgh, and they've been guid meetings. Guid enough, but not extraordinary, mind. Until tonight. Tonight Mr. Campbell preached as fine a sermon as I've ever heard and then there was a great, mighty outpouring of the Holy Spirit. And then we continued with a kitchen meeting in a house across from the church. People praying. That's all, just simple, honest prayer."

Faye jabbed me in the ribs with her elbow and rolled her eyes. "What did I tell you? He's come to make us pray."

In spite of the restlessness in the room, the minister persisted with his story, "And my dearie wife here, in the middle of the praying and the weeping and the singing, she looks across the room, and what does she see? What does she see, indeed, but the twa pipers who were to be playing at this very hall tonight, weeping and praying and breaking their hearts. And she says to me, 'Those were the twa pipers who were to be at the dance in Carloway tonight. They've advertised that they'd be at the dance, but here they are, crying to God for Mercy.' And I said to her, 'We'll go home to the parish and report what has happened.' And that's what we've done."

Murmured confusion and louder scoffing met the announcement. Pipers—breaking their hearts in prayer? What could he mean? Nonsense. Stuff for old grannies. Not for grand Highland pipers.

The preacher held the floor. "When we came in here just now there was a lass singing a Gaelic tune. She had a lovely voice. Why don't you all join me now in singing a Psalm?"

It was fortunate that the invitation was general, not directed to me, because I would have been incapable of replying. What on earth did one say to such an unheard-of request?

And no one else seemed to know what to do either. As the murmur in the hall grew it was clear that this suggestion had caused more consternation than the first announcement. Psalm-singing at a ceilidh? It was bad enough that they did that dreary business in the kirk. No need to be bringing it into the hall.

"Well, if ye start, I'm sure you'll get quite a number to follow you." Mrs. McLellan's words to her husband were soft and encouraging. But firm. Not a voice to be disobeyed.

"From Thy spirit whither shall I go?" the minister began.

His wife joined in, "Or from Thy presence fly?"

Around the hall a few voices joined in tentatively. "Ascend I to heaven, lo, Thou art there; There, if in hell I lie."

I shivered at the sentiment, but I felt obliged to join in. My lips moved with the words, but I didn't give the effort my full voice.

> If I take the wings of the morning,
> And dwell in the uttermost parts of the sea;
> Even there shall thy hand lead me,
> And thy right hand shall hold me...

Most of the hall had joined in, but Faye pinched her lips firmly together. I turned to give her an encouraging nod when Faye jumped to her feet and ran from the hall.

At the end of the psalm the M. C. strode back onto the floor. There were several gasps from those who caught the look of steely intensity on his face. Hitting a minister would be unthinkable. Little Mrs. Macarthur, Alan Ian's mother, grabbed her son's arm just before he reached Mr. McLellan.

"It's all right, Mam," he said, then turned to the preacher.

"I apologize. I was wrong." The words sounded jerked out of him. He rushed from the hall and onto one of the busses waiting to return the revelers to their homes.

Slowly the hall emptied as, one by one or in groups of two or three, the revelers went out to the busses—not to go home, but, unthinkably, to pray. I sat in a quiet corner of the deserted hall feeling dazed, trying to figure out what was happening. I didn't feel any different, but the atmosphere in the hall seemed strangely transformed.

I turned at the sound of high-heeled shoes clattering across the floor and saw Faye running in, her hair askew, her cheeks streaked with tears. "Aileana, Aileana, you've got to help me. I've looked everywhere. I went onto all those busses of praying people. Euan isn't anywhere. But I did find Janet, his little sister. She said she hasn't seen him since yesterday. He wasn't at home at all to eat or dress for the dance or anything.

"I know something awful has happened. He wouldn't miss the ceilidh. He wouldn't. He was as excited about it as I was. We were—Oh, Aileana, I've got to tell you or I'll die! We were going to run off to Stornoway tonight and be wed."

"You were going to elope?"

"Yes! Don't you see, that's what the new dress was all about. But I couldn't tell you. I wanted to. And I was so happy. And now it's all gone wrong." She burst into tears.

I gathered her into my arms and held her shaking body. When the barrage finally calmed Faye managed to sob, "Something terrible has happened to him. I know it has. I just know it."

Chapter Eight

By mid-morning the next day Felicity was again heading to the backside of the island. She had slept poorly the night before, so allowed herself a slow start. Now, though, rejuvenated by Anna's hearty cooked breakfast, which this morning included crispy fried black sausage with tangy mustard and porridge that had achieved maximum creaminess by being soaked overnight and cooked slowly in milk, along with more than one slice of granary toast slathered with Dundee marmalade, she felt ready to face the world.

When Isla heard Felicity's research was taking her to see Aileana's home in Port of Ness, she suggested that, if Felicity didn't mind having them tag along, this would be a good opportunity to take Teddy to the nearby Eoropie Dunes playpark. Felicity welcomed the suggestion as she had been feeling tiny pangs of guilt at leaving him for another day. Only the tiniest corner of her mind held a thought that after Antony's warning she would be glad to have her son nearer her with Isla's eyes to keep watch as well. The idea that she could be taking him into any kind of danger was not to be considered. Any inkling of skullduggery was beyond credence in this wide-open, green, windswept land beneath the clearest of blue skies.

They were a mile or so north of Barvas when Isla suggested

from the back seat, where she had chosen to sit next to Teddy, who was firmly strapped into the booster seat provided by the hire firm, that they take a wee detour to see the Truishal Stone. Isla seemed to be surprised at Felicity's blank-sounding "What?"

"Have you not heard tell of it? It's the tallest standing stone in Scotland—the only remainder of a great circle built something like five thousand years ago."

To American Felicity, anything older than a few hundred years still seemed incomprehensible, even though she had lived in Britain long enough that she should be accustomed to it by now. When she saw that the narrow road Isla pointed to was the same one she had taken to Donald Smith's home in Ballantrushal the day before, she was doubly happy to turn aside.

Felicity parked behind another car at the side of the road, and they all got out to stand across from the other visitor, all gazing upward at the giant monolith. She snapped a picture of Teddy looking duly impressed by the great metamorphic stone towering twenty feet above his head. She snapped three angles, then texted them to Antony, sure the pictures would reassure him of their safety. While she was doing that Teddy happily joined Isla in a race around the base—a useful exercise for getting wiggles out before completing the twenty-minute ride on to the top of the island.

As she drove on, Felicity hoped the day's jaunt would prove useful to her research. She wasn't sure how much there was available on her subject to add substance to yesterday's interview, but she was hoping that seeing the home Aileana Mackay had fled from, and then was so abruptly drawn back to, would help bring her journal alive. Hopefully getting to know Aileana better would make Felicity's talk more concrete—not just a nice, theoretical spiritual concept from a past event, but something that happened to a flesh and blood woman they could identify with.

In addition, taking the picture of Teddy gave her a new idea. She would take pictures—lots of them—and illustrate her talk.

Thank goodness she had photographed Donald John Smith and his home yesterday. They could stop and get photos of the Barvas church on the way back today. This was what she needed—the untold story of a young woman who lived it all, and photos to show that it was all still there. Just like the people her fellow spiritual directors might be working with right now. She headed for the top of the island with new enthusiasm for her project.

It was fortunate that a bit of internet research had yielded the fact that Cliff House, the former Mackay home, was still standing and, fortuitously, was for sale, although the realtor's listing mentioned that it had been remodeled more than once since it was built in 1919. Still, it didn't seem that things on the island changed very rapidly.

At the tiny Port of Ness village—primarily a few shops and a scattered double row of houses lining the road until it ran into the ocean—she turned onto a narrow, winding lane to the harbor. "Oh!" Felicity blinked when she stopped and looked up at the impressive white house standing on the green cliff above her. The phalanx of houses they had passed between had been mostly grey or tan roughcast bungalows. Felicity had been expecting to find something similar, or smaller, perhaps dilapidated, since Aileana had been so anxious to get away. Nothing in Aileana's journal had prepared her for this house, standing alone with its three steeply roofed gables in the upper story, its large windows facing the wide bay. Did the young Aileana sit behind one of those bare glass panes staring out across the water, longing to take a boat to the mainland on the other side? Or did she run with the wind, down the long flight of stone steps between the tall grasses leading to the perfect crescent of white sand beyond the breakwater with dreams of the future filling her vision? Felicity noted the cluster of boats sheltering behind the breakwater. Surely, in Aileana's day that would have been a fishing fleet?

While Teddy and Isla enjoyed the pristine silvery sand, Felicity took pictures for the newly inspired aspect of her project. Now she wished she had made arrangements with the realtor to view the interior of the house, but she would make the most of what she could see.

Fortunately, she had snapped a good selection of views before a small voice called to her from the beach, "Mummy, look!" A very sandy and very proud Teddy held out both hands, filled with a collection of seashells. Isla trailing behind him, her hands equally full and an equally satisfied smile on her face.

"What a wonderful collection! Well done both of you. Let's find a bag to put them in." Felicity led back to the car.

"Mummy, I'm hungry." The plaint came as soon as the beach-combing treasures were safely deposited.

Both women agreed whole-heartedly. The combination of fresh sea air and mild exercise was enough to make even Anna's substantial breakfast seem a thing of the past. "Playpark next?" Felicity suggested.

A five-minute drive took them to a broad green expanse leading to a tempting glimpse of blue water and white surf in the distance. Closer was an area offering swings, slides and various imaginative bits of play equipment as well as picnic tables, all surrounded by a rust-red fence. Felicity and Isla even managed a few quiet minutes enjoying the contents of the tea flask while Teddy, who had made quick work of three Scotch eggs, explored with a little blond girl just taller than himself.

Felicity basked in the breeze ruffling her hair, the sun warming her head, the wide unspoiled views under a pellucid blue sky, and the sound of children's voices mingled with seabird calls. "I've learned that one of the unexpected pleasures of traveling with children is that they take you to places you would never see otherwise."

Isla laughed. "Yes, and you see things in entirely new ways. I think I want to be a pre-school teacher."

When the mother of Teddy's playmate called her daughter to

go home, Felicity realized it was time for them to move on as well.

"You mentioned a lighthouse near here?" she asked Isla.

"Yes, just up the road a wee bit." Isla said, then paused. "Well, twenty minutes or so. But the views are stunning. And it would be a shame to come so far without seeing the very tip of the island. We might be able to make out the Faroes."

Felicity laughed. "If you don't become a preschool teacher, you can always work for a tourist bureau."

They were barely back on the main road when Felicity spotted a sign pointing down a dirt path to a low, oblong building built of the odd-sized stones Felicity had learned the Scots called random rubble. "St. Moluag's Church, Scottish Episcopal" it said. She had to think—almost count on her fingers—to be sure, but, yes, tomorrow was Sunday. She had given no thought to worship, but this looked charming. Whoever Saint Moluag was. She made a mental note to ask Antony.

As their narrow road continued northward, Felicity was surprised at how the entire island seemed to look the same—flat, green land that the Scots called machair dotted with small tan bungalows lining the road. And she was surprised at how many houses there were. "What do people do for a living clear out here? Is there farming?"

"Aye, sheep farming. We've a lot of small crofters. And fishing. A lot of weaving, too—home industry. You've heard of Harris tweed? A lot is actually made on Lewis. Shipped all around the world, it is. And, of course, with remote working some are employed by companies around the world but never leave their homes. I have a cousin in Carloway who works for a company in Japan."

Felicity nodded, then her attention was claimed by the tall, red brick lighthouse that sprang to view. Teddy saw it at the same time and pointed from his car seat. "Look, Mummy. Can we go up?"

"Och, I'm sorry," Isla answered. "I'm afraid not. It's all locked up."

Teddy's face fell. "I want to go up," he repeated when Felicity pulled into the car park.

"Sorry. No one does that now. But we can still explore from the outside."

"Is it still working?' Felicity asked.

"Aye, the light still shines, but it's automated—monitored remotely from Edinburgh now. No one goes in at all unless there's need for repairs."

They observed the towering structure, surrounded by well-kept white buildings, and Isla continued, "It's a radio control station now. They supervise all the radio stations in the North Minch. Perfect use for it, since it's nearly 37 meters high."

Felicity struggled to translate. Maybe more than 120 feet? But any attempt at calculation was whipped from her head as she stepped out of the car. "Oh," she gasped and struggled to tuck the ends of her long hair into her jacket to keep it out of her face. Even then, though, she hadn't realized how strong the gale was until Teddy decided he wanted to circle the lighthouse. They had been somewhat sheltered by the buildings closer to the parking lot and the low stone wall surrounding the enclosure. Then they stepped onto the green machair leading to the cliff edge. When she got her breath back Felicity squealed and grabbed at her light jacket to keep it from being blown off her back. "Teddy, hold my hand!"

Isla laughed. "I'm sorry. I forgot to warn you. The Butt has the dubious honor of being the windiest spot in the Hebrides."

"Can we go closer, Mummy?" Teddy tugged her toward the jagged black rocks extending beyond the smooth turf.

"Only if you hold my hand. Tightly." Felicity raised her voice and used her most no-nonsense tone to be certain her son knew she meant business.

In spite of the buffeting, however, the whipping of the wind, the menacing rocks, and crashing waves just a few yards beyond them all added to the exhilaration of the moment. There was nothing to do but give in to Teddy's insistent tug on her hand and her own instinct for exploration and follow the jagged coastline, watching the flocks of seabirds soar and swoop overhead.

Gulls were the only ones Felicity recognized from her childhood family vacations on the Oregon coast, but Isla pointed out plovers, shearwaters, and fulmars. Felicity wasn't sure which was which until a gannet made its spectacular arrow-like dive for a fish. She stood, rapt with fascination, as its winged fellows followed, making similar high-speed plunges into the surf. They never failed to come up with a flopping fish in their bill.

On around the edge of another jutting finger of land Felicity stopped to study the cliffside of the neighboring headland extending into the water. A gaping black hole in the face of the rock brought to mind Catriona's mentioning cave tours around the island. She hadn't considered before that the entire island must be ringed with caves. The thought caused a niggling itch in the back of her mind, but she had no time to connect the dots before Teddy was tugging again.

"Look, Mummy, it's that boat."

"What boat?" Teddy's pointing finger directed her gaze further out. Had he spotted one of the CalMac ferries with their distinctive red funnels?

Then she saw where her son was pointing. A sleek white yacht with a prow as sharply pointed as a gannet's dive. "Yes, that does look like the boat Daddy's friend..." She started to say there were probably a lot like that, but then it turned toward the back of the island and Felicity saw the name written in large, black script: *Selkie*.

Surely Antony's quirky student was still on Iona with him? It must belong to someone else—a friend who just gave him a ride to his seminar. But no, Antony had definitely referred to it as Roger Wellman's boat.

"Let's race it!" That time Teddy's jerk almost released him from Felicity's hold.

"No." Felicity was suddenly cold. She'd had enough blasting by the wind, enough of threatening terrain, enough of swish ships that looked like they could be used as an attack weapon. "We're going home."

A quick, hot supper and warm bath for Teddy, then she could cuddle in her eiderdown and return to the world of Aileana's story...

I held my sobbing sister in my arms all the way up the island in the back seat of Struan's car. The storm of tears had quieted by the time we reached Cliff House, so I was able to slip Faye up the stairs to our room without waking our parents.

I closed the door and pushed my sister towards the bed. "You've got to sleep, Faye. Here." I pulled the flannel nightie from under her pillow and held it out. Faye was like a rag doll, but I managed to get her into bed without waking our light-sleeping mother in the room down the hall.

I was certain Faye would sleep until noon, but morning sunlight was just piercing the dawn haze and streaking through our dormer window when I felt myself being shaken awake.

"Faye, go back to sleep. It's barely morning." I attempted to roll onto my side, but Faye was insistent.

"No. I can't. You've got to wake up. You have to help me."

I groaned. "What?"

"I've been awake for ages. I've tried to think of everything. I know Euan wouldn't have missed last night for the world. You have to help me find him. He must be sick or hurt or something. I've heard of Nazis hiding out in remote places like this rather than go back to Germany. Maybe Euan was captured—held at gunpoint..."

"Faye, stop! That's nonsense. There are no Nazis hiding on

Lewis." I made myself sound confident. But, really, what did I know?

"Well, something happened! You have to help me."

I pushed myself to a half-sitting position. "What can I do? What can you do?" I sighed. I didn't want to upset her further, but Faye needed to face the truth. "Look, darling, I know you're fond of Euan—"

"Fond of him? Fond? Aileana, I love him. I'm going to marry him. I don't care what Mam and Da or anyone says. I know what I feel!"

Faye was clearly working herself into a state. I put a calming hand on her arm. I knew that to remind Faye that she was still young, or that Euan was her first boyfriend, would just incite more fury. But certain facts had to be faced. "Fine, fine. But you need to think." How could I put this without making things worse? "Euan is fond of his pint. Maybe he snuck off to a—a howff with the lads, or even went to Stornoway to a pub, and—"

I had almost forgotten the term for a secret drinking place on this side of the island where prohibition held sway. But it made little difference what I called it, my sister wouldn't listen.

Faye gave a snarl of disgust and stomped across the room to her bureau. She yanked open a drawer and began pulling out clothes. "You're as bad as Mam. I'll do it myself."

I could hardly let my little sister traipse off alone in this state. I pulled myself out of bed. "A'right. Go put the kettle on and make us some toast. I'll be down in a minute." It was certain I'd get no peace until Faye faced the fact that her boyfriend had deserted her. Little wonder that Euan would get cold feet at the thought of marriage. I was quite certain he didn't have a steady job. So, if he did run off, where would he go? Would he have enough money to get to the mainland? His parents were small crofters near Barvas, but his sister said he hadn't been home...

I was still trying to think of something useful to do when

I sat across the table from Faye, spreading marmalade on my toast. Faye's drawn face and red eyes looked so desperate I knew I had to come up with an idea to give my sister hope—even if it was sure to be an empty dream. "I suppose we should start at the last place we know he was. When does the bus go down the island?" There would be no sense in asking to use the family car. Not as long as petrol rationing was still so strict. Da needed every gallon—"even the fumes," as he was known to say—so he could carry on his work as a builder.

"No bus till evening on Saturdays, but we can ride down with the postie and get the bus home. He should be along soon. What do we tell Mam?"

"Tell Mam about what?" Our mother bustled into the kitchen and pulled a cast iron skillet from the rack above the stove. "I'll have sausage and fried bread for you soon."

I took a final gulp of tea and stood up. "Sorry, Mam, I know I just got home, but Faye promised Janet McLeod she would help her today, and I need to talk to some people in Barvas." I thought fast. "Now that I'm home I'll be needing to get a job. Faye's going with me. She knows some people there. I have to get my bag." I flew up the stairs. If I got caught up in a debate with our mother...

Mam was still protesting when we pulled our coats from the peg by the door and fled into a frosty December morning. We didn't have long to wait until the small van trundled up our lane. The advantage to living at the end of the road was that the postman turned around and headed straight back down the island from our home. And the trip down was always quick because Angus would have stopped at all the crofts lining the road on his way up. Angus, who had delivered our post since I was a wee'un, greeted me and readily assented to giving us a ride to Barvas as he had done for as long as I could remember.

"It's a grand thing to be seein' ye, young Aileana. Had yer

fill o' the big city have ye? Or did ye come back for our meetings? Ye heard about our grand meetings even in Glasgow, then, did ye?"

It was obvious Angus was a proponent of these strange events that had conspired to deprive the youth of Lewis of our pipers. "I've heard some about them."

"Aye. Ye must attend. Fine, they are, but better felt than telt." I didn't know what to say to that and Faye, huddled in a corner, was no help at all. But Angus didn't seem to need any encouragement. "Start at the Barvas church, they do, every evenin'. Aye, that Duncan Campbell, he's a gallus preacher. Busses come from all over the island. Jammed to the rafters, the church is. Then cottage meetings after. Different home every night. Ah, it's guid. Plenty of young'uns—ye'll be wantin' to join 'em."

The silence required a response. "Um, cottage meetings?" That was the best I could do.

"Ach, aye. Folks are hungry, ye see? Hungry to hear the Word. Just hear the Word and sing and pray together. Goes on until all hours of the night or early morning. Homes are filled with people. Not joost the front room where the speaker is, but every room. People sitting on the stairs, the floor, people listening at the windows. All informal and sae friendly, just goin' on all night. Sometimes till mornin'" He shook his head and laughed. "Aye, ye joost don't want to leave. I got home at six this mornin'."

Angus drew a breath to continue but Faye pulled herself up and pointed to a dirt track turning off the main road that traversed the island. "Here, Angus. Let us off here. My friend lives just down here."

"Aye, the McLeod croft." Angus gave a satisfied nod.

We thanked him and fled up the path. Janet, just a year or two younger than Faye, answered the door. "Faye, Aileana! Er—come awa' in." She was obviously surprised to see us.

Faye rushed in ahead of me. "Is Euan here? Have you heard

from him? Why wasn't he at the dance? I don't know what to do—"

Mrs. McLeod stood at the kitchen door at the end of the hall holding a big brown teapot. "Come awa' in, girls. Have some tea."

I noticed that Euan's mother didn't seem overly concerned about her son's disappearance. We sat at a big, scrubbed oak table in the center of the kitchen and accepted steaming cups of tea. As soon as Mrs. McLeod picked up a bowl of kitchen scraps and left to feed the chickens, Faye practically pounced on Janet. "Euan—where is he? He promised me. Last night, he said. He promised." When Janet looked blank and shook her head, Faye rushed on, "You must have some idea. Have you checked with his friends? Did he go somewhere to look for a job? Have you checked with the Cottage Hospital?"

Janet gave a small chuckle. "A job? Aye, that would be a fine thing. How well do you know my brother? I don't think—"

I saw that Faye was on the verge of blurting out that she loved Euan and was planning to marry him—indeed, would be married to him already if he hadn't disappeared. Certain that wouldn't be helpful at the moment, I interrupted. "I hardly know him at all. Tell me about him."

Janet smiled. "A charmer, mo bhràthair, full of jokes and dreams. But nae sae steady."

"But he's missing!" Faye insisted.

"Aye. That's what I'm tryin' to tell ye. Are ye not hearin'? He's nae missin'. He's joost Euan. He goes his own way. Does his own pleasure. He'll nae dance to any piper."

"So, you've not been to the polis?" Faye didn't wait for Janet to reply. "And you've not reported him missing?" Her voice rose with each question.

"Who's missing?" Mrs. McLeod returned from her chickens with an empty bowl.

"Euan was meant to take Faye to the dance last night," Janet explained. "He didn't turn up. She thinks we should go to the polis."

Mrs. McLeod smiled. "I'd not be botherin' the polis. He'll turn up. He always does."

I was poised to calm my sister, but there was no need. Faye stood, stiff with controlled dignity. "Thank you for the tea. We'll be going now." She led the way to the door.

We were barely out of hearing of the house when Faye exploded. "They think it's a joke! Like—like Mary's little lamb, 'Leave him alone and he'll come home, wagging his tail behind him.' There's something wrong and I know it! I know him better than they do—I know the real Euan..."

I put an arm around Faye's shaking shoulders and urged her along the lane to the road. "Come on. The police are just up the road. We'll go there. Struan will help us."

In spite of being able to see our breath on the frosty air, we managed to walk fast enough to be comfortably warm when we arrived at the small, grey building that provides police protection to the little cluster of buildings comprising Barvas village and a wide surrounding area. The black and white Gaelic sign over the door read Stèisean Poileis.

"Fàilte!" I was startled, but not displeased by the warmth of Struan's greeting as he looked up from his desk and came around the counter to greet us. His wide smile made me want to step into his open arms with relief, but I restrained myself. "Tha seo na thoileachas."

"Not pleasure, Struan." I tried to sound stern. "Business."

"Oh, aye. Business, ye say?"

"You know. You were there! Euan McLeod is missing. You've got to find him. Something terrible has happened—"

"Wheesht!" Struan cut off Faye's torrent. "The chan eil e math has nae turned up yet, ye say?"

"He's no—no ne'er-do-well!" Faye's face was alarmingly red. It was time I intervened. "Struan, you can see Faye's upset. Truly worried, she is. There must be something you can do." Struan shook his head. "There's been no official report filed. He's an adult. It hasn't even been twenty-four hours yet…"

Faye jumped in again, "No—Janet hasn't seen him since the day before yesterday—she said so."

"There you have it, the family haven't reported him missing." He took a step backwards. "There's nothing I can do. You'll have to wait for him to turn up."

I didn't wait for Faye's outburst. I took a step towards Struan. "Nothing you can do—officially. We understand." I hoped Faye wouldn't contradict me. "But unofficially, couldn't you help us look—ask around a bit? Give us some ideas what to do?" I dropped my voice to a whisper. "Please, Struan. Faye's desperate."

"Aye. Right ye are. Have ye asked his mates?" He gave a dubious grin. "Or maybe he's off to a prayer meetin'—seems half the island is nowadays."

I started to thank him, but he stopped me with a hand on my arm. "I'm off duty at noon. I could take you around a wee bit. Places we used to go. Mayhap he went off to have a think—see the stanes at Calanais, or some such?"

It was clear Struan was making that up as he went along, but I realized anything to keep Faye occupied would be good—no matter what Struan's ulterior motive might be. I nodded and accepted the bill he pulled from a wad in his pocket with instructions to buy picnic fixings, then asked, "Unofficially speaking, where might he have gone for a wee drink with his mates?" Euan would have been unlikely to have the petrol to take him across the island to the nearest pub in Stornoway, but everyone knew there were plenty of secret howffs the police would turn blind eyes to on this side of the island.

Struan named two shops. "But don't go to the backdoor at

this hour—just enquire of the proprietor quiet-like on the side." He paused. "You didn't hear this from me, ye understand."

I nodded, then steered Faye towards the door. "We'll ask around for Euan, then get sandwich makings and come back here."

Struan's ready agreement did little to put my mind to rest. His warm greeting was pleasant and his willingness to help much appreciated—really nothing one wouldn't expect from an old friend. And yet—I couldn't help feeling his response was something more. And whatever "something more" might be, I was not ready for it. I was here as a result of what turned out to be my own overblown sense of duty, but I was in no way ready to acquiesce to sinking back into my old island life. Calum and my life in Glasgow were far too alive to be buried in a morass of the past. It almost seemed that the more I saw the twinkle in Struan's blue eyes, the more I missed the warm brown glow of Calum's—even when the warm glow turned to enraged fire.

Still, I was glad to see Faye looking more hopeful as we approached the fishmonger, which I considered the most likely location on Struan's list of possibilities for an after-hours drinkery. The best I could do, though, was to enquire as to whether Euan McLeod had been there late Thursday or Friday evenings. "His mam is worried," I lied, hoping that might move the stern-faced fishmonger to a softened answer.

"Oh, aye? If she is it'd be a first. Our Euan's his own man, as I'd think ye'd ken."

Faye's steps were dragging as we moved on up the street to the greengrocer. I received a similarly unhelpful answer, but Faye's fervent plea, "Mas e do thoil e, please!" in a voice near to choking, softened the grocer's wife standing nearby.

"We've nae seen yer young man for that many days. Or his mates. Off to the fancy high life in Stornoway, if ye ask me. Regular-like, he goes. Brags about it to his mates. You'd do best to look for a nice quiet lad instead of that tearaway."

My mind boggled. A jaunt to Stornoway? Frequent ones? But that would involve a vehicle, petrol, at a minimum money for bus fare. Where did Euan get such means? And now I thought again of the silk dress Faye had worn so proudly to the ceilidh. How did Euan come by such a thing? What was he involved in to have such resources at his disposal?

At least the grocer was able to supply us with oatcakes, cheese, and bottles of lemonade—and even a string bag to carry them in. When we returned to the station Struan was waiting for us. He pulled a brown paper parcel from under the counter. "A wee contribution to the picnic fixin's."

I laughed at his exalted description of our meagre provisions, then gasped in amazement when I undid the wrapper. "Chocolate! Struan Macaulay, where... how...?" I couldn't remember the last time I had seen a chocolate bar.

"Ye're best not asking." He tapped the side of his nose.

I smiled and added the rare treat to my bag before taking the passenger seat next to Struan. He was doing his best to be an entertaining host while Faye sat tense and white in the back as we headed down the island. I couldn't help thinking of the contrast we made to the easygoing teens we had been in that long-ago, halcyon summer before the violence of war shattered the world and changed life forever. Even though today's frosty weather did little to evoke memories of the picnics we had shared in more carefree days of the past. I couldn't resist losing myself in recalling a time of endless blue skies and warm days...

"Dinna fash yersel', Struan, they lassie's joost bein' coy. I'm certain she finds yer story enthrallin."

"Oh!" Struan's ironic, talking-to-himself comment brought me back to the present. A present with cold, grey skies, a ruined career, and a distressed sister. "Struan, I am sorry. I was thinking about the past—when we used to make this trek in Hamish's jalopy—that last summer with Jamie..."

"Och, aye. And yer wee sister and who-all else. How did we ever manage to cram so many in that old banger? Hamish'd only had his license about a month."

I made an effort to match his joviality. There was little to be gained by dwelling on past losses. "You'd be writing the neds tickets now."

The ploy worked and Struan carried on reminiscing about the happy times we had known when life was simple and both of our big brothers were so full of life—before German bullets ended them. I didn't even mind that he embellished it all a great deal and made us sound closer than we actually had been. I certainly had no memories of pairing off with Struan in our games of hide and seek, although I had enjoyed playing such games in and out around the ring of standing stones. The question was, did I want to make a pair with him now as he seemed to desire? He was certainly good-looking, helpful, friendly... but when I closed my eyes and thought about him, it was Calum's image that filled my mind. And made me shiver when I saw his scowl.

Aileana, my girl, you have to get over him. That's in the past. Put Calum Finlay Alexander right out of your mind, I told myself sternly.

My steely resolve was interrupted by a sob from the back seat. I looked up and saw we had reached the village of Carloway. The little white church with its flat, empty bell tower stood on the gentle rise above the road. And surprisingly, even now, midday on a Saturday, a group was gathered around waiting to get in. Was this one of those meetings everyone seemed to be talking about? Or were they praying? No—stranger yet—they were singing.

I rolled my window down an inch and let a few of the strains float in before I rolled it up again almost in disgust. Surprised by my own reactions, I considered. It wasn't the sound of the music. The light, sweet melody floating on the air wasn't off-putting. Nor could I claim my reaction was solely to the blast of sharp air that hit me in the face. I refused to consider the possibility that I closed the window against any desire to join in singing with them.

And it was just as well, because now Faye's single sob gave way to a flood of tears and I realized my sister's reaction had not been to the church, but rather to the village hall behind it. Less than twenty-four hours ago Faye had been ecstatically planning her elopement. If Euan had turned up at that hall last night, Faye Mackay would now be Faye McLeod. I was hardly convinced that would have been the best outcome for my sister's future, but I understood her heartache at the moment.

Fortunately, we arrived at the great circle of standing stones within minutes and Faye seemed willing to be distracted from her dismal thoughts. "We had some grand times here, didn't we?" Struan said, perhaps more heartily than the moment merited. He jerked his door open. "Race you to the centre!"

Suddenly, even Faye seemed to be swept back ten years or more to when she was just entering her teens, back past all those years the war and the continuing hard times of rationing had stolen. Back to a carefree summer of explorations, games, picnics, and long, golden evenings. I gave a shout into the wind and was off after Struan, following the stone avenue to the great dance of prehistoric monoliths circling the turf above Loch Roag with the hills of the Isle of Bernera in the background.

I reached the circle, panting for breath, and for a moment felt disorientated. I had been following Struan, intent on catching up with him, but now he had disappeared from sight. "Struan?" The only reply was the wind whipping off the loch and past the western stones. "Struan, where are you?" Now my cry was louder.

Standing still, I felt the bite of the wind, so I started following the uneven circle of jagged stones. "Help me find Struan," I called to Faye as she entered the circle from the avenue. Some of the stones were tall and thin, almost like trees; others, more squat and wider. Some the width of perhaps three men—plenty of room to hide behind. Beyond the circle another avenue, this one a double row, stretched nearly a hundred yards to the north. I had no desire to search behind every stone. I was cold, hungry, and out of breath. Definitely in no mood to be playing childish games.

"Struan, come out! Stop being a dobber! I want to eat!" I started towards the wide, central monolith.

"Aileana, stop." Struan rose up seemingly out of the ground and walked towards me.

I realized he hadn't been playing hide-and-seek behind a standing stone, but rather, kneeling in the chambered tomb to the east of the central stone. And his voice told me he had not been enacting a foolish game.

"What?" Instead of stopping as ordered, I increased my pace.

"Aileana..."

But before he could stop me Faye rushed up from behind a nearby stone, running straight towards the tomb. "What is it? Have you found Euan?"

Struan reached out to stop her, but she eluded him. She came to an abrupt halt at the edge of the stone-circled depression forming the tomb, then drew back from the rusty brown stains on the flat, rectangular stone beside the trench leading from the earthen bowl. And screamed. Struan was beside her in a moment, his arms around her, pulling her back. "Come on. It's a'right. Hush."

"But that was blood! Is it—was it—what...?" She ended in a strangled sob.

"Dinna be a ninny. It's nothing."

"No! I saw. That was blood."

"Maybe. Unlikely. If it is, it's from some poor animal—some scallywags playing at Druids like we used to do. Remember?"

He attempted a smile as he turned her around and propelled her forwards. "We'll eat in the car. It's too cold here." It came out as more of a command than a suggestion.

We made quick work of the oatcakes and cheese, washed down with our bottled drinks, before lingering over Struan's chocolate. It felt like we would never make up for its scarcity during the war—and even now it was hard enough to come by. When the last morsel had been devoured, we headed back up the island with somewhat lifted spirits and at a faster pace than we drove down. No one talked much as Struan was obviously concentrating on his driving. When we passed the Carloway church, though, I did notice an even larger crowd of people had gathered.

Back at Barvas, Struan parked beside the police station. "I'm sorry, ladies, I'd love to run ye home, but, uh, I've some work to do and it'll be dark soon." I took that to mean he wanted to investigate his findings further. Had he secured a sample of the bloodied rock for analysis? Surely modern science could tell him whether the blood was human or animal. Please, God, let it be animal. Some numpty with a chicken playing at being a Druid.

"Just time to catch the bus." I jumped out and began running towards the junction where the bus from Stornoway would stop on its single journey up the island for that day. Faye and I were standing in the wooden shelter, panting, when a thought struck me. I had barely caught my breath when the big ivory and maroon bus stopped to let out three passengers laden with bundles. As soon as I paid our fares, I asked the driver, "Were you driving yesterday and the day before?"

"Certain. Drive every day except the Sabbath, don't I?"

"Did Euan McLeod ride with you? Do you know him?" I started to describe him, thinking maybe Euan wasn't flush with money and ration coupons. Maybe just anxious to get away.

The driver's negative reply quashed that idea. "Certain I know him. I know my people—that's the job." He shook his head.

"I've nae seen the young scamp for a twelve-month or more. Above public transport, that one."

Faye's brief flashes of relief from anxiety seemed to fade and the winter sun sank further with every mile the bus lumbered up the island. The world was deep in a December dark by the time we arrived back at Port of Ness and we were both chilled through by the time we walked from the bus stop to the white house on the cliff above the harbor.

The warmth of the house and the familiar deliciousness of Mam's rich fish stew and fresh oatbread eaten around the family kitchen table worked their magic. I began to feel the stresses of the day fading. I was sufficiently mellow that even Da's evening reading from the big, black Gaelic Bible didn't set my teeth on edge like it usually did. I suppose I actually found it comforting to enter again into the long-buried rhythm of my childhood: Morning and evening every day of my life until I escaped to Glasgow, one chapter, Da's voice rising and falling in the musical Gaelic cadences. No need to focus on the words, just let it float over you like a soothing melody. It wasn't that my parents were particularly religious—for all their adherence to the tenets of the Wee Frees—the Free Kirk o' Scotland. This was simply life on the island. The practice proved you were a God-fearing family. Upright. Reliable. Near-to every household on Lewis would be doing the same. It made you part of the community.

That's what made Mam's words so shattering when Da closed the Bible. "We are going to a meeting tonight." She held our eyes, emphasizing the first word: "We are going." Then even more squarely at Faye and me in that penetrating way only my mother could look. "All of us."

I was baffled. Had my parents been attending these strange meetings the past week? In spite of the fact that The Reverend

Duncan Campbell, who seemed to be the focus of the whole thing, was from the Faith Mission—which was scandalously interdenominational in Wee Free ideology?

Whatever our parents were up to, there was certainly no reason for Faye and me to pay it much mind. Like everyone, the Mackay family had always made perfunctory attendance at the kirk down the road. But we never considered ourselves religious. "Joost be a guid person and get on with it. Ye know wha's richt. Do it." That was the philosophy of Skeena and Tavish Mackay. And it had always worked just fine. Religious fervor had nothing to do with any part of our lives.

Now, though, the pronouncement hung in the air, leaving no room for questions. Mam was known the length of the island as a determined woman. Jamie used to say, "The only reason Rome wasn't built in a day was because Mother was not there."

Still, I tried. "I don't have any clothes." It was true enough. I had asked Moira to send the things I left behind in her Glasgow flat, but they had not arrived yet. The outfit I borrowed from Faye fit me poorly.

"They are all laid out for you on the bed."

"But I don't know when to stand and when to sit."

"Just do what the rest do. You just come with us, for we are not leaving you here to make this place a synagogue of Satan."

I barely managed to stifle my gasp. How did Mam know that when they were away I would settle back with a book and turn up the Scottish dance music on the radio? That was her idea of a synagogue of Satan. Still, I knew when I was beaten.

Chapter Nine

Felicity set the notebook aside, metaphorically shaking her head at how times had changed since the middle of the last century. Now, such behavior as the Mackay's would be scorned as hypocritical. But she wondered, were we right to dismiss such attitudes with our air of modern superiority? Perhaps. But on the other hand, even the form of religion apparently provided a stable framework for their society. There appeared to have been true social cohesion in the community. And it seemed to have provided a structure for a deeper experience when the time was ripe.

Or maybe not. Maybe the form without the fire explained why the young people of the island had so firmly turned their backs on any aspect of faith. But then, our pious spurning of hypocrisy hadn't kept the same thing from happening today. Felicity was still pondering how this story could be useful to spiritual directors working in today's very different environment when her phone vibrated.

She grabbed it and ran into the attached bathroom so as not to disturb her sleeping son. "Antony! Oh, I'm so excited to hear your voice! I've got so much to tell you and so much to ask you and I want to hear all about your day, and I hope you can talk for hours! Please tell me you don't have to rush off to another meeting. Can't you miss Compline tonight—Oh, please!"

"Wait, wait!" The laughter that followed was wonderful to hear. "You haven't heard my voice yet."

"Oh, sorry." She bit her lip.

"The retreat house director is leading Compline, and I can talk all night—or at least until my battery runs down. Now, take a breath and do tell me about your day."

She had been so wrapped up in Aileana's adventure she started to tell him about the Callanish Circle, then realized, no, it was the Truishal stone they had visited, which made her ask, "Oh, did you get my picture—of Teddy with the stone?"

"Uh, sorry. I didn't think to check for messages—I was busy all day. Just a minute, I'll look." A pause, then a chuckle. "Oh, that's grand. Teddy looks so little next to that giant stone."

"Scroll, I sent three."

"Oh, yes. It looks—" He paused suddenly. "Felicity, did you take a good look at the third shot?" An odd tension had come into his voice.

"No, I just loved the first one of him looking up—"

"Look at it."

She pulled the photo up. "Oh, yeah, not so good. He was distracted by that guy coming around the stone."

"Not Teddy. That man. Enlarge it."

She did. "Yeah, bright shirt, no wonder it took Teddy's attention. And all that red hair. It was a windy—"

"Doesn't that look familiar?"

She thought. "No, should it?"

"I probably wouldn't have remembered either, but it's even the same shirt." He paused. When she didn't reply he added, "And you're supposed to be the one with the photographic memory."

"Sorry, must have run out of film."

"Our hike on Iona. The ravine with the dodgy diesel."

Now she remembered. Little wonder she didn't recall a lone hiker after what she had just seen in that crevice. Besides, it seemed so unlikely—impossible, really. "You're serious? You think it's the same man? Suddenly showing up on Lewis?"

"Look carefully. Think."

Felicity obeyed. "Mhhh, yeah, maybe... But this is Scotland—redheads are thick on the ground here." Still, she felt a niggling worry at the back of her mind. And there was something else she was going to tell Antony—another coincidence... But it was gone.

"You could be right. I hope you are." But he didn't sound convinced. Still, he went on to another topic, "Where are you going to church tomorrow?"

"Oh, yes—I wanted to ask you—we found the most charming little church up at the top of the island—Saint Moluag's. A sign said tomorrow is his feast day and they're having a special commemoration. I thought it would be fun to go there, but who was Saint Moluag? Have you ever heard of him?"

She should have known better than to ask. "Ah, 'Moluc pure—fair son of Lismore, of noble Scottish extraction' according to Butler. Educated in Ireland under Saint Brendan the Elder. In the middle of the sixth century, he evangelized Argyllshire and visited the islands as far north as the Hebrides."

"So, he was real?"

"Oh, yes, undoubtedly real—but obscure. Would you like a bedtime story? Are you sitting comfortably?"

"I would love it, but I'm not at all comfortable. Wait. I'll just go cozy back down in bed and listen to every word, but I won't say much because I don't want to wake Teddy." She scrambled back to the bed and plumped her pillows. "Now," she whispered and hugged the phone to her ear...

Born in the cradle of the Gaelic lands, he was known by many names: Luan or Lugaid, a beacon of light amidst the darkness that cloaked the land; Moluoc or Moluag, an affectionate name for the beloved Bishop of Lismore, Apostle of the Picts, and Patron Saint of Argyll.

When Moluag's studies in Ireland were finished, he, filled with a heart aflame for evangelism, chose twelve companions to accompany his mission back to his homeland. Tradition would have it that the very rock on which he stood by the Eireann shore detached itself from the Irish coast, and he was carried up the Sea of the Hebrides to the island we now know as Lismore, in Loch Linnhe.

Here he founded his community—on the island sacred to the Western Picts. Here, on the most important religious spot to the people he would evangelize, he would take his stand. A supremely desirable site it was, hallowed by pagans as the burial site of cremated Pictish kings from ancient times. This was to be his first centre, for did not Saint Brendan himself teach the importance of focusing on the similarities and the continuity between early Christianity and paganism rather than the differences between them? A building block from which to carry his hearers forward into the full Truth.

This would be Moluag's model, following the tradition of Saint Paul who told his listeners in Athens, 'For as I walked around and observed your objects of worship, I found an altar with this inscription: to an unknown god. Him I declare unto you.' Such would be the spreading of the northern light—a conversion process of proclamation and education rather than confrontation. Gradual and loving it would be.

But legend would have it that Moluag was not always so patient. It was the case that the sainted Columba, he also of Ireland educated and now evangelizing in the Inner Hebrides and Highlands, had, as Moluag, a desire to take the message to the farthest out, most northern islands of the land we now know as Scotland. And so arose the most famous of the legends that grew around Moluag. The two saints agreed a pact. They would not argue over the land. They would race for it.

So it was, the two missionaries, intrepid sailors both, set out in their coracles, determined to sail to the farthest island, and he who reached it before all else—who first touched the soil—would be the one to establish his mission work there. They sailed up the water we know as the Little Minch that separates the inner and the outer Hebrides, straight up to the northernmost plot of land—that known now as the isle of Lewis and Harris. From early morn, when they left the back of Columba's Iona, until late in the evening, rowing their tiny coracles like the valiant and hearty men they were, the two held course. The sun warm on their half-moon tonsured heads, the breeze whipping their homespun robes; sails set, oars dipping. And sometimes Moluag led, and sometimes Columba, but both steadfastly resolved.

As the sun sank in the west, the sky a glow of God's pink and gold, the seabirds calling them alike onward to victory, the tip of the highly prized island rose into view. And then it was that, with a mighty gathering of his muscles, Columba dug his oar deep into the waves, the wind billowed his sail, and he surged ahead.

Moluag likewise, gathered his best effort, adjusted his sail, plied his oar. He raced beside Columba for a time. Neck and neck, oar dipping beside oar. The land loomed a few yards ahead. Verdant green turf covering land with great outcroppings of sturdy stone structures. Certain to be peopled by those of equal heart. Hearts soon to be warmed by knowledge of the true God. The goal so near. Victory in sight. But it would be victory for Columba as he pulled to the fore. Inches only—but it would be enough.

Until Moluag drew his well-honed knife from his belt, severed the tip of his finger, and flung it ashore. Moluag's touch on the land was first. He would establish his centre here.

In spite of her determination not to wake her sleeping son, Felicity burst out laughing. "You can't be serious."

"Well… Remember, hagiographies are as much poetry as historical biography. They were written to tell the truth of the person, to exemplify their spirit, not to report the accuracy of the events. Look for the symbolism."

"Ah, yes. I remember my Church History lecturer giving the same advice." She smiled at the memory of sitting in his classes, rapt with her fellow students as Father Antony brought the ancient saints alive.

"Clever chap, he was. I hope you took his advice to heart."

"Every word." And she had.

"So, in Moluag's case," Antony continued, "the floating rock that carried the saint from Ireland to Scotland could be a lyrical way to express his enthusiasm for his mission, or the strength of his calling, or maybe his impatience—as the flinging of his fingertip well might. Or his determination, or his ability to think outside the box—or outside the coracle in this case.

"Whatever the details, we know that he travelled widely and was highly regarded as the Apostle of the Picts. By the time of his death in 592 he had established over 100 monasteries. He became the patron saint of the Royal House of Lorn and of the Kings of Man."

The next morning candles glowed beside the altar and morning sunlight streaked through the small square windows into the tiny chapel, warming the grey stone walls with a golden glow appropriate to the missionary known as bringer of light to the Picts. The pews of the little chapel, where services were offered only on special occasions, were comfortably filled. The responses to the prayers echoed from the walls as if the spirits of long-ago worshippers had joined them. The hymns included the familiar Old Irish hymn "Be Thou My Vision", and the new-to-Felicity "Alone with none but thee, my God", which she was surprised to see was attributed to Saint Columba.

The minister from St. Peter's Scottish Episcopal Church in Stornoway led prayers, then delivered a sermon relating the journeys of St. Moluag to those of St. Paul. The commemoration liturgy followed: "Let us remember before God His servant Saint Moluag.

The righteous live for evermore;"

"Their reward also is with the Lord," Felicity responded with those around her.

"O God the King of saints, we praise and magnify thy holy Name for all thy servants who have finished their course in thy faith and fear, especially today for thy righteous servant Moluag; and we beseech thee that, encouraged by his example, we may attain unto everlasting life; through the merits of thy Son Jesus Christ our Lord."

"Amen."

The small but wholehearted flock were dismissed with a Scottish blessing:

> *May the blessing of light be on you—light without and light within.*
>
> *May the blessed sunlight shine on you like a great peat fire, so that stranger and friend may come and warm himself at it.*
>
> *And may light shine out of the two eyes of you,*
> *like a candle set in the window of a house,*
> *bidding the wanderer come in out of the storm.*

Feeling truly warmed, Felicity walked across the machair to where Isla and Teddy were kicking a ball that, despite her years in Britain, Felicity still called a soccer ball. She gathered her son in her arms and swung him up in the brisk air.

"He'll be a right footballer, that one will," Isla said as she jogged across the field to them.

"Thank you so much, Isla." Felicity set Teddy on his feet with a small oof of relief. She wouldn't be able to do that much longer. "His wiggles would have been too much for that tiny chapel space."

She turned to her son. "Go get your ball. We're going to the beach." Teddy shot across the turf with a shriek of delight.

Through the past days Felicity was beginning to feel at home on the island. The presence of so few roads meant driving the same route repeatedly—a blessing for one whose sense of direction was not her strongest point. Today she felt herself to be among old friends at the sights that were becoming familiar to her as she drove past the turn-off to Donald John Smith's home where she had gone on her first day. Then the Barvas church on the rising ground to her left just before the turn eastward to Stornoway. At Carloway she spotted the community centre where Aileana and Faye had waited for the pipers that never turned up, then on to Callanish. Felicity smiled at the poetic imagery of calling that great, solid stone circle a dance. Still, she had to admit she couldn't think of a better term than dancing when she thought of running after Teddy among the monoliths.

In terms of a straight distance, they now weren't far from their goal of the Uig beach, but Felicity had learned that in Scotland, even more so than in England, distance must be judged by time, rather than miles. Here, the duration of a journey entirely relied on the number and length of the lochs one must travel around to reach their destination. And on the west coast of this sea-battered island, the lochs were many and long. In the distance the mountains of Harris rose, beckoning to them in slate blue ridges, some with their tops obscured by a swirl of cloud.

Since turning off the side road—narrow enough itself—the way became more threadlike until it barely accommodated her tiny, hired car. She could only hope she didn't meet anyone. She wasn't sure which would be worse—having to back up until she came to one of the little square, white signs marking a passing place, or having to face-off another driver.

Verdant green covered the rugged land with turf that encroached both sides, and tufty emerald patches dotted the center of the tarmac. A sturdy wire fence bordered the road keeping it clear of sheep. Yellow and white wildflowers blew in the wind everywhere, and enormous, rugged, moss-covered boulders were strewn about as if a team of giants had suddenly abandoned football practice.

Around a bend in the narrow lane and there, to the side of the road, sat a sturdy wooden carving of Uig Beach's claim to fame—one of the Lewis Chessmen. A decidedly Nordic looking king, his proud head atop a squat, stunted body, he sported a lush, drooping mustache, a long, bushy beard and a magnificent crown. Felicity stopped momentarily to point it out to Teddy, although a statue which would be taller than himself seemed destined to confuse a child's understanding of an object that in life was perhaps two or three inches tall.

Still, as she drove on, she tried to explain. "That funny-looking man is to let visitors know why this beach is famous. That statue is a very big version of one of what are known as the Lewis Chessmen. You know what chessmen are, don't you?"

"Like Daddy's. He said he'd teach me to play when I'm six."

"Exactly." Felicity smiled and for a moment she was back in her father's study, playing chess with the gentle, soft-spoken Andrew Howard. The remembered wood and leather smell of a small room filled with shelves of old books hit her so hard she almost gasped. And soon now Teddy would be playing with Antony. Truly, *one generation passes unto another*. Maybe she could get a replica set of the Lewis men for Antony for Christmas. What a delightful thing for Teddy to learn on.

They parked at the campsite at the end of the road and followed the trail over the rise. The first glimpse of Uig beach was breathtaking. A vast crescent of pale golden sand curved to both right and left. Felicity had read that here the rugged Atlantic coast was at its most dramatic with myriad islets and cliffs interspersing the sweeps of pristine sand. It was all of that, certainly, and yet, in spite of the weather-beaten harshness of the climate, her first impression was that all it lacked was palm trees to make the scene stretched before them look like a South Sea Isle. Well, that and warmth.

She pulled her jacket closer around her and took off after her son to the beckoning sands. The beach was so wide they could hardly see the ocean beyond, but water was not at the top of anyone's mind—food was. Breakfast had been little more than tea and toast for Felicity, and that hours ago. The eggs mayonnaise, apple slices, and packets of crisps Isla had packed to help keep Teddy amused on the drive down the island were long gone.

"Can we find a more sheltered place to eat?" Felicity suggested. In spite of her hunger, she had no desire to have sand blown into her food. Isla pointed to one side of the irregular bow-shaped beach where a formation of rocks offered an angled recess. "Perfect!" Felicity took Teddy's hand, and they jogged across the sand.

When the first half of her bap stuffed with whiskey-cured salmon had assuaged her initial ravenousness, Felicity turned again to the story she had begun in the car—the story that made her choose this beach above all the many others Lewis offered for their Sunday excursion. "So, I didn't finish telling you… That funny chessman we were talking about—lots of pieces, really—was made a long, long, time ago." She paused—how did you convey a concept of the twelfth century to a child? "Ah, back when there were knights and dragons like in other stories."

"Like King Arthur." Teddy got the reference immediately and Felicity resisted the impulse to be side-tracked by a more accurate attempt at dating.

"Close enough. And in a country a long way away called Norway." She pointed vaguely up the island behind her, hoping she was aiming approximately to the northeast. "The Norsemen were great sailors and carvers. They even carved dragon heads on the front of their ships. But the ocean voyages were long, so they had lots of time to play games—and chess was one of their favorites.

"Well, apparently, one of those dragon-headed ships pulled ashore right here." Now she gestured out to where the surf ran up onto the white-gold sand. "Because a long, long time later there was a violent storm here one night. The winds were so fierce that they blew the ocean surf right up onto the beach and washed away some of the banks around the edge. The next morning a crofter—a man who lived nearby in a little house—came down to the beach.

"Maybe he was looking for treasure after the storm, we don't know. But guess what—the wind had dug up a whole pile of these little chess pieces: kings and queens and bishops and knights and warders—what we call rooks. But he didn't know he had found treasure. This was back when people believed in faeries and gnomes and sprites—and that's what he thought they were. So, some people say he ran away, but others think he was brave and captured them."

Teddy thought for a moment. "I would have been brave."

Isla laughed. "Aye, you would have been, Master Ted the bold. How's that?"

He jumped to his feet. "Let's go explore."

"Your mother hasn't eaten her lunch yet. Shall we climb over these rocks while she finishes? There's another beach on the other side and some caves beyond that."

"I'll be done in a minute. I'll meet you on top. Don't go any further without me," Felicity ordered around a bite of her sandwich.

A few minutes later she tucked the remains of their picnic in Isla's bag and scrambled up the sheltering bank to encounter the wind on top again. She spotted Isla and Teddy right down at the tip of the promontory looking out to the rolling waves. Teddy ran to her, "Mummy, we saw the boat again." He took her hand and tugged her toward the edge of the cliff where foaming water crashed against the rocks.

"What boat?"

Isla answered. "The one we saw at the lighthouse. It did look like it, but we only saw the back."

"You know, Daddy's friend's," Teddy insisted.

Felicity nodded and smiled but regretted that she had failed to ask Antony more about his yacht-sailing student. She would remember next time they spoke.

"Can we go to the caves? Isla says there's lots of them." Teddy pointed to dark openings in the cliff wall on the far side of the tiny beach below them. "Please, Mummy. Maybe we'll find treasure."

"Well, I don't know. Are they safe?" She turned to Isla.

Isla nodded. "Safe as houses when the tide's well out, but I wouldn't like to take a chance when it's coming in. You could get a right drenching at best." She led to the tip of the promontory and gazed down at the white surf breaking on the rocks. "We'll nae be going on over today, Master Ted the bold. The sea has us cut off."

A gust of wind whipped Felicity's long braid and chilled the back of her neck, making her shiver. "How about going back down to our own beach—we haven't explored the other side of it. Then we need to be getting back."

Teddy turned and headed off with Isla close behind him. For the thousandth time Felicity shot a thank you prayer heavenward. She couldn't imagine what she would do without Isla.

A short time later Felicity was back behind the wheel, driving around the lochs and up and down the steep, rocky hills till they reached the wide, flat moor on top, then on to Stornoway. It had been a perfect Sunday, her "day off" with no real research, just fun. But when she got back tonight, she would at least continue her reading—after she called Antony to see what she could learn about his mysteriously unconventional student, he of the swanky white yacht.

As it turned out, by the time she had Teddy fed, bathed and satisfied with a second telling of the Lewis chessmen story, she found a loving, but frustratingly brief voicemail from Antony letting her know that he missed her but would be leading Evensong and Compline both tonight, so had turned his phone off. She sent him a brief text, then turned to Aileana's story…

Chapter Ten

Our family walked the two-and-a-half miles to the church with me pretending to be in a towering rage and storming up every step of the road. To tell the truth, I had begun to feel a bit of curiosity about what I would encounter. What was it that had drawn all those people we saw outside the Carloway church at a time when they would normally be working or visiting a neighbor or in some way tending to their own business? And, stranger yet, what had drawn my parents to attend these meetings that were such a deviation from their life-long practice of attending church twice on Sundays, then considering that a quite sufficient contact with the Divine—saving Da's after-meal Bible reading which was a matter of family pride and education.

When we got there, I was even more mystified. Even from the outside there seemed to be an atmosphere around the whole area. And inside was even stranger. It would have been spooky if it hadn't felt so, well—warm. Still, it was odd. In a church bursting with people—young and old—there was no conversation. Complete silence, filled with a sort of quivering expectation, was unbroken as people eased themselves into their seats.

Then they started singing. I had never heard singing like that. All my life I had heard Gaelic psalm-singing. Thin and unharmonious—drab I always thought. Tonight, they were still singing psalms, but from their hearts. The words rose to heaven like they had wings. Wings of fire. It went right through me and sent shivers up and down my spine.

The preacher stood and walked to the pulpit. People listened intently, glued to every word. There was a sense of something... something so tangible I thought I should be able to touch it. But I couldn't even think of a word for it. I didn't want to listen, yet there was no escaping it.

I walked home afterwards encased in a little ball of my own silence. Yet even then singing surrounded me—just floating on the breeze from other groups of walkers ahead and behind us.

"Well, Aileana, how did ye like the meeting?" my father asked when we were home.

"I did not!" I stormed up the stairs to bed without my supper, far too confused to eat.

"Are you going to the meeting tonight?" Faye asked me the next morning.

"I am not." I put all the scorn I could muster into my voice.

All day my head declared staunchly, No. I'll not go. Never again.

I was determined not to go. Yet that evening when the others left, my feet just walked along with them. In the best island preaching style the minister thundered forth his message: Eternal damnation to the lost, blessed salvation to the penitent. I could say one thing for him—that preacher believed what he said. The Gospel rang forth—the glory of redemption, the wonders of heaven. It was terrible and thrilling. Hell to shun; Heaven to gain. Concepts I had heard since my childhood, but now it seemed that an awareness of eternal things followed me. There was a canopy of God-consciousness over the whole area. I could not escape it. Not just in church. It was everywhere. He was everywhere.

By the third morning, I was desperate to break out. But

where could I go? What could I do? The meetings were all anyone talked about. Except Faye. All she talked about was Euan—who still hadn't shown up. I had been surprised when she continued going to the meetings, but I noticed she was distracted, not really listening to the preacher. Instead, she would spend her evening scouring the congregation, even turning in her seat to scrutinize every face. "Faye, sit still," I had nudged her the night before. "What are you doing?"

"I'm looking for him. Euan."

The desperation in her voice and the anguish on her face was still with me the next day. Then I realized how I could keep everybody happy. I found her at the breakfast table toying with a bowl of congealing porridge. "Faye, I just realized that's brilliant—what you said. That's what we can do. Everyone on the island is going to meetings. Every night. And our parents insist that we go whether we want to or not. So, we'll go."

My sister's sorrowful eyes clouded with confusion. "Why? What are you talking about?"

"Oh." I realized I had been recalling our whispered exchange the night before so vividly it felt like Faye had just spoken. "Last night. You said you were looking for Euan. We'll search for him—all over the island. In every meeting. Everyone will be happy because we're going to meetings. I can even ask Struan to take us." It would give me an excuse to go, but something else to think about when thoughts of God and Heaven and Hell got too uncomfortable.

Faye threw her arms around me. "Oh, thank you, thank you! I didn't think you cared." She started sobbing.

"Here." I thrust a hanky at her. "Mop up. I'll go tell Mam." That gave me pause. What would I tell our mother? "I'll say we want to hear the famous minister in Barvas tonight. We can take the bus. Struan will bring us home."

That evening it appeared that my plan was working perfectly. The bus arrived in good time and when we walked into the police station Struan seemed delighted to see us—and even more delighted to promise to take us home. He apologized for not attending the meeting since he was on duty—although he didn't sound so very sorry. But he would be "Verra, verra happy" to see us home after.

I appreciated his readiness to assist my scheme, but I would have been more comfortable if he hadn't ended with a suggestive wink.

Things only started going wrong when we arrived at the church. We were well ahead of the appointed time, but the church was so full we couldn't get in. It seemed everyone wanted to hear the famous Duncan Campbell, come all the way from Edinburgh. A large crowd of regular parishioners stood around the iron-railed stairs leading up to the arched, red front door. All around, people were complaining that their church was so filled with strangers they couldn't get in.

It seemed there was nothing to do but sit in the empty vehicles and wait for the church to empty so they could take a turn at holding a meeting. At first, I was dismayed. We couldn't wait for a second service. Mam would be worried sick if we arrived home so late. Then I realized, this provided a perfect opportunity. We could go from one bus to another, talking to people. We knew some of Euan's mates, and if none of them had come to a meeting—which would hardly surprise me—we could at least ask young men of his age if they had seen him.

I explained my plan to Faye. "You take the lorries. I'll take the busses. There should be enough time to talk to any likely looking lad. Then when the others come out, we'll watch for Euan until Struan comes to take us home."

Faye looked doubtful. "I won't know what to say."

"Say his mother is worried." Faye bit her lip. Her reluctance irritated me. "Look. We're doing this for you. Do you have a better idea?" She shook her head, making her blond curls bounce. "Right. Start with the big blue one over there." I pointed to the lorry with people huddled close together for warmth on its cargo bed, then turned to the first bus which had now filled with waiting worshippers.

In the third row back, I spotted a likely looking chap who wasn't caught up in the hymn-singing that was starting in the back of the bus. He scooted to make room for me to perch on the seat. I gave him a tentative smile and plunged. "I'm sorry to be a disturbance, but I'm looking for," I paused, "my friend's brother."

"Oh, aye?" He looked skeptical.

"Yes. Do you know Euan McLeod?"

He raised one eyebrow. "Only by reputation. Ye'd be better off with me."

That was hardly what I expected from someone waiting to go to a meeting. I hoped he'd get converted—he obviously needed it. I moved on down the aisle of the bus, apologizing for interrupting the singing when I spotted someone I felt I might have seen Euan with in the old days. He nodded at my query. Yes, he knew Euan McCleod but hadn't seen him since the war. And that was as much information as anyone seemed to have.

I was beginning to regret my clever idea by the time I had worked halfway down the aisle of the third bus. This one was even worse than the first one. Here the people had chosen to pray rather than sing. If I wanted to ask a question, I had to put my mouth close to the person's ear and whisper just loudly enough to be heard above the murmurs of invocations being sent to heaven.

I actually did find a schoolmate of Euan's who said he remembered him well but hadn't seen him for years. The woman sitting next to him stared at me until I stood up and started to the back of the bus, trying to decide whether or not to abandon the whole idea.

I had half turned when I saw someone I remembered. I had met Artair during the second summer I spent as a volunteer errand girl at RAF Stornoway. When I was sent with a message to the RAF Police Station, I was flattered by the attention from the young aircraftman in his distinctive red cap that marked the military police. Later though, he was altogether too friendly when I helped out at the canteen where my mother volunteered.

Now, he looked up and gave a little wave from the last row of the bus. He had either forgotten the cold shoulder I once turned on him or was willing to let bygones be bygones. He indicated the empty spot on the bench beside him.

"It's grand to see you, Aileana." I was surprised that he remembered my name, but he had always been good at that sort of thing. At least, this bus was less crowded than the others and it was easier to talk here at the back—as long as we kept it to a whisper.

"What are you doing back on Lewis? Are you still with the RAF?"

He shook his head. "Not so much call for military police these days. I'm with the Ministry of Fuel and Power now. They sent me to Stornoway to follow up on a case that appears to have links to Lewis. It was a natural since I'd been stationed here."

We spent a few minutes catching up. Then he asked, "Have you been attending the meetings?"

"A few." I tried to sound nonchalant. "Tonight, I'm trying to help a friend, though. Janet MacLeod." I thought I might as well try to make this sound good. "Do you remember her?"

He thought for a moment. "Little kid in plaits and glasses? A few years ago, anyway. Her brother spent some time in our detention cells, and she pestered us about visiting him. We couldn't allow it, of course."

"In a cell? You arrested Euan?" This was worse than I had

imagined.

"Not as I remember. I don't think it came to that. We detained him pending further investigation as I recall. There were accusations of some of the Air Recruits stealing petrol from the base and selling it on the black market, but nothing was ever proved." He shook his head. "That was, what? Four, five years ago? I may be remembering wrong." He shrugged.

"We are talking about Euan McLeod, right?" I needed to be sure before I told Faye this.

"That sounds right. Is he in trouble again?"

I sighed. "I don't know. He's disappeared. We're all worried." Now I wasn't fudging. I was getting worried. It did sound likely that Euan would have been mixed up in something more serious than a lad's lark during the war. And now? Maybe he never stopped.

The elderly couple on the far end of the bench joined in the prayers energetically enough to make conversation difficult, but I was lost in thought anyway. If Euan had been involved with black-market petrol during the war, might he still be? Fuel was still severely rationed, and that would explain his willingness—and ability—to drive all over the island. And his access to sufficient cash to buy a silk dress for Faye. Maybe even to consider getting wed—if he had been serious about that.

Unlikely as it seemed, this opened a whole new explanation for his disappearance...

My thoughts were interrupted by movement from the front of the bus. People had begun coming out of the church. There would be a scramble among those waiting to get seats inside. We both stood up. "I can ask around a bit for your friend," Artair said as I began moving slowly up the aisle. "Are you on the telephone?" I shook my head. "Well, give me your address. Or check in with me at RAF Stornoway." He winked. "Just like old times."

Still too full of himself, I thought, but I thanked him, mum-bled something about it being nice to see him again, and hurried off the bus to find Faye.

She stood to the side of the waiting crowd. In a sea of happy faces, some glowing ecstatically, others serenely peaceful, her misery made my heart ache. Her lowered head and slumped shoulders told me she hadn't learned anything. Not anything good, anyway.

I hugged her. "We'll keep looking. There're meetings all over the island. We've barely even started." I hoped I sounded more optimistic than I felt.

Chapter Eleven

Felicity put the manuscript aside with difficulty. Only the knowledge that her son would be bouncing on her bed at the break of dawn—which came incredibly early on this far-north island in midsummer—forced her to turn off her light. She was really beginning to identify with Aileana now.

The whole thing she had been reading about Aileana being raised with the cultural observance of church ritual chimed perfectly with Felicity's background. Her family, too, were regular church attenders—every Christmas and Easter. She hadn't encountered real belief until she went off to study in a theological college in Yorkshire.

Felicity smiled at the memory of being thrown together with her church history lecturer over the murder of her favorite monk. And her irritation at Antony's insistence on the life-changing reality of encountering God through faith and prayer. Until she faced instant death at the barrel of a gun and found that all those stories of ancient saints Antony kept boring her with held true for today as well.

Life-changing, indeed. Like Aileana, Felicity had abandoned her own career plans. She smiled. How thankful she was now that she hadn't carried out her scheme to become an activist for political justice through a role as priest. In those days when she thought she knew everything she hadn't even heard of spiritual directors, let alone considered becoming one. Helping people one life at a time was a far cry from the rallies and marches she had dreamed of leading. And far more satisfying.

Even the hints of problematic petrol in Aileana's journal seemed to carry echoes of Antony's report of dodgy diesel. What if…

A few, brief hours later, Felicity's dream of being tossed by wind and rain in a small boat in a loch ended abruptly when she realized it wasn't a Hebridean storm—it was her five-year-old son. "Teddy, Stop!" She fought to sit up and force her eyes open. Then she discovered her storm-tossed dream hadn't been only Teddy. Rain really was battering her window. She recalled the driving, horizontal rain she had experienced on pilgrimage in Wales. That was in June, too. Did it rain like that in the Hebrides, as well? Probably worse, her mind answered. Thank goodness she had arranged local interviews for today. This would be no day for driving across a peat bog or exploring a beach.

She reached for Teddy's jeans and the heavy, knit jumper left by his bed the night before. "Let's get you dressed, and you can go get a start on that nice bacon I can smell Anna frying for you. Tell her I'll be there as soon as I've rung Daddy." *And had a long, hot shower,* she promised herself as she guided her son to the door. Thank goodness their B&B hostess was great with kids and kept a supply of her own children's outgrown toys for visitors. But the thing that would really keep Teddy occupied was Orion, the family's big black dog.

Occupied for the moment, that is. She recalled Isla mentioning a place called Adventure Island for indoor play. She looked it up on her phone. Perfect. Isla and Teddy could spend the day there. That settled, she tapped on Antony's number.

He came on immediately. "Good morning, I was just going to

ring you."

"Lovely. Great minds and all that. I can't wait to tell you all about our day yesterday. I'm so sorry I missed your call last night. I want to hear about your day, too. But Saint Moluag's was lovely and then we went to Uig. Teddy loved the story about the chessmen. And we think we saw your student's boat—strange, that. But first, what do you know about the black market? It seems like there's something going on from RAF Stornoway and..." She paused for breath.

"Black market? What are you talking about? I thought I was used to your *non sequiturs*, but there's no black market that I know of. Isn't RAF Stornoway closed? I thought it was just an airport now." Antony sounded even more confused than Felicity felt.

Then she realized the source of her disorientation. "Oh, sorry. No. I mean, yes. It's Stornoway Airport now. I fell asleep reading Aileana's journal last night. And it seems like there was some black-market activity on Lewis. Right alongside this amazing revival that was sweeping the island—isn't that odd? Or maybe not—light and dark side by side—I think you said it's always like that."

Antony laughed. "You don't know how much it pleases me to know that you actually listened to my lectures—and better yet, remember them."

"Of course. How could you doubt me? Still, though, it does seem like an oxymoron. But the thing is, reading about that stuff made me think of the dodgy diesel you mentioned."

"You think there could be a connection between barrels of contaminated diesel on Iona today and black-market activities on Lewis in the 1940s?" The skepticism rang loud and clear in his voice.

She sighed. "No, not really a connection. It just seemed coincidental that we should encounter such similar things so far apart and they sort of got tangled together in my mind. Aileana's journal is really quite engrossing..."

"And you have a very active imagination." She could hear the smile in his voice now. "Still, I get it." He paused. "Maybe it's not so coincidental, really. That is—remote islands, times of economic stress, locations readily accessible by boat, plenty of hidden caves—the perfect ingredients for nefarious activities. Rum-running, contraband luxuries, moonshine… It's been that way throughout history."

His mention of boats and caves reminded her. "Yes, that's the other thing I wanted to tell you—well ask you about really. We saw that boat—yacht—*Selkie*—at the lighthouse the other day. Then yesterday at Uig again—at least Isla and Teddy said it looked a lot like it. So, that non-traditional student of yours, you did say he owns that yacht, didn't you? Not just sailing with a friend? Do you think he might have loaned it to someone or something? Is he still there with you?"

"Yes. No. No. Yes. I think that's the right order. It is definitely Roger's boat. He tries to maintain a suitable humility, but he really is inordinately proud of it. And it's not quite as frivolous as it sounds. He belongs to some sort of Christian boating association that does charity things."

Felicity started to laugh, thinking of a single friend of hers who wanted to start a ministry to hunks. Then she recalled the Countess of Huntingdon who used her Park Avenue mansion so effectively to share the Gospel with her aristocratic friends. Maybe not as self-serving as it first sounded.

Antony continued, "If you're thinking *Selkie* might be being used for gun-running or something, let me put your mind at rest. I heard Roger give his captain a strict reminder. It seems his oldest son Roger *fils* is something of a tearaway. He used to have a great time on Daddy's yacht until Roger *père* discovered the drug bashes young Rog was hosting. Roger was furious—banned his son's use of the *Selkie* and cut his allowance."

"Does he have other children?"

"Not sure. I think so, but are you sure you saw *Selkie*? Roger mentioned she was going to some marine engine place for a repair."

"And you heard that yourself? I mean, that's really strange, but I definitely saw her—I read the name clearly. Second time, not so sure, but Isla seemed pretty sure." She told him about the sightings in more detail. "And one more thing. This coast is riddled with caves. Some are rather famous and get a lot of tourists, but others could be really hidden..." When Antony was silent, she said, "I know. Over-active imagination. Never mind."

"No. That's not what I'm thinking. I'm thinking I wish I were there with you. Can you leave now?"

"Leave? I have interviews scheduled all day here. There's a new library that should be excellent for local history. My work is really coming together. I just need a bit more to round out what I'm getting from these journals. Besides, I'm not at all sure any ferries will be sailing for a while—we're having a doozie of a storm."

"Are there police there?"

"Yes, of course." She thought it a strange question until she remembered that there were no police on Iona.

"Then tell them. I don't like this." He sounded authentically worried.

"Okay, if you think it's important—"

"Tell them about Iona and the man you saw both places—show them your photo." His voice was thick with worry. "I would come to you if I could."

"What nonsense!" Felicity forced herself to sound brighter than she felt at the moment. "You have a job to do there. I have a job to do here. We'll stick to our plan and meet in Glasgow when we're done. Your students—"

"My students are adults. They are set to do independent research on Celtic Christianity and work with the Iona Community for the rest of the week. I'm just supervising. No one's going anywhere in this storm—we have it here, too—but when it finishes..."

"Antony, don't be silly—I'm fine. There's no need..."

"Mummy, Anna says do you want breakfast?" Teddy stood in the door with one arm around Orion.

"Yes, darling, tell her I'll be right there."

"Time for Morning Prayers here, too," Antony said, but he sounded reluctant to hang up. "You'll remember? You'll do what I said?"

"I will, I promise. I love you."

She pushed the end call button, then stared at her phone for a moment. What had she promised to do?

"Mummy—"

She sighed, at least a good breakfast would help her face going out in this storm. She mentally ran over the list of all she had to do that day, then started to the door after giving Aileana's notebook a lingering glance. It would be a perfect day to stay in and read—if only... *Later*, she promised herself.

Chapter Twelve

But after breakfast the fury of the storm, and Teddy's contentment playing with Orion, convinced her to allow herself just a quick dip into the journal. Then, she promised herself firmly, she would take teddy to Isla and get on with her interviews.

"Oh, why did I ever undertake such a crazy scheme? I'm exhausted. And we've barely begun. Just look at this!" I slapped the unfolded paper on the bed beside me.

Faye glanced at me with that perpetually distressed look she had worn since Euan's disappearance. "It's a map of Stornoway. So?"

"Faye, there's just no way we can do it—attending meetings in hopes of finding Euan is a fool's errand. Every village on Lewis is holding meetings. In the unlikely event that Euan is going to meetings—and do you really think that's probable?—what are our chances that we turn up at the same one?"

"What? I thought this was your idea. And we have to do something, or I'll go spare. We could maybe try just the big ones. The ones Mister Campbell preaches at, maybe." Faye's words barely phased me, but her voice nearly broke my heart. My frolicsome little sister, pleading like she was staring into a great, dark pit.

I sighed and tried to sound reasonable. It was the best I could do. I couldn't manage encouraging. But she was right. I had suggested it. This was my own fault. "I suppose we can try. But even then, it's no easy thing. Duncan Campbell preaches in one church at seven o'clock, in another at ten, in a third at twelve, then back to the first church at three o'clock in the morning. And cottage meetings continue in homes after most services."

The silence echoed in our room. Then it was shattered by the ringing of the doorbell.

It was obvious Faye wasn't going to move and Mam had gone to the market, so I rushed downstairs, not sure whether I was relieved by the interruption or irritated. More irritated, I think. I yanked the door open.

"Calum!" I took a step back and blinked. "Calum Finlay Alexander. Is it really yourself?"

"And who else would you be thinking it is?"

"A ghost from another world." Even my voice sounded spectral in my own ears—like it, too, had come from somewhere long ago and far away. I stepped back to let him in before the winter wind chilled the whole house as it had already chilled me.

"Tea. I'll make tea," I managed and gestured for him to sit on the sofa in the front room. Instead, he followed me to the kitchen and sat at the table.

When the kettle was on the stove I turned to him. "I never thought to see you again."

"Then you reckoned without Great Auntie Ida."

That rang a faint echo. Maybe he had mentioned having an aged relative here. I was far too focused on other things when I lived in that fantasy world they called Glasgow. The kettle boiled and I turned back to the stove, glad to have something routine to focus on.

"Two great aunties, actually. Christine and Ida Smith."

I gawped. "Ida? Everyone here calls her Peggy. And Christine? They're your aunties?" I still couldn't take it in. "The Praying Sisters? The ones who started all this—" Words failed me. I circled my hand in the air.

"The same. Insisted I come, they did. I ignored the first two telegrams. I was careless with the third—left it on my table and my mam saw it when she stopped by to visit. Family duty to the old dears and all that—so here I am. Why being ancient and blind gives a person the power to order people about I'm not sure, but it works."

I set the big brown teapot on the table with a jug of milk alongside cups, saucers, and spoons, then took a seat across from Calum. Ony when I sat down did I realize how weak my knees were. I hoped my hand wouldn't shake when I poured the tea.

In contrast to the state I was in, Calum seemed perfectly at ease, as if his icy rage at the station had been only in my imagination. "Moira told me your parents survived." He even managed to say it without sounding accusing. Or adding I told you so. "How have you been?"

I took a gulp of my tea. Only when it scalded my throat did I realize I had forgotten to add milk. When I finished coughing, I still didn't know how to answer him.

"A'richt. Never mind that. Then tell me about these meetings. I'm going to have to go with the aunties and I want to know what to expect. Do you attend?"

"We've been going every night. Faye and me. The whole island goes. I'm exhausted..." I realized I wasn't making sense. I took a deep breath, then a sip of properly prepared tea. What were the meetings like? How could I put my jumbled feelings into words? Truth to tell I was spooked by them—by my feelings even more than by the meetings. Wanting to be there, but hating them; trying to stay away, but always going. I just shook my head.

Calum tried again. "Why do I have the feeling I keep asking

the wrong questions? Let me start over. Have you been singing?"

I was still far from calm, but at least my heart wasn't pounding so loudly I couldn't hear my own voice. I had tried so hard to put Calum out of my mind, out of my heart... I took a deep breath. "Sing? We don't do anything but sing. Walking to meetings. At the meetings. Walking home from the meetings. The whole island. You can hear people singing from one village to the next. It really is remarkable."

"That isn't what I meant."

"I know it isn't. But everything's so strange. Right at first— one night. I did sing at a ceilidh. I thought I'd never sing again, but I couldn't help it..." And then I was telling him everything. It was such a relief just to let it all pour out. The pipers who got religion. Euan who disappeared. Faye's distress. Our attempts to find him. Struan's help. The blood at Callanish. Everything.

Calum had poured himself his third cup of tea and my cup was stone cold by the time I got to describing our attending meetings in an attempt to look for Euan, and my meeting Artair who I had known during the war, and what he told me about Euan being suspected of sneaking petrol from the air base to sell on the black market... "And nothing makes any sense and I'm so tired and Faye is desperate, and I don't know what to do." It took every ounce of willpower I could summon to keep from bursting into tears and flinging myself at Calum for comfort.

He just nodded his head. "Aye. Puir wee lassie." The fact that Calum had reverted to a deeper Scots than he used in Glasgow indicated that my tangled tale had moved him. Did someone actually understand? "And ye've no one to help ye?"

"We can't really talk to Mam and Da. Struan, he's the local polis and an old friend, sometimes he takes us to the meetings. The police can't do anything official because Euan's family won't file a report, but Struan seemed to give a thought for the blood at Callanish." I shivered at the memory.

"So ye cog Euan just got caught up in the ecstasy of these meetings? Without even going home to eat or sleep or change clothes? Is that likely?"

Even for a barmpot like Euan I knew Calum was right—the whole thing was an unrealistic grasping at straws. I'd known all along. I sighed. "No. It's far more likely he's gone off on a bender. But I have to do something for Faye. And it keeps the parents happy because we're at meetings."

Calum smiled. "Oh, aye. I know. Now I have to keep the aulds content, too." He drained his cup, and I poured fresh ones for both of us. "But does anyone have any serious theories about what could have happened?"

"Serious or sensible? Euan was always a wee gadgie and he never grew out of it. He never worked, but always seemed to have money." I told Calum about Faye's silk dress. "He could be stealing, running from creditors… or maybe the idea he was taken by the Nazis is plausible. And then Artair said he was accused of stealing petrol for the black market during the war…" And this was the man my sister was in love with. I shook my head.

"Nazis? Are there Nazis hiding here?"

"Theories. Rumors. What they're calling the Ministries Trial at Nuremberg—some say leaders in the party hierarchy are hiding in remote places. Well, we're remote, I'll give them that. Who knows?"

Calum thought for a moment. "Black market sounds more likely to me."

"But the war's over."

"Rationing isn't, though. Most people still want more petrol than their coupons will buy. That's why Parliament passed that law last year requiring red dye in commercial petrol to prevent its resale for private use."

"But would someone buy red petrol? Wouldn't they be arrested or fined or something?"

"Aye, indeed, they would—that's why thieves do things like filtering it through charcoal, or dissolving aspirin in it. Washing it through bread is the easiest. I'm hearing a good Scots wholemeal loaf is the best. But then with the rationing off bread so recent, folks are still more wanting to eat their bread than muddy it up with red dye."

"Calum, how do you know all this?" I hoped my frown was fierce.

"I've plenty of mates from the back streets of the Gorbals. A canny lot they are. Ye pick up plenty in the pub." He grinned and winked, then turned serious again. "I'm telt that washing petrol is actually getting more difficult—The Min of Fuel and Power are a canny lot. Changed the formula for the dye. Since then, evading rationing has focused more on counterfeiting."

How did one counterfeit petrol? But before I could ask, the kitchen door opened, and my mother blew in with the wind. Calum jumped to his feet to help with the shopping she carried. "Mam, this is Calum from Glasgow—he's a nephew of the Praying Sisters." I introduced them formally.

"It's a pleasure to meet you, Mrs. Mackay." Calum looked at his watch. "I need to be getting' on—The Aunties, you know. Mayhap I'll see you at the meeting tonight?" He looked at me. "I'd offer to come for you, but I'll have the aunties."

"Oh, there's no need. Struan will take us."

My answer must have been too quick—or too enthusiastic— because Calum's curt nod indicated he wasn't best pleased. He turned to the door without another word. Why couldn't I understand him better?

Faye was waiting for me in our room. "Who was that? Was it someone who knew something about Euan? I was afraid to come down. If it's bad news I don't think I want to hear it."

I gave her a brief hug. "You are a goose. It was an old friend from Glasgow. I think I mentioned Calum. He's here to take his auld aunties to the meetings." Faye was in dire need of a distraction. It would be a perfect time to take her for a walk, but the weather was Baltic. I looked around for an idea and spotted the Bible I had purchased at Mam's direction lying by my bed unread.

I had to smile at the memory. I had carried it to the next service after I got it. A lot of the young folk were going up to Reverend Campbell and asking him to sign their Bibles and write in them. I joined the queue arguing with myself. What if he refused? But why would he? He wouldn't write a greeting to someone unconverted. But then, he didn't know I was unconverted. Of course he would autograph my Bible. But how embarrassing if he wouldn't. The worry remained. After all, ministers were away in their own important world, a world from which I was completely excluded. Who could tell what they knew?

I decided to give it a miss. I started to dart out of the line when the young woman in front of me stepped aside and I was face to face with the great Duncan Campbell.

He smiled. A truly warm, genuine smile, and held out his hand for my Bible.

I don't remember what he said, I had worked myself into too much of a state. He must have asked my name, because he signed it: To Aileana Mackay, it says. I just remember being overwhelmed by how human he was: so nice, so approachable, so kind. I was very glad to have his name in my Bible.

But I had never read it. Faye, likewise, had a Bible by her bed. Never opened. "Let's read our Bibles."

Her face registered shock at my suggestion. At least I had managed to distract her. She looked around as if to figure out what I was talking about. "But what if someone comes in and sees us? We'd look right numpties."

I pulled two issues of the popular magazine "The People's Friend" from a stack by the window. "Here. Open it to one of their grand love stories. If there's a sound on the on the stairs, put it over your Bible."

We had planned to go to a meeting in Kinlock that evening, but Struan was late calling for us, so we agreed to go to the meeting in Barvas rather than arriving late at our planned destination, even though it was unlikely Euan would be anywhere so close to home if he was hiding, and we hadn't been to Kinloch yet.

As usual, Faye spent the first half of the meeting twisting in her seat and craning her neck. Then slumped into a morose little lump for the rest of the service. Tonight, though, she sat up when Duncan Campbell took to the pulpit. He announced his text: "Thy word is a lamp unto my feet, and a light unto my path." He held his open, big black Bible up with both hands. "This is the lamp of God. Its eternal words are the Light of the World for all people."

Duncan Campbell returned his Bible to the pulpit and leaned forward, towering above the congregation. Then he pointed right down at us—right at Faye and me. "You've got 'The People's Friend' in one hand and the Bible in the other."

My gulp was so loud I'm sure the people standing outside heard it. I slid down in my seat and wished I could go clear through the floor. I don't remember another thing about that service.

I was still stunned when the meeting ended. I just wanted to go home. Since the ground had refused to swallow me up, going to bed seemed like the only option left. But Faye wasn't giving up. "Let's go there." She pointed across the road to a group that was forming in the field beside the loch. "He might be there."

I wanted to scream at my sister's obstinacy, but it was easier just to follow along. Struan made it clear that he had no objection as he smiled and took out his police-issue torch to guide us down the slope. Still, I dragged my feet.

By the time we joined them, most people were singing a Gaelic hymn. It was dark, but most folks carried torches because they had walked across the moor to the meeting. Still, it was too dark and there were too many people, and it was too cold. Faye would never find Euan. Even if she borrowed a torch and shone it in the face of everyone here. Even if Euan were here—which I was quite convinced he wasn't.

A group near us quit singing and began praying. Loudly. Across the field voices mingled and carried on the night air. Singing. Praying. Crying to heaven. Then Duncan Campbell, who had followed the group across the field from the meeting, extended his arms and began to speak—whether to God or to the people, I didn't care. I just wanted to go home.

Of a sudden a light flared in the window of the croft behind the minister. A moment later the door opened, and a small woman swathed in a black shawl slammed the door back against the wall. She banged her walking stick on the floor for attention. "Wheest! Will ye stop this stooshie? Haud yer tongues, the lot o' ye. Can a body no get her sleep?"

The minister turned and extended his arm towards her. "Awa' w' ye, Mother. Ye've been asleep long enough."

Amazingly, the woman closed the door of her croft behind her and joined the group as the preacher began admonishing his avid listeners on the dangers of being asleep spiritually.

"Struan, let me borrow your torch," Faye begged. "I need to look..." Her voice trailed off. Apparently even she realized the hopelessness of her boundless tenacity.

Struan appeared reluctant, but before he could answer a familiar male voice spoke over my shoulder. "Here, use mine. I take it this is yer sister, Aileana?"

"Calum. What are you doing here? I thought you were with your aunties?"

"Needing their beds, they were. Auntie Christine's arthritics were playing up something fierce. I saw the auld dears home, then thought I'd join the group." He grinned. "Glad I did. If you hadn't been on the edge of this curn o' folk I'd never have spotted ye."

"You mean—" I started. Was he looking for me? But Struan cut me off.

"It's time I was getting you two home." He jerked my arm almost roughly.

As much as I agreed with the sentiment, I dug my heels in. I would not be dragged about. "Struan, this is Calum. From Glasgow." I turned. "Calum—Struan, an old friend."

Their acknowledgement of the introduction seemed to be a mutual glare. But maybe it was just the dark that made it seem so.

I continued. "Faye, I told you about Calum."

She didn't wait for the second half of the introduction. "Oh, yes, I'm Aileana's sister and thank ye ever so much! I'd be most grateful for the loan of your torch." She held her hand out. "I have a friend... that is, I lost... I'm looking..."

Calum extended his elbow rather than the light he held. "How about borrowing my torch with me attached?"

"I'm taking the lassies home now." Struan sounded more like he was pulling a drunk from a stramash down the pub, than escorting two girls from a prayer meeting.

"No, please—" Faye began.

"I'll bring her home." Calum said it to me, ignoring Struan.

I nodded. "I'll tell Mam and Da you've stayed on at a meeting and ye're getting a ride with a friend."

At least Faye was happy. The men still glared at each other and I—how did I feel? The meetings were bad enough. The same confusion I'd felt ever since I attended that first meeting just kept getting worse. I was frightened and drawn at the same time. It was like being pulled—and repelled—by a strong magnet. And now—Calum. Why did he have to show up just when I was beginning to come to terms with having cut my ties to all thoughts of a singing career? All thoughts of escaping to the big city. All thoughts of Calum. Struan was my knight errant now—complete with all the reassuring comfort of my childhood memories. Of the home I thought I'd left behind.

And yet...

Chapter Thirteen

"Oh, aye. I was just a bairn, but I remember it weel." The small, wrinkled face split with a dreamy smile and the blue eyes took on a faraway look. "Seventy-five years ago, that was."

"What can you tell me about it, Shona?" Felicity prodded, her pen poised over her notebook. By the time she arrived at the second care home she was scheduled to visit the rain had settled from furious deluge to steady drencher that gave a staccato background to her interview.

The head of wispy white hair shook from side to side and Felicity's heart sank. "Don't you recall anything?" She meant to ask gently, but she was afraid she sounded desperate. This was her third interview from a list of names the librarian had supplied her with when she enquired about people she might talk to—people who experienced the Awakening in person. The first one had dementia, the second was profoundly deaf. Shona Macritchie was her last hope.

The surprisingly clear eyes looked straight at her. "I said I remember it weel. Putting it into words is a different matter. It was a feeling over the whole island. A body couldn't escape it, whether ye wanted to or no. Like most of the young people, I wanted to. How do you describe a feeling? It was just there—like you could touch it."

Shona set the rockers of her chair going. Back and forth, three times, up and down. Then she spoke in rhythm with the motion. "One night I attended the regular meeting I always went to. That's what you did. There wasn't anything else to do. Didn't matter whether you were converted or no. You just went.

"After that meeting, off we went to another about nine miles away. The preacher preached on the marriage feast of the lamb, and I realized: *I want to go there.* It just washed over me. Like heaven was bending down over my soul. That was it. It was like telling a friend you accepted their invitation to their birthday party. Or their wedding. I was so happy. I felt so light I hung onto the pew so I wouldn't float off.

"After that we all climbed back aboard the coal lorry with all our friends. It was regularly washed down to take people to the meetings, ye ken? When we got home, we all thought, what a shame to go to bed. We didn't want to part. We wanted that glorious night to go on and on. So, we walked along the shore."

She smiled, then closed her eyes and Felicity was afraid she had drifted off. Shona spoke softly. "Such a lovely moonlight night, and this group of young yins walking along the shore. Jesus with us—just like He must have walked with the disciples by Galilee. We began to sing above the sound of the waves."

And she did. Her old voice soft and light, a whispered memory:

> *A nis cha'n urrainn neach air bith ach Criosd a shàsachadh,*
> *Gun ainm eile dhomhsa,*
> *Tha gaol is beatha, is aoibhneas buan,*
> *A Thighearna Iosa, a fhuaradh annad.*

Shona smiled at Felicity's bemused look and switched to English.

*Now none but Christ can satisfy,
None other name for me,
There's love and life and lasting joy,
Lord Jesus, found in Thee.*

"'Weel, we had better go to bed,' someone said at last. 'It's a waste of time, but we'd better go.'

"Then someone else said, 'We'll pray first.'

"But none of us had ever prayed out loud before, so we just stood there on the seashore, a little group of teenies with bowed heads. Not a sound except the sound of the sea, and silently lifted up our hearts, all thankful-like."

Shona opened her eyes and grinned at Felicity. "Ye nae thocht I could forget all that, now, did ye?"

Felicity was still smiling as she awaited her gammon and cheese bap in a nearby sandwich shop. She couldn't speak for Shona's memory—but she knew that she would never forget that interview.

She was happy now with the material she had gathered for the historical part of her talk; her only trouble would be squeezing her information into the allotted time. That was the inspirational part was well seen-to. But what about the workshop she was to lead afterward? What did she have of practical advice for her fellow spiritual guides? Could she really draw lessons for today from all she had learned? *Wash down your coal lorry? Carry a torch to meetings?* She was immediately ashamed of her flippancy, but it did seem her mind worked that way.

Well, she still had her afternoon. It would be back to the library for her. After another cup of tea before heading out into the continuing rain.

The librarian had assured Felicity this morning that she would have a stack of books on the revival waiting for her when she called back. Lissy, her brown hair pulled back in a neat ponytail long enough to swing across the back of her thick Aran sweater, led Felicity to a quiet corner where a pale pinewood table held three stacks: pamphlets, paperbacks, and a few serious looking hardbacks.

The pamphlets and paperbacks were mostly eyewitness accounts and testimonies—all stories adding detail and color to those she had already encountered. None, of course, in the detail of Aileana's notebooks. Felicity made a mental note to encourage Wendy to consider donating these treasures to the library archive. Felicity looked at the rather forbidding stack remaining.

Nothing in any of the accounts she had read so far had given any hint of a missing young man—although almost all of them made reference to the story of the Carloway Pipers. And sure enough, she found other mentions of the 'People's Friend' sermon and the ancient crofter being told she'd been asleep too long. It was good to have Aileana's account corroborated, but she needed more. Should she explore the red petrol situation? No—surely that would be a rabbit trail. Her fellow SpiDir members would expect practical helps for today's spiritual seekers, not interesting history or intriguing mystery. Our world seemed so different now. So removed by far more than just time and distance from the post-war Isle of Lewis. Technology, values, ideas…

And yet, she knew peoples' hearts, emotions, and basic desires and needs remained the same. She opened her notebook and began a list. What did people today need the most? Want the most? To know they are loved and to be able to give love; safety, physical and emotional; a sense of their place in this confusing world… her pen flew down the page.

When the flow of ideas stopped, she looked back at the top. How different were these from Aileana, Faye and her friends? Very little, indeed. And what had the Awakening done to fill those needs? Individually it opened to each person the reality of something bigger than themselves. It brought them into contact with the Divine. It set them on new paths in harmony with the order of the universe. In modern terms, opening themselves to the Holy Spirit had put them in sync with the cosmos and its Creator.

But it wasn't just individuals. It was the whole island, and those all around, the whole of the Western Isles. It created Community. Felicity smiled, thinking how much Antony would love this. All his work with the Ecumenical Commission had been to that end. To break down barriers, to bring people together. By bringing them to God.

Community. She circled the word. So important—and so lacking in the modern world. But still alive, even today, in the way she had seen people working together here in this small dot in the North Atlantic. She felt comforted to know that in many ways the long-ago event she was studying still bore fruit today. Could it happen again? In other places? That was the sort of thing those attending her class would ask. And if so, what could they do?

Felicity sighed and took the top book from the stack. She worked down the pile, reading, skimming, jotting notes. By the third volume the repetitions seemed to be forming a pattern. But that wouldn't do at all. It was too obvious. Too simple. There was nothing new, startling, exciting. Her class would want—

She smiled and dropped her pen as the realization struck her. Spiritual directors had the same problems as those they were seeking to guide. The same problem she had—always looking for sophisticated answers. Always wanting something new, something exciting. And the answers were so old, so mundane. And so vague when people wanted clear, step-by-step directions. What do you do if you want to help your community or an individual seeker find awakening, peace, the Divine?

Still wanting to resist, telling herself it wasn't enough, Felicity shook her head and picked up her abandoned pen. Her entire workshop would consist of three lines:

Prayer, constant and fervent, individual and communal, spoken and silent, formal and spontaneous.

Obedience, to Scripture and to what the Spirit told your spirit. Felicity started to mark that out. Too spooky. Too wishy-washy. Too self-abnegating. Too counter-cultural. Not popular qualities in current times. The line remained.

Openness, to God and others, willingness to believe and receive and follow. *Physician, heal thyself,* Felicity thought. But when she remembered how rash and stubborn she had been a few years ago, maybe it wasn't so hopeless. She still had her moments, but she did stop to think more often now. Formation, the monks at The Community of the Transfiguration would call it.

She sat for some time staring at her notes and at the books and pamphlets covering her table, but not really seeing anything. At last, she shrugged, well, there it was—that was all she could do. Maybe lightning would strike, and she would get some earth-shattering insight. But she had a sinking feeling that she had her answer.

A glance at the window told her the wind had picked up. It was driving rain horizontally against the windows. There was no chance of Antony getting to her today. And Teddy would be happy at his play center with Isla. Teddy loved ball pits, and their website had featured a super-looking one. So, she might as well stay put until the rain let up at least a little. Surely that much fury couldn't last very long. It was summer after all. She could wait it out reading the journal she had tucked in her bag before leaving her room that morning. She hoped they would find Euan, but it did seem hopeless.

She stuffed her materials in her bag and abandoned her workspace for a comfy looking bright orange easy chair against the wall. Before she could pull out Aileana's journal, however, she spotted a stack of newspapers on a low table beside her chair. She glanced at the paper on the top of the stack. As always, war, royals and sports captured the headlines, followed closely by political squabbles and assorted scandals. Felicity sighed, *As it was, is now, and ever shall be.* But pictures of the elegant Princess of Wales were always worth looking at. She picked up the paper and scanned a couple of pages. Then a headline caught her eye, an announcement of a Polish company producing a revolutionary new biofuel from waste products. "This alternative fuel is known for high calorie content, great quality, efficiency and low ash content." That sounded good. But, the article continued, concern existed that importing such products from Poland at severely low-priced levels could damage the local biodiesel economy.

Felicity wasn't sure what the problem with lower fuel prices would be, but apparently it was all speculative anyway. She started to turn the page when she saw a related article: "Paraffin in Diesel Blamed for Widespread Lorry Breakdown". Wasn't that what Antony said the police on Iona were investigating? She read on:

"Authorities believe a criminal network may be responsible for the widespread incidence of lorry breakdowns in Scotland. Over 15,000 incidents of blocked diesel filters have been reported in Scotland in recent months, according to the Department of Transport. Paraffin in the fuel is blamed for the blockages which are causing mayhem on motorways with traffic pileups and crashes resulting in injury and death.

"High diesel prices have driven motorists to seek out bargain fuels. Paraffin, at about half the price of diesel, is a frequent choice for an additive. Adding paraffin to petrol for economy and higher performance has a long history, but modern engines are increasingly sensitive to contaminated fuel. A vehicle might run for some time on such contaminated fuel, then suddenly break down. Scotland's recent unseasonably cool weather makes the paraffin solidify more quickly, increasing the risk of breakdown and damage to the motor.

"Under normal conditions paraffin added to diesel improves viscosity and lubrication. However, when temperatures begin to fall, the paraffin thickens and turns into a cloudy mixture. This is known as fuel's 'cloud point'. The wax can clog fuel filters and solidify until the fuel no longer flows and renders the engine useless."

The article went on to recount how paraffin, which Felicity reminded herself to read as kerosene, was used as fuel for engines as disparate as jets and lawnmowers. It could serve as an inexpensive and efficient fuel in the right circumstances. The article then undertook an analysis of percentages of kerosene to petrol and various formulas that made Felicity go cross-eyed. She had hated high school chemistry and time had not improved her affinity for the subject.

The next paper in the stack was a tabloid noted for its sensational journalism. Below a report of a Member of Parliament clubbing with a nude model, a war scare, and the latest suspected bribing of a top footballer were the headlines: "DoT says Dodgy Diesel is Murder". Felicity scanned the article declaring that anonymous sources believed a vicious criminal ring was smuggling cheap foreign diesel into Scotland, cutting it with kerosene and passing it on to unscrupulous venders. They quoted an unnamed Department of Transport official saying that "Scotland has sustained 174 traffic deaths in recent months, a 17% increase over the year before. Many caused by illegal practices. Additionally, Scottish motorists suffered 1,556 serious injuries, a 2% increase over the previous period."

The paper then called for an immediate, full-scale investigation by law enforcement to crack down on such illicit practices. Followed by a list of severe criticisms of the efficiency of the Scottish Police Authority. Then a rant about the environmental disasters caused by fossil fuels such as paraffin in terms of greenhouse gas emissions, non-renewability, and associated extraction impacts.

Anonymous sources, unnamed official. Felicity shook her head and thrust the paper back on the table with disgust. Until she realized that was no way to treat library property. She retrieved the crumpled pile and repentantly smoothed out the creases, folding properly on the original lines. As she did so, she thought again about the first article, cheap refuse-based diesel from Poland...

She pulled out her phone and consulted her favorite information-in-a-box—*What port in Poland is closest to the Isle of Lewis?* she asked.

The answer appeared instantly on her screen: *The port in Poland that is closest to the Isle of Lewis is the Port of Gdańsk. It is one of the largest and most significant ports in Poland, located on the southern coast of the Baltic Sea. It is a major hub for maritime trade and transportation.*

Felicity considered. A busy, international port, sure to be closely regulated, was not a likely choice for ne'er-do-wells, was it? She typed another question: *What about a smaller, more private port?*

Again, a hair-trigger response: *A smaller, more private port in Poland that is closer to the Isle of Lewis would be the Port of Świnoujście.*

Another option could be the Port of Kołobrzeg, which is also a smaller port situated on the Baltic Sea. Kołobrzeg is known for being less congested and might offer a more private and quieter docking experience.

A quieter docking experience would certainly be what someone attempting to smuggle cheap Polish biofuel to the UK would want. She opened a map on her phone and looked at the route from Kołobrzeg to the Port of Ness, which she had witnessed to be a very quiet port, indeed.

A bit of time checking maps and staring at formulas of how to estimate time and distance for a private yacht brought Felicity the unhelpful information—well, estimates, really—that it was about 800 nautical miles from Kołobrzeg to the Port of Ness and it would take several days to navigate it. But, of course, one must consult up-to-date weather forecasts and tide charts and consider other variables. She sighed and closed her phone.

Well, she supposed it didn't really matter where it might come from; the fact remained—it was possible to ship cheap fuel into the Hebrides. Then adulterate it with cheaper yet paraffin? Then what? Sell to an unscrupulous supplier to cause economic and mechanical mayhem? And death?

She unfolded her carefully refolded newspaper and scanned the article again. Yes, she had remembered correctly, it wasn't only death from motor crashes. Air pollution from dodgy diesel emissions were estimated to cause premature death for 5,000 people a year. Murder, indeed.

And those making money from such corrupt practice would certainly be willing to commit actual murder. She shivered.

Squeezing her eyes shut against the memory only made the image sharper: a scuffed hiking boot, a rumpled khaki sock, a stretch of hairy, heavily-muscled, male leg disappearing into the gorse covering the side of the gully... sun glinting off the rims of metal barrels beyond... Gulls swooping overhead...

Not a simple misadventure for a hiker who then got up and walked away.

She jumped to her feet. Lissy was at the information desk. "Where is the police station?" She had promised Antony, then forgotten all about it.

"Up the street, left on Church Street. A three-minute walk. The librarian pointed. "But you don't want to go out in this do you? It's stoatin' doon."

Felicity pulled her rain hat from her bag. She was clear to the door when she realized she hadn't even said thank you. And, no, she didn't want to be out in this monsoon, but she was driven by a far more compelling urge. At least, once she turned the corner, the wind was to her back. Never mind that the rain soaked through her mac in moments.

"You need to contact the police on Iona." The young constable at the desk looked startled—whether by her abrupt words, or the fact that she was dripping water all over his papers, didn't matter.

She had his attention.

"I'm sorry, lass. Iona doesn't have a police station. We're the headquarters for Police Scotland in the Western Isles." His voice held a ring of considerable pride.

"No. I mean, Yes, I understand." She pulled off her hat and raincoat, abandoning them to a puddle on the floor, but at least the precipitation on the constable's desk stopped. "There are police there now. From Glasgow. That is, there were a couple of days ago. Investigating—" What? Smuggling? Murder? "Investigating. I have information for them."

He looked skeptical, but her urgency must have communicated itself to him, if not her sense. "Would you like to step in here, Miss?" He picked up a notepad and nodded to a woman officer who took his place at the front desk.

The room was just large enough to hold a table with a chair on each side and more folding chairs stacked against the wall. "It's been really strange—" Felicity started as soon as they were seated and Sergeant Macabe, as his name badge read, had taken out his pen. Did all surnames on Lewis start with M? It seemed so.

Sergent Macabe held up a hand. "If I could just get a few details first, Miss."

"Oh, yes, of course. It's Mrs. actually." She rattled it all off as fast as he could write: her name, contact information, then the discovery in the gully on Iona, her suspicions from reading the newspapers, the yacht *Selkie*, the man from the trail on Iona who suddenly appeared on Lewis… "Wait, I've got a picture." She took out her phone and scrolled through her recent shots, then held it out to the officer.

After a quick glance he reached into his pocket, pulled out his own phone, and gave the screen a few taps. "Can you airdrop that to me? Here's my contact."

Felicity followed his precise instructions and a moment later heard the satisfying whoosh that meant Sergeant Macabe now had the photo she had inadvertently taken of the man at the Truishal Stone. He returned his phone to his pocket without looking, but she assumed he would later.

"You'll let them know all this? The police on Iona? My husband's there. They talked to him—" She felt compelled to relate her anxiety to this officer. He was so calm, so methodical. Couldn't he see—this wasn't just a matter of routine? "You've got to understand. The body was gone. They think he just slipped and was dazed a bit, then walked off. But I saw him—the seagulls had pecked. The flies—" She covered her eyes with her hands momentarily. "He was dead. Murdered. I know it."

"Yes, Miss, er—Mrs. We'll take care of it. Thank you for your help. Would you like a cup of tea before you go?"

"No." Felicity shook her head emphatically. The sergeant's placidity increased her sense of urgency. "Teddy. I've got to get back to Teddy." She fled to the reception room, barely pausing to stoop down at the front desk to retrieve her soggy rain gear.

"Stop that! Behave, George." The female voice behind the counter was accompanied by a giggle and a playful slap at the sergeant standing very close beside her. Felicity rose, clutching her still-dripping garments. And came face-to-face with the very head of red curls she had just seen again in her photo. Wearing a police uniform.

Chapter Fourteen

"Felicity, what on airth?" Only when Catriona cried out at her appearance did Felicity realize the state she was in. Panting for breath and soaking wet, she had run all the way from the police station, oblivious to the weather and to anything but the primal instinct to get to her child and protect him.

She only eased up on her gripping hug of Teddy's soft, warm five-year-old body when his cry told her she was frightening him. "Oh, sorry, darling." She sat back on her heels. "Mummy missed you so much today." She forced her voice to sound calm, bright, normal. "Tell me—what did you do?" Then she saw the wet patch she left on his shirt and accepted the towel Isla held out to her.

"After the ball pit Isla made play dough—not out of a can. I stirred the pot and it was warm and squishy."

"How lovely, what did you make out of it?"

"Stuff we saw. Caves, boats, the lighthouse, that big stone—I forgot its name."

"That's lovely, darling." But she was concentrating more on drying her hair than on Teddy's prattle. Once she was reasonably dry and had changed into the warm skirt and jumper proffered by Isla, it took little persuasion for her to accept the invitation to stay to dinner and partake in Catriona's cottage pie and freshly baked bread.

On their second cup of tea, with Teddy happily watching a "Bob the Builder" rerun on the telly, Isla asked, "Now tell us, what possessed you to run like a skarrit hare through that downpour? You were in a right old state."

What could she say? *That man you didn't even notice at the Truishal stone, but happened to get in my photo, he's the same one we saw on Iona maybe going toward what turns out to be probably a stash of dodgy diesel and then after I had poured it all out to the police, what did I see but that he was a policeman, and I don't know if he's working undercover or if he's bent or if I'm going crazy, and I simply panicked, and...*

She sighed and shook her head. "I don't really know—it's probably nothing. I saw someone who looked really threatening and, well—I do have a very good imagination. Besides, I was missing Teddy and with the rain and everything..." She shrugged, realizing how lame it all sounded. And then she realized—her car was still in the car park by the library.

"Ah, you wee pet." Catriona was in her most motherly mode. "Don't be shy of telling us you're missing your man." She reached across the table and squeezed Felicity's hand. "I know all about that with Cameron off on the oil rig for weeks at a time." She sighed.

Felicity nodded and did her best to produce a brave smile. Warm and dry, with a full stomach and congenial company, it was easy to believe she had overreacted and that there was a simple, logical answer to all her questions. That officer the woman at the desk called George was probably on Iona and at the Truishal Stone for entirely innocent reasons. Policemen did take holidays, didn't they? Go on hikes? Sight-see? Or it was all a case of mistaken identity? Maybe he even had a twin brother. One saw a lot of curly red hair in Scotland... She continued to argue with herself.

"Why don't you stay here tonight?" Catriona offered. "You can ring your B&B so Anna won't worry. Anyone would understand your not wanting to go out in this blattering."

Isla laughed when Felicity blinked at Catriona's term. "Heavy rain that makes a lot of noise," she translated.

That was exactly what it was. Felicity was delighted at the idea of staying put for the night and accepted gratefully—after somewhat shame-facedly asking Catriona to take her back to retrieve her car.

Once Teddy was tucked in bed and his heavy breathing told her he was asleep, she slipped to the now empty living room to call Antony. She had so much to tell him. As her phone rang, she began running through all she wanted to say, so that when it switched to voicemail she just carried on talking in the middle of where her thoughts had taken her. Never mind wasting time telling him how frustrating it was to have to talk to a piece of technology when she wanted her flesh-and-blood husband.

Deflated, she crept back along the hall, slipped into bed beside her sleeping son and took Aileana's journal from her bedside table. Once she'd read of Calum's return she simply couldn't stop…

A few weeks later, with our subdued Christmas observances thankfully well behind us, a morose Faye and I were just finishing washing the supper dishes when there was a knock at the door. Faye gave me that apprehensive look that had become so characteristic with her of late—half hope of good news and half terror of bad news. "I'll get it," I said.

"Kirsty Anne, thank goodness." Here was someone who might be able to cheer Faye up. She and Kirsty Anne, who lived just down the road, had been freens since infant school. I led the way to the kitchen, hoping to see a smile from Faye.

Instead, her frown deepened. She took one look and sighed. Her tone was caustic, "I see you've got it."

Kirsty Anne flew across the room and threw her arms around her friend. "Faye, don't you understand anything? I don't have

'It'—I have 'Him'. Come to the meeting with me tonight—I can't explain it, but you'll see..."

I turned from the room in disgust. I was determined. No more meetings for me. If Faye wanted to go with her friend, it would be on her own head. And I had no desire to wait around to hear Kirsty's story. What was one more conversion? By now I felt like I'd heard it all. Revival was the talk of the island. Go where you would, they'd be talking about what had happened the night before, or the night before that, when so-and-so had come to the Lord. 'Did you hear, Mr. X, who has been such a drunkard, is now praying in the cottage meetings?' And so it went on. And on. And on.

The worst was Mam's betrayal. At least, that's what it felt like to me. It would have been all right if this conversion business hadn't come to our home. Attending meetings was one thing. Getting religion was another matter entirely. It was good for some. But not in our home. All along there had been fear in my heart lest any of our family became concerned for their souls. We're good people. Respectable. We never hurt anyone. Wasn't that enough?

Just three nights ago I should have been watching out for Euan, but instead, I was keeping my eye on Mam who had taken the daft notion of sitting down at the front. For all her insisting that Faye and I go to the meetings, and her and Da attending regularly, she had remained her stoic self. Perfectly happy to observe the conventions without making any personal commitment. But she seemed different that night. She never chose to sit in front before. One of the back three rows of pews had always been good enough for her before, thank you very much. But now she was intent on the preacher's words.

To my consternation, I saw her take out her white handkerchief and wipe the tears from her eyes. Then she buried her face in her handkerchief. And worse—far worse—frighteningly, I felt a solemn sense of God come over my soul.

When we arrived home that night, Faye and I hardly knew how to speak to Mam or what to do. We trod softly and moved quietly. A sense of awe had come into our home. Here was a situation we couldn't handle. The solemnity in our home seemed to be everywhere.

And then Da. The very next night, I was passing my parent's room, and I heard my father, a big, strong man who had been a seaman in his youth and now a hard-working builder, weeping as if his heart would break. He cried out, "Oh God, be merciful to me a sinner!" If the fear of God hadn't already been in my heart, that would have put it there. Worse, when he was leading family worship last night, right in the middle of his prayer—a formal sort of prayer that he repeated often—his voice choked. He finished the prayer in an entirely different way.

I knew before he spoke that we were in serious trouble. Sure enough, he had realized what he called the truth of a personal salvation. He said the light just broke through as he prayed. "I knelt a burdened and convicted man. I rose from my knees saved by grace. I jest want tae go out into the street and tell everyone I find that I'm saved."

I just wanted to go to my room and put my pillow over my head. Which I did. Oh, why did I ever leave Glasgow? Why did I come back to this awful, threatening place? I'm trapped like a bird in a cage. Well, that's it. No more meetings for me. I was absolutely determined. Faye could go with her friends. She didn't need me. I pulled my comforter over the pillow already covering my head.

I don't know how long I stayed there. I must have slept.

"Aileana. Are you asleep, Aileana?" I hadn't even heard Faye come in. I ignored her.

"Aileana, please. I need to talk to you." She shook my shoulder.

I sighed and threw the covers off. I could hide from God—try to, anyway—but I couldn't hide from my sister. "What is it? I want to sleep."

"I've got news—after the meeting tonight—"

"What?" I wanted to yell. Didn't she have any idea what was going on? Our family was in crisis. How could she be thinking about anything else? "Faye, stop! If this is about Euan, forget it. I'm through. I'll not go to another meeting. I'd leave the island tonight if I could, but I've nowhere to go. Just forget Euan and... And read a story in the 'People's Friend'." I started to put the pillow back over my head.

Faye grabbed it and threw it on the floor. "I can't! I can't! Oh, Ali..." She burst into tears and just crumpled right down on the floor. I hadn't heard my childhood name for years and years. It softened me more than her tears.

I reached down and tried to pull her up. But she resisted, so I sat on the floor beside her and took her into my arms. "There, there, Foo," I used her baby name. "It'll be alright. You'll see. You'll—"

"No, it won't. You don't understand. You don't know anything!"

I waited, afraid whatever I might say would just make it worse, and I didn't want her sobs to bring Mam and Da in. That was the last thing we needed.

Finally, the cloudburst subsided. I pulled a hanky from my pocket and gave it to her. She didn't even bother to mop up the tears still rolling down her cheeks. Her lips barely moved. It was as if the words were so awful breath wouldn't support them.

I wasn't sure I had heard her at first. Then I wished I hadn't. It couldn't be true. My little sister couldn't be with child. That did not happen in our respectable world. It would kill our parents. It would kill Faye.

"We were as good as married," she pleaded. At least she had found her voice. "What can I do?"

I couldn't think of a thing that could be done. Who could help us? We couldn't ask anyone. No one must know. Absolutely no one. I certainly didn't want to involve Struan or Calum in anything so personal. So sordid. So shameful. Besides, they were doing all they could to help look for Euan.

There was nothing I could say, so I just sat there, holding her.

"Say something," she pleaded after ages.

I groped through the fog in my mind. If we went back to before Faye dropped her bombshell maybe it wouldn't explode. Maybe this conversation wouldn't have happened at all—just disappear like the nightmare it was. "Let's start over. You said you had news."

"I saw Artair. After the meeting."

"Artair? How did you know him? Did I tell you about him?"

"Janet did. Kirsty and I, we met Janet at the meeting. Janet introduced him and he said he knew you. Why didn't you tell me you saw him weeks ago?"

I shook my head. It was too complicated. Too long ago. "It doesn't matter. You wanted to tell me something,"

"But it does matter! It matters a lot. You didn't tell me a man you used to know promised to look for Euan."

"He said something vague like he'd keep an eye out. I didn't expect it to come to anything. Why? Did he find something?" Now she had my attention.

"Not really. Nothing that means anything, but he said to tell you. He's been looking at some old records—from the war. Apparently, Euan was involved in freebooting that boatload of whiskey intended for Nazi troops. The one that ran aground off the coast. Everyone was talking about it at the time."

She paused with a stifled sob. "And maybe in illegal slaughtering of sheep on Harris—some black-market ring selling the meat on." She gave a shuddering sigh. "But those are in the past. Years ago. They can't have anything to do with what's happening now. Nothing to do with Euan's disappearance?" The last came out like a question. Like she was begging me to agree with her.

What could I possibly say? "I don't know. I just don't know anything." I pulled myself to my feet and a ragdoll-like Faye after me. "Go to bed. We'll talk in the morning." I picked up my pillow, but I didn't put it over my head this time.

I was exhausted. Every part of me ached. But most of all my brain and my heart. Still, I couldn't sleep. I tried to think, but my thoughts made no sense. Images of drunken Nazis and blood-streaked sheep running across the machair filled my mind, interspersed with visions of my parents standing in a radiant aureole of light. I wasn't sure which was the worst.

Well after midnight two thoughts became clear. Everything Euan had been suspected of in the past had involved others. Whatever he did, he was just a dogsbody. And he still would be. Whatever he was involved in that made him disappear, he would be part of an illicit ring. But what could it be? And who would be head of it?

One thing was clear to me, though. I couldn't refuse to help Faye. Whatever wild goose chase she wanted to go on, I had to follow. If only to be there to pick up the pieces when we knew the worst—whatever it was...

Sure enough, I felt like I had barely fallen asleep when Faye was shaking me awake. "Aileana, wake up. I've got an idea."

I sighed and sat up. The morning sun dazzled my eyes. We hadn't closed our curtains the night before.

"We've only been looking on Lewis. The revival has gone farther: Harris, Berneray, clear down to Benbecula..."

I groaned. It was as I feared. My sister did want to go haar hunting. I was not going to Benbecula. That was right down at the south of the chain of islands making up the Outer Hebrides. It would take hours even if one did manage to hit the timing right to catch the necessary ferries. "I suppose I can ask Struan if he'll take us to Tarbert." At least the main village of Harris wasn't far south of the imaginary border with Lewis—and there was good road all the way. Still, even that would mean more than an hour each direction. I calculated the travel time. Struan would not be pleased to be asked to close the station early to make the drive, even though there had been virtually no crime on the island since what they were calling the Awakening kept everyone occupied in prayer meetings. I could ring him from the phone box next to the Port of Ness post office, but this would be best done in person.

I gave an inward groan. "We'll get the bus down to Barvas. If Struan won't take us, there might be a lorry going that far." I shrugged. It was very unusual for visitors to throng to a church in another district, but I heard it had been happening lately. People were so anxious to attend meetings that groups would crowd into busses or lorries and go considerable distances. Sometimes two or three meetings in one night. I shook my head at the very thought.

I could tell that Struan wasn't best pleased when we turned up at the Barvas police station a few hours later asking him to take us to Tarbert that night. "What? The meetings closer to home aren't fine enough for ye?" He looked at his watch and I hoped he wouldn't say he didn't have enough petrol, although he never seemed to be short. I suppose the police wouldn't be.

I think he was ready to refuse. Then he looked at Faye. There wasn't a man in the world who could say no to those pleading-spaniel eyes.

"A'richt, but I've nae had my tea. See ye bring a hamper."

I held up the basket I'd come prepared with.

We drove across the moor towards Stornoway then turned straight south for the journey down the island. Faye's hopefulness at going to an area we hadn't searched before was a healthy counterbalance to Struan's morose resignation. I tried to make it up to him. "Thank you for this, Struan. It means a lot to Faye."

"And to you, too, I hope."

What could I say? "Yes, of course it does. You've been such a help. I don't know what we'd have done without you."

"And is that all?"

I wasn't sure whether he was disappointed or angry. I didn't want him to be either. "All my life…" My mind filled with memories of those shared, carefree days before the war. Struan carrying me home when I sprained my ankle in a mad race to the beach. Dragging me to shore when I over-swam my strength in the cold waters of a loch. Sheltering together in a ruined blackhouse when a sudden rainstorm interrupted our picnic. That had been the first time he kissed me… "Struan, you know it isn't." I left my feelings undefined. It was the best I could do.

A glum silence filled the car. I turned my head and focused on watching the scenery—not that there was much to look at. Miles of machair—winter brown just hinting at a coming green—crossed by strips of dark brown trenches where peat had been cut. It wouldn't be long until the new cutting would begin. In April the moor would be dotted with people in colorful jumpers wielding their traditional tairsgeirs, forming piles of long, narrow, dark brown bricks with their peat cutters—just as generations before them had done. And piles of peats, stacked in a herringbone pattern to dry, would appear behind the crofts and cottages of those who knew that next winter they would be glad of fuel that cost them nothing but labor.

After Stornoway we turned straight south. Leaving the brief, comforting sight of buildings, bushes and even a few green pine trees behind us, we were again crossing another peat bog. The sun was sinking fast into the west by the time we neared the hillocky, loch-strewn terrain of the bottom of Lewis. Bare, turf-covered landscape peppered with dark gneiss and slashed by gullies surrounded us on both sides, but, at last, I saw in the distance the sight I had been waiting for—the mountains of Harris, their peaks lost in cloud, rose purple in the late afternoon light. Even Struan seemed to relax.

After Loch Seaforth we were officially in Harris and had less than twenty minutes to go. I hoped to goodness this fool's errand Faye insisted on would be worth it. The road curved around past the shoulder of Clisham, the highest mountain in the Western Isles, and innumerable puddles, ponds, and running burns testified to the fact that, indeed, spring was coming. Someday.

At last Struan heaved a grudging sigh and pointed to a tan, harled building. "Well, I hope ye're happy."

The first thing I noticed was that the flat, open bell tower over the front door actually had a bell in it. A rare thing on this island where such amenities are considered too showy. The next thing I noticed was the sizeable crowd milling about. "Oh, no! There's no room left."

I wasn't sure which was louder, the grinding of Struan's teeth or his gears as he thrust the car into reverse.

"No, wait!" Faye cried. "We've come all this way—we've got to search the crowd. At least these people standing outside. Maybe I can just squeeze in the door and take a peek, too."

Struan edged his car to the side of the road since the car park was full. Faye opened her door. "Aren't you going to come help me?" Struan and I obediently opened our doors and followed some distance behind her.

Faye hurried ahead to the waiting crowd, most of whom were singing a Psalm in Gaelic, but a few were rapt in prayer. A moment later Faye turned back with a look of consternation. "They're all auld." This was unusual. One of the most surprising things about the meetings was how the young people of the island flocked to them. Then I saw the logo on the side of the nearest bus that read Caraidean na h-aois. Friends of the Aged was one of the biggest groups for the elderly on the Isle of Lewis. You had to laugh—we had arrived at an old folks' outing.

"Well, I'm going to see if I can get a look inside." Faye walked on. I had to admire her determination.

A far different figure caught my attention, however. I hurried to the back of the crowd. "Calum, what are you doing here?"

He spun around, looking equally surprised to see me, then leaned down to speak to the tiny old lady clutching his arm. They both turned to me. "Aunt Ida, I want you to meet my friend Aileana. The one I've told you about who sings like a lark."

I was completely overcome by the warm smile that split the lined face of the frail, bent woman. "Oh, my dearie." She took my hand in both of hers. I could feel the gnarled bones beneath her flesh, but the skin was soft and warm. "Sing. Sing for the Lord." Then she turned back to her own singing as if she hadn't spoken.

Her nephew, however, remained focused on me. "I can't tell you how glad I am to see you."

"You are?" I hadn't seen him since the meeting in Barvas. I didn't even know he was still on Lewis. "I thought you had completely washed your hands of me."

His reply was a quick peck on my cheek.

My hand flew to the side of my face. "Calum! Not in public. I think they arrest people for that here."

"We're leaving." Struan's look made it clear that, indeed, he would like to arrest Calum.

Faye returned, shaking her head and Struan bundled us into his car.

All the way back up the island I kept rubbing my cheek. I wasn't sure whether I was trying to rub the feel of Calum's lips from my face or his aunt's touch and strange words from my hand and my mind. But one thing I couldn't erase was the sound of the singing. How could those quavery, raspy voices of a busload of old-age pensioners sound like silver bells?

A WIND IN THE HEBRIDES

And how could everyone be feeling so much peace and joy when all I feel is turbulence?

Chapter Fifteen

Felicity sighed and set the journal aside. She had hoped reading of long-ago times on the Isle of Lewis would give her some perspective on what was going on today, but it only seemed to complicate things. On the one hand, it gave her more to worry about. Euan's disappearance, Faye's predicament—unwed motherhood was a shameful thing in those days. What would happen to her in that strait-laced society? Would she be cast out? Made to wear a scarlet letter? And Aileana's confusion over the two men in her life…

On the other hand, reading it at this distance in time gave Felicity some perspective. It would all have felt life and death to them at the time, but now the real menace Felicity faced in the here and now made the journal seem like a storybook. Had she really stumbled on some finely tuned smuggling operation—an enterprise some were willing to murder to protect?

How much credence could she reasonably give to the idea of having discovered some criminal plot? As a teen she had loved novels about romantic freebooters versus the law-and-order revenuers—Winston Graham, Daphne du Maurier… And yet, she couldn't seem to put events down to a novelist's imagination and let it go at that.

Worse, as much as she would like to go to sleep and escape it all, she felt wider awake than ever. Shivering when her bare feet touched the floor, she pulled her bag from the corner where she had dumped it and began digging. From the bottom she pulled out her own notebook, only slightly damp from the downpour she had carried it through earlier. She had hoped to talk to Antony about all this. He could always help her make sense of the most difficult situations. But she was on her own, so maybe putting it on paper would help. She had to do something, and this was the best she could think of.

In spite of her desire to be organize her thoughts into some kind of logical precision, her questions simply spilled out on the page, just as her free-association ramblings that always brought a bemused smile to her husband's face.

Police, she wrote at the top of the first page.

George—at diesel dump on Iona? Involved with body? Turned up on Lewis.

Was he watching her? Teddy? Were they in danger?

What would the young officer do with all she told him? And the photo she gave him?

Was it all a dodgy diesel scam as the evidence seemed to point to?

Was George bent? Or on holiday? Or was he the same man at all?

If he was bent and following them earlier to see what she knew, was she in danger?

Or was it good that she had reported it? Either way, what should she do?

Body, she headed the next page.

Who was it? Where did it go? Did George move it?

Did Lachlan and the search team overlook it?

Did the hiker waken from the stupor of a fall and simply walk off?

Selkie topped the third page.

Instead of writing she reviewed the pictures in her mind. At the dock on Iona; streaking through the blue waters off the Butt of Lewis, long white wake streaming behind, then turning to round the point and exhibiting the name in its elegant black script; Teddy's report of seeing it again near the Uig beach... All while the yacht was reportedly undergoing an engine repair.

Was Roger Wellman somehow involved? Using his Christian ministry as a cover for nefarious activity? Had the reprobate Rog Junior somehow got around his father's injunction against his use of the boat? Had Wellman's trusted captain, or a crew member, somehow highjacked the boat for their own nefarious purposes? Or merely a bit of a lark?

Argh! This was impossible. Endless questions. Absolutely no answers. Felicity felt like she was digging a deep, dark hole with every question she jotted down. She headed a fourth page *Dodgy Diesel*, added a few notes, then just stared at the blank space until she felt herself going cross-eyed. Was there any connection to all this? Or was she mixing her situation with thoughts from Aileana's journal? Red petrol, black-market fuel; barrels hidden on Iona, breakdowns on Scottish motorways...

The notebook slid to the floor.

When Felicity woke in the morning the storm had stopped but the dreich sky and drizzling rain outside her window was almost as bad. If only the sun were shining. She would love to take Teddy on a picnic and forget all about the arcane plots of smuggling and piracy she'd been cooking up. Like something from a florid novel set in the eighteenth century, she told herself.

Teddy still slept, a warm, soft lump of pure relaxation and innocence. She smiled, glad that he was getting some extra rest, and slid soundlessly out of the bed. Until her foot crunched the page of her fallen notebook. She picked it up, smoothed out the crinkled page and frowned at her notes. What had she written? Something about biofuel in Poland—yes, she remembered reading about that in the library. Then Norway, Europe's largest petrol producer. Under that, the scrawl was completely illegible.

She sighed. Just as well. It couldn't have been worth much anyway. Still, her nighttime scribbles had shown her how much she still needed to know—if she were to make sense of what was going on. If anything was going on. She supposed she should be concentrating more on the Awakening. There were undoubtedly still details she could dig out that would enrich her talk and workshop. To be truly honest with herself, though, she needed to admit that most of all she wanted to make sense of more immediate events—if only so she could dismiss them from her mind and stop her disorienting and distracting habit of mixing events past and present.

Even more pressing, she was uncomfortable about that body. Soothing as the idea of him coming around from some sort of blackout and continuing a stroll around the island was, she found it too much to swallow. Not that she was likely to learn anything about that in the library. Still, she needed a plan for the day and going there seemed the best she could think of.

Felicity had just finished pulling her clothes on when Teddy turned over, stretched and sat up—tousle-haired and grinning—immediately bright-eyed and ready for the day as he always was. "Are you hungry, darling? I expect Catriona has a bowl of lovely porridge for you."

Teddy bounced out of bed, made quick work of dressing, and headed toward the kitchen with his mother right behind him. They were halfway down the hall when Felicity stopped. "Wait." She took her son's hand and listened. Yes, she was right. She did hear a male voice. Should they burst in on their hostess if she had company?

Just then the kitchen door swung open, and Isla came out. "Guess what? Da's home. We didn't expect him for a couple of weeks yet."

"Oh, how lovely."

"Yes. It can be a long gap between shore leaves."

Felicity struggled to remember. What did Isla's father do? Was it the Royal Navy? Something to do with the sea. Then she remembered. Offshore oil—that was it. Worked on one of those platforms in the North Sea. And then she knew, that was what she had scribbled last night...

Isla held out her hand to Teddy. "Hungry? Come on."

Felicity followed Teddy and Isla into the kitchen. A large, sandy-haired man, balding a little on top, stood and extended his hand. "Hello, Felicity. Welcome. Welcome. I'm Cameron. Catriona's been telling me about your work. Nice that our Isla can help you out."

His handclasp was warm, his voice more booming than most Scots Felicity had encountered. She supposed that came of working on an oil rig that must be incredibly noisy with the constant running of heavy machinery. She said the proper things to acknowledge his effusive greeting.

Then turned to Isla who was making toast for Teddy to accompany the bowl of porridge he was already tucking into with one hand while he sailed his play dough boat around his lighthouse sculpture. "I don't want to take you away from your family today, Isla. I can take Teddy with me. I thought I'd go back to the library. They have a good children's department—I can get books to entertain him." She struggled to sound more enthusiastic than she felt.

"No, no. It's no problem at all. Da will be immured in his office all day anyway, won't you, Da?"

"The lass has the size of it. The idea of time off when ye're on shore leave is fine for some, but when it comes to OIMs it's a matter of no rest for the wicked. Forms stacked to the ceiling, there are—compliance reports for Health and Safety, logistics coordination with other rigs, statistical data on production... you name it—they all have to be filled out in triplicate..."

Felicity accepted a bowl of porridge and seasoned it with salt and butter in the way she had observed most Scots doing, although Teddy stuck to his traditional milk and sugar. "That must be fascinating work. Where are you located?" Felicity had heard of offshore oil rigs all her life but had very little concept of their workings. "There are a lot of them, aren't there?"

"One hundred eighty-four in the North Sea."

Felicity considered that such a number justified the ring of pride in his voice. "Which one do you work on?"

"The Schiehallion—a deepwater field—just over a hundred miles west of the Shetlands."

Felicity struggled to make sense of that. She had a vague idea that would be about halfway between Norway and the Isle of Lewis. She nodded as if she were following him perfectly. "And what did you say you do? OI something?"

He grinned and Felicity saw immediately how much Isla looked like her father. "OIM—Offshore Installation Manager—the guy that stands around all day in a hard hat carrying a clipboard. Ensuring operational continuity and safety is the theory. Filling out forms, it mostly comes down to. If anything goes wrong the higher-ups have someone to blame."

Catriona looked more worried than her husband sounded. "Has anything gone wrong? Is that why you're home ahead of schedule? Has production fallen off?"

"Nae, lass, nothing to worrit about. It's good, actually, just the nuisance of training a new assistant."

"I thought you just did that a few months back."

"Aye. I thought so, too. That daft lad Kenny Shea hared off on shore leave—bragging about the POSH yacht his rich friend was taking him sailing on. Hasn't bothered to come back. If it weren't for the inconvenience, I'd say good riddance."

He carried on grumbling about the aggravation caused by his underling's failure to return, but Felicity's attention turned to Isla when she asked Teddy. "How would you like to go to a Castle today?"

Felicity remembered seeing the stone towers and fine, crenelated turrets rising above the grove of leafy green on the hilltop when the ferry sailed into Stornoway harbor.

"They have a room where you can dress up like children who lived on the island hundreds of years ago and you can play with the kind of toys children had then."

Teddy looked a bit unsure, so Felicity encouraged him. "That sounds lovely. And if you don't want to play like an island boy, you could be a Medieval knight—or a Viking like one of the chessmen."

She wasn't certain how much of that the five-year-old grasped, but he smiled.

"And if we're lucky, the storyteller lady will be there—she does a grand job," Isla added. Then she turned to Felicity. "Why don't you go with us? You might find something useful, too. They keep an extensive archive." She grinned. "And there's a brilliant caff for lunch."

Felicity glanced at the grey clouds which seemed lower than ever. And the wind had picked up—it didn't look like the ferry would be likely to or from Iona today. The idea of going off to the library by herself held little attraction. "Sold," she said.

Around the far side of the harbor the road started a gradual ascent through dense greenery—leafy trees clasping branches to form an archway overhead with banks of ferns underneath. "Watch carefully, Teddy. You should be able to spot big clumps of mushrooms in the undergrowth," Isla instructed.

Obediently, Teddy pressed his nose against the window to peer into the woodland world. The road ahead was shiny with the misting rain; the dark clouds overhead seemed to be just clearing the tops of the trees. It all presented a verdant lushness that gave Felicity the feeling of being on an altogether different island—or back in the heart of England.

"The Woodlands Centre," Isla said with a sweep of her arm at the green panorama. "Not a stick of it's native to Lewis, of course. Mid-1900s Sir James Matheson bought the whole island for half a million pounds. Threw himself into improving everything—agriculture, drainage schemes, road construction… The roads we've been driving on all week are down to him. He built the castle and laid out the grounds in a manner befitting the Laird of the Castle. All very nice, I'm sure—just too bad about the 500 families that had to be cleared off the land." Her voice held a ring of ironic resentment. Then she shrugged. "But then, he arranged their emigration to Canada, so maybe they got the best of the deal in the end."

They topped the gradual incline they had been ascending and drove around a gentle curve. The medievalesque stone walls and turrets sprang into view. "Is that a real castle?" Teddy asked. He had tromped over many a ruined castle in his native Yorkshire with his history-loving father.

Isla grinned. "Well, it's the closest we've got to offer anyway—even if it is got-up Victorian." To their left was the covered entrance porch Sir James built for the comfort of his guests arriving by carriage, but Isla carried on around behind the castle to the parking lot which faced the museum extension.

"Can we go in the castle?" Teddy asked.

"Doesn't look like there's a wedding or anything going on today, so we should be able to walk around the ground floor," Isla said. "There's a shop and café. Maybe we can peek in the ballroom—it's very grand, but there's really more to do over here in the museum." She led the way through a rain far gentler than the downpour of the day before.

Inside the low, metal-plated building extending from the castle like a modern armor-clad knight, Isla pointed Felicity to a glass door through which she could see a book-lined room with worktables in the center. "That's the reading room. It's by appointment only, so I rang them before we left. Rather last-minute, I'm afraid, but they said they'd have someone there to help you." She held out her hand to Teddy. "Let's go get you a backpack—they have coloring sheets, I Spy cards, discovery trail maps—all kinds of stuff."

They started off, but Felicity stopped them and dug for her coin purse. She had seen the signs saying entrance was free, but donations much needed. Inside the reading room she apologized to the attendant for arriving on such short notice.

"It's nae problem, we're happy to welcome readers." Marie Morrison, according to her nametag, was a woman of obvious efficiency and professionalism. Her neat navy-blue skirt and cardigan over a crisp white blouse seemed to reflect the care she took in all areas of her life. Felicity found this both comforting and worrying. She wished she were better prepared for this visit. "It's just if we have more notice, we can have materials ready for you. What are you researching?"

Felicity blinked. So many questions had been competing for attention in her mind: The Awakening, of course—that was what brought her to the island, after all. But equally the missing body, the contraband fuel... current events pushed their distracting questions forward. "Several things really," she began, then realized she needed to focus. "Post World War II island history, mostly. The Lewis Awakening..."

Marie Morrison nodded her neatly bobbed brown hair. "Interesting fact about that phenomenon is how it completely bypassed Stornoway. Still, the general spirituality of the island affected everyone, I suppose. I'll be happy to bring you what we have in our archives." She indicated a table where Felicity should sit. "I trust you brought your own pencil? We don't allow pens around our manuscripts, you understand."

"Oh, yes, always." Felicity was thankful for her past experiences working with valuable historic papers—sometimes even actual medieval documents.

"If you would just care to sign our register and then wash your hands before you begin," Marie pointed to the book on the counter, then to a door marked washroom. "I'll fetch your documents. They aren't extensive, I'm afraid."

The pile of manuscripts, when it arrived a few minutes later, was not large, but to Felicity's delight, it was material she had not seen before. A collection of hand-written manuscripts by a number of people giving first-person accounts of their experiences of the revival. Just looking at them made Felicity think of Aileana's extensively kept journals. Perhaps this well-kept archive would be an even better repository than the library when it came time for Wendy to donate them. How happy Antony would be to see such respect for local history.

Felicity was soon writing busily with her trusty pencil, making a list of the unique features of these experiences that she thought her fellow SpiDir members would find interesting—and possibly useful—in their counseling. The most important thing for a spiritual guide to keep in mind, she felt, was to treat each one who came to her as an individual; there were no stock answers in this business. And that was what these stories told. Occurrences of the Holy Spirit working with each individual as an individual, starting right where they were in their everyday lives.

She liked the story by Big Sandy McLeod who recounted that his minister declared with confidence weeks ahead of the actual beginning of the Awakening that "The Lord is about to do a great work in our midst." He proceeded to hold meetings in accord with what he knew was coming. Felicity labeled her notes on that story Confidence.

The next account was of a pastor's wife. Scandalized to find her husband and a visitor laughing when she took a tea tray in to them in the pastor's study, she issued a sharp rebuke. "How can you laugh when you see the state of the world?"

"Oh," said her minister husband. "You just exercise a little patience."

"Patience?"

"Yes," the visitor agreed, "Have patience."

"You must be patient and leave it to the Lord," her husband added.

Two weeks later the visitor returned. When the minister's wife came in with the tea he couldn't help remarking on her obvious change of demeanor. She told him about great improvements in her family since the last time. "Now I have reason to be happy."

Her minister husband nodded and turned to the visitor, "I told her she must be patient. She had been looking at the dark side, but I saw the promises of God dispersing the darkness and I knew it would happen soon in reality."

Felicity wrote Patience and underlined it.

Her third point was Unity after reading about the results of services based on the theme "How good and how pleasant it is for brethren to dwell together in unity."

Another recounted experiences of singing, always in the traditional Gaelic way based on the Psalms. Then, a final report stressed the centrality of prayer. Felicity came to the bottom of her stack and pushed it away with a smile and sigh of satisfaction. She felt her research was complete. She had what she needed for her conference.

Besides, she was hungry. She thanked the archivist who seemed equally happy to be freed for lunch, and asked if, after lunch, she could look at anything they might have on the effect of oil and gas production on the island. "Er—I mean petrol," she amended. Then added quickly, "Or diesel—any fuel, really."

Marie's crisp nod settled the plan. And Felicity went off in search of Teddy and Isla.

She found them in the children's activity room. Teddy was happily dressed as a Viking with horned helmet and plastic sword stuck through a leather belt. Isla wore a Harris tweed jacket over a homespun shirt and a distinctive cap with a soft crown like a Tam o' Shanter and a peaked front like an English flat cap.

"What are you playing?"

"I'm the Viking who played chess on the beach," Teddy announced proudly.

"And I'm the crofter who found them," Isla added. "We started out playing chess" she pointed to the board on a table, "—then Teddy got the idea of hiding the men and I find them."

"What a great treasure hunt! And what is your cap? I've never seen one like it."

"It's called a crofter's bunnet. Very traditional."

"What fun. Is anyone ready for lunch?"

"She hasn't found the chessmen yet," Teddy objected.

It took Isla and Felicity working together several minutes to locate the clutch of plastic replicas that Teddy had buried under a box of building bricks intended for constructing a model of Lews Castle.

When the costumes were back on the rack, Teddy proudly showed his mum the replica of the Lewis lighthouse he made from a tall red plastic cup, complete with bricks, blue door, and windows carefully indicated by marking pen, brought to life by a battery-powered candle under a clear cup on top.

"What a successful morning you've had!" Felicity held out her hand. "Now, let's go see the castle."

Teddy was happy to skip down the long hallways of highly polished floors lined with Ionic pillars, stare at the crystal chandeliers and highly colored ceiling of the ballroom, and walk through the gift shop, but his interest came alive when he found the replica chessmen. "Which one would you like?" Felicity asked.

It took careful deliberation, but the choice fell to the knight on his short-legged pony, a choice with which Felicity heartily agreed. With his trophy clutched happily in his hand, Teddy reminded his mum that he was hungry.

"The Storehouse is on around the corner," Isla pointed. "Or we could go to the Woodland Café—it's just a five-minute walk, and the sun has come out." Isla glanced out a window. "Well, nearly."

Felicity was more than happy to agree. Fresh air and, hopefully, lower prices were both appealing thoughts. And a few minutes later she found that, in spite of the trees still dripping on them, the smoothly paved path through the lush greenery was just what she needed to clear her head after her time spent struggling over hand-written documents, some in faded ink and some in awkward penmanship, indeed.

Lunch was a matter of soup and toasted sandwiches in the glass-walled room in the middle of the woods. After finishing off with two cups of tea and a piece of the ubiquitous Scottish shortbread Felicity was ready to go back to work. "Thank you for suggesting the archive, Isla. They have some original documents I couldn't get anywhere else. And what are you two going to do this afternoon?"

Isla looked at Teddy. "How about the I-Spy wildlife trail? I think you've got a map in your pack."

Teddy dug in the museum-supplied backpack and triumphantly produced a colorful map of a well-marked trail, complete with a magnifying glass to examine bugs, bark, and wildflowers.

Felicity laughed. "I think that's a yes. You two go on. Just come get me in the reading room when you're ready to go back."

The efficient Marie was waiting for her with files of information pertaining to the petroleum industry in Scotland, most of which appeared to be newspaper clippings and government documents. Felicity thanked her. Marie nodded, but replied, "You'd do better at the public library for information on the oil industry, though."

Felicity was afraid she was right. "There was one other topic—" Vague, disjointed ideas had been bouncing around at the back of Felicity's head. Perhaps she could find something here to help bring the shards together. "Uig beach."

The curator looked puzzled. "You want information on the

chessmen? We have plenty of that."

Rule number one: refine your search, Felicity reminded herself. "I was thinking more of the beach itself, the geology. As to the oil industry, do you have maps or perhaps tables of Scotland's offshore locations and maybe something including Poland or Norway? I'm thinking mostly of refineries." Still ambiguous, she realized, but Marie gave a nod and turned to her backroom stacks.

In less time than Felicity could have hoped the librarian was back. "We have some quite good geological survey maps and leaflets on Uig beach—there is considerable interest, due to the chessmen, you know." She placed a small bundle in front of Felicity. "I only found these two information pamphlets that mark offshore drilling and refineries in the locations you mentioned. Of course, the closest refinery to us is in Grangemouth, near Edinburgh, so it's not particularly relevant to our collection." She ended the delivery of her information with a definite sniff that seemed calculated to let Felicity know that Marie Morrison did not hold with oil production or refining.

Felicity understood—in spite of all the conveniences attached to life with gas and oil, climate change was a real concern. She put her pencil down and considered. She should have thought of this before. Could that possibly be what any of this was about? She thought of the protesters she had seen in Glasgow.

Could eco-warriors be trying to cause havoc in the oil and gas industry with dodgy diesel, promoting trouble with offshore drilling? Who knew what else? Would they even be willing to commit murder? The demonstrators she had noticed looked peaceful enough—uni students mostly, with a good sprinkling of grey beards. Still, some extremists might be prepared to go further. She shivered. She was all for taking care of our planet and being careful with resources. But within legal bounds...

Felicity struggled to think rationally. If there was anything at all to her ideas of the body on Iona being connected to smuggling fuel for the dogy diesel problem—and her only reason to think that, was the proximity of the body to the barrels in the ravine on Iona—smugglers would only be interested in refined oil, not crude. So, would someone like Cameron's troublesome former underling have industry connections that could lead to supplying illegitimate operations?

She shook her head at the realization she was grasping at straws and turned to a map on the top of Marie's bundle. Big red dots marked the major oil processing plants in Europe. A legend gave details on their production. If she was reading this right Mongstad, in Norway, refined about 230,000 barrels of crude oil every day.

Numbers weren't Felicity's strong point, but those statistics sounded impressive enough that a few barrels secreted away by a ring of smugglers might not be noticed. But they would have exceedingly strict controls, she reminded herself, thinking of the stacks of forms Cameron had complained about that morning.

Competing theories debated in her head. Surely those numbers would be sufficient to bring out demonstrators, too—even in a nearby country.

She frowned at the map, then went to the desk and asked Marie if she perhaps had a ruler Felicity could borrow. Success. Now she could calculate that by water, Mongstad, near Bergen, was perhaps about 370 miles from Lewis.

She turned her focus to Poland. The largest refinery was in Plock in central Poland, producing 343 barrels a day. The other refinery, in Gdańsk near the Baltic Sea, produced about hundred barrels a day less. And all that about 800 miles across the North Sea. Surely that would make Poland an outlier in the smuggling stakes?

Marie had said Grangemouth, near Edinburgh, was Scotland's only crude oil refinery. Felicity studied the information on the map: approximately 200,000 barrels per day of products, including petrol, diesel, and jet fuel. But Edinburgh was... Hmm, 150 miles by land, including two ferry crossings to get to Iona. No, very little chance the fuel for the dogy diesel found in those barrels on Iona came from that direction.

Okay, interesting, and perhaps helpful for narrowing her thinking a bit, but Felicity certainly didn't feel she was any closer to answering the vexing questions she struggled with. She turned to the file of newspaper clippings. The biggest one, near the bottom of the file, meaning it was several years old, still made interesting reading. The headline proclaimed: Global Climate Protests from the Small Sun-drenched Inner Hebridean Island of Iona to the Packed Streets of Central London.

She skimmed the article: Biggest-ever environmental protest the UK had seen, 300,000-350,000 participants; more than 100,000 in London...

She slowed her reading when she came to Edinburgh: A huge crowd marched from the Meadows, down the Royal Mile to the Scottish parliament. They were clapped and cheered by onlookers, saluted by a bagpiper and entertained by a percussion drummer and jazz bands.

Felicity pictured it in her mind: Chants of "Hey hey, ho ho, climate change has got to go!" filling the streets, tens of thousands of people, bearing hand-painted signs: "33.2C in Scotland. Time to panic!" "Sea levels are rising. So are we!" "You'll die of old age. I'll die of climate change."

She carried on, sifting through the carefully compiled collection, trying to focus on organizations and demonstrations that were specifically related to the oil industry. She jotted the names of some of the organizations that seemed to be the most active: Climate Camp Scotland, End Fossil Fuels Scotland, Just Stop Oil, Extinction Rebellion...

She scanned the photos of demonstrations and noted some of the slogans: "End Fossil Fuels", "North Sea Fossil Free", "Stop Fueling the Flames". She was pleased to see the banners calling for

"A Just Transition for Workers".

A large article reported on a protest only a few months ago. "From babies to bagpipers, hundreds of thousands filled the streets in more than 200 rallies. Climate activists stage protest dancing to 'Stayin' Alive' by Bee Gees in Edinburgh.

"Protesters said they are aiming to 'highlight the flawed climate risk models used by pension funds and to call on the funds to stop investing in fossil fuels.'"

She smiled at photos of young people, some in neon-bright wigs, performing well-synchronized dance moves. It was difficult to imagine any of these earnest activists committing murder. The focus of their protest seemed to be to get pension funds to divest from fossil fuel companies and to reinvest wisely. Since people voted with their pocketbooks, that was probably a good approach for a persuasive campaign.

Apparently, even the Hebrides, peaceful and out-of-the-way as they were, had been home to plenty of protests—as least as far as Iona, but searching more carefully through the file for such activity on the Isle of Lewis, the most she could find were protests over the closing of a bank and of disrupted ferry service. But then, maybe that lack of focus would make it the perfect choice for an operation that dealt in contraband fuel?

Felicity glanced at the clock on the wall. She had been here for more than an hour already. Surely Isla and Teddy would be coming to collect her soon. Her remaining item was the geological survey information on Lewis. Felicity hadn't had a clearly defined idea in mind when she asked Marie for information on Uig bay, but as she looked at the pamphlets spread before her, some of the blurry edges of her thoughts seemed to harden. If—and it was a huge if—fuel for the dodgy diesel was coming to Lewis to be mixed with kerosene, then smuggled to irresponsible garages on the mainland, it would be coming by boat—and she had, more than once, seen a boat off these shores that its owner thought was off somewhere being repaired—the many caves around the shoreline of Lewis would be most fortuitous assets. And, on Teddy's sharp-eyed testimony, the last place they had seen that boat was at Uig Bay.

That did it—she finally realized what had been tickling at the back of her mind like a persistent itch that she couldn't scratch, Aileana had written about the myriad, secluded caves, many practically inaccessible. Was that to do with Nazi whiskey? She couldn't remember. Could some ring be hiding their black-market booty in such a place today?

She unfolded a pamphlet and here before her was a detailed map of Lewis from the Scottish Cave and Mine Database. It showed a nearly solid trail of red balloon markers circling the coast, each one indicating the presence of a cave. And, sure enough, one of the heaviest concentrations circled the promontories facing the open sea below Uig Bay. Felicity closed her eyes and saw again that wide, white crescent of sand, herself sitting comfortably finishing her smoked salmon bap and reveling in the quiet while Teddy, with Isla right behind him, headed straight toward the location of those red markers.

"I found all the Xs on the map, Mummy."

It took Felicity a moment to realize that the small voice at her elbow wasn't in her memory, but rather came from her son holding out the nature trail map which he had successfully conquered with Isla's help. She took a deep breath to help her refocus.

"That's brilliant, darling. Let me just thank Marie for her help today and you can tell me all about your adventure on the way home."

She did want to hear details of her son's nature walk, but more than anything, she wanted to get back to the quiet of the B&B and call Antony.

"Antony, Oh, I'm so glad you're there!" Felicity felt the tension drain from her body at the sound of her husband's voice. It felt like it had taken hours to get Teddy fed, bathed and settled so she could finally pour everything out to her husband. "Please don't tell me you have to rush off. I have so much to tell you."

She could hear his smile in his voice. "It's grand to talk to you, too. Have I mentioned that I miss you?"

"Oh," Felicity fought against choking up. When she set out on this adventure, she had no idea being apart would be so difficult. "How's the seminar going?" She'd try for something neutral while she got her equilibrium back.

He told her a bit about the activities and comments of some of his students. She noted that Roger Wellman, he of the sleek yacht, was still there—apparently deeply absorbed in Columban history. "So just two days and we can rendezvous in Glasgow—assuming this wind goes down. Now, you said you had a lot to tell me."

Where to start. She couldn't remember what she'd actually told him and what had been merely imagined conversations in her mind. "I may be repeating myself—tell me if I am…" In her jumbled-together, run-on way she recounted going to the police station, then discovering that the man in her photo at the Truishal Stone was a police officer they called George. "And I'm sure he's the hiker we saw on Iona, and I don't know if that means he's one of the ring or that he's working undercover, so now I don't know whether or not I can go back to the police with the information I've dug up. Of course, it's all theory, and there may be other explanations, but it scared me so bad I ran all the way—"

"Whoa, whoa, wait a minute," Antony managed to interrupt her flow. "What are you talking about? What ring?"

"The smugglers that made the dogy diesel that are causing all the lorry breakdowns like we saw in Glasgow, that they found in the barrels in the ravine. Smugglers bring the diesel in from Norway and hide it in caves on Lewis, and they killed that hiker I saw that disappeared, and they're probably using Wellman's yacht. I read all about it, and…"

"Felicity!" She startled at the sharpness in Antony's tone. "Stop.

What are you saying? You read about Norwegian fuel in caves on Lewis?"

"Oh, well, not exactly." She forced herself to think before speaking. "I've been reading reports and newspaper clippings and it all makes sense. Really, it does—even if I'm not. And if there is anything to it at all, it has to be a ring because it's a really big operation—it would take a lot of organizing. And we do know for certain that the dodgy diesel exists." She stopped short and bit her tongue. Was she making any sense? It had seemed rational in her mind, but now, out in the open, put into actual words...

"And I do know what I saw in that ravine. Nobody takes a rest with their head down in a gully and flies buzzing around open wounds."

"All right. Yes, I accept that you know what you saw. I'll admit I think the just-taking-a-rest explanation is pretty weak. So, somebody moved him after we were there. I get it. That does sound like it was unlikely to have been a case of his tripping and falling. But that's still a huge leap to some sort of international fuel-running scam."

As always, Antony was being rational; she needed to be, too. "Well, I did have one other idea. There have been a lot of really big anti-fossil fuel demonstrations—even at least one on Iona. They look peaceful enough, but some extremist eco-warrior could have gone too far."

"Felicity, why are you doing this at all? If there is a problem the police will take care of it. You reported what you knew—or thought you knew—to the police. Now let it go. I grant that the business about the body in the ravine is disturbing, but it's not your problem. Isn't that something counselors tell their directees—define whose problem it is?"

"Oh." Silence. He was right. "Yeah."

"Okay. Good. Now, how has your preparation for your conference gone?"

"Brilliant. The journals Wendy gave me are amazing and

I've seen almost all of the places she tells about, and I've talked to people who were actually here at the Awakening, and I found more personal accounts at the castle, and yeah—I have more than enough for my speech and I've got my workshop outlined.

"Oh, and today we went to Lews Castle. They have a really good archive about the island's history in their museum—that's where I found the hand-written eyewitness accounts, and I realized what a great place that would be for Wendy to donate her great aunt's notebooks. They would be really looked after there."

"That is brilliant. So now you take a day off, and we'll meet in Glasgow on Friday."

"Antony, I love you." She couldn't begin to tell him how much better she felt, but she was sure he could hear at least some of it in her voice. Her shoulders relaxed and she could breathe freely.

He chuckled and told her he felt easier, too. "I love you, too. Now get a good night of sleep and have fun tomorrow."

"I will, right after I read another section in the journal. It's my bedtime story."

They signed off after another exchange of I love yous. What a wonderful realization that this wasn't her problem. She had probably just been channeling Aileana for whom helping Faye was her problem. But Felicity was free to forget all about it—the troubles of the oil industry—smuggling, adulterated products, eco-demonstrators—all of it was interesting to read about, but like most of the world's problems, beyond her job—or ability—to solve. Thank goodness.

Tomorrow the sun would shine. She would take Teddy on that picnic she'd been hoping for. And the next day they would get on one of those little planes at the Stornoway airport and she would fly back to Antony.

She picked up Aileana's notebook and settled back on her pillows with a soft smile playing around her lips.

Chapter Sixteen

I wasn't feeling any better the next morning. I went down for breakfast hoping a cup of hot, strong tea would revive me. Faye was sitting at the table bent over the same map of Lewis I had found so discouraging when we started this whole farce. Her finger traced a pattern from one tiny cross marking a church to the next. Well, at last she had seen how hopeless it was. I supposed that was progress.

"I know it's hard to give up, darling, but, really, it's for the best."

As if I hadn't spoken, Faye tapped a spot on the map with her finger and looked up, almost glowing. "Here! We haven't tried this area at all yet."

Yet? She thought we were still going on with it all?

"Callanish. We'll go to Callanish tonight."

I shook my head. In despair, not disagreement. There was no use arguing. I could refuse, but she would go on her own. I sighed. "It's no good asking Struan to take us. He made that clear enough last night."

"Maybe Mam and Da? They'll be going somewhere."

"They'll go wherever Duncan Campbell is preaching." My sister was fine with concocting hare-brained schemes—and insisting on carrying them out. But the logistics were always up to me. "I suppose there might be a lorry going." Faye brightened at my suggestion, but my heart sank. Even if one found a lorry going to Callanish, just the thought of riding close to an hour in an open lorry bed made me shiver. Spring was coming, but it wasn't here yet.

Faye jumped up and hugged me. "Yes! Of course. There are always lorries from Barvas because way more people show up for the meetings than the church there can accommodate. They go all over the island!"

If only I could share my sister's blind optimism.

I was feeling no more optimistic as we began the ten-minute trudge from the Barvas bus stop back up the road to the church. I had seen the three lorries parked around the church, waiting to receive the overflow once the church was crammed. They looked no more comfortable than I was expecting. I didn't even look up when a car passed us. But I did when the driver reversed and called out his window. "Going somewhere?"

Faye reacted first and ran to him. "Struan! We're going to Callanish. Faye said you wouldn't take us, but I knew she was wrong."

"Callanish?" He shook his head. "Yer sister's got the richt of it."

"You won't take us?"

He reached back and opened the rear door. "Hop in. I'll take ye to the church. That's as far as I've petrol for. Been out searching fer our village daftie all afternoon. Wandered off again. His mam was in a state. My tank's on fumes."

I was happy enough for a lift even as far as the Barvas church. I hopped in. "Did you find him?"

"Oh, aye. Headed to the moor with his tairsgeir. Thinking to cut peats."

"I didn't think the polis ran out of petrol coupons," I said.

"Nah, plenty of those—petrol station's closed, isn't it?"

At the church Faye jumped out and ran to the closest lorry

driver. I saw him shake his head at her query—which was undoubtedly if he was going to Callanish. She had no more luck with the other two and turned back towards the car with slumped shoulders. Then she shouted and darted forwards. A bus was just pulling into the car park, the same bus we had seen before with its Friends of the Aged logo emblazoned on the side.

The bus had barely come to a stop when Faye was banging on the door, and a moment later running back to us with a smile that reached from ear to ear.

"They are! They are! And we can go if we have a pensioner with us." She looked around as if she would grab the closest granny and drag her onto the bus with her.

Several aged people who had obviously been waiting for the bus made their way across the car park, most with the aid of sticks, but not seeming in need of a helper. The bus wasn't full, but Faye bounced from foot to foot with jitters. Then she was darting off again, but away from the bus. And I saw what she was headed for: Calum ushering his Aunt Ida from the car.

Calum nodded at Faye and seemed to be agreeable to whatever she was proposing to him. She turned and beckoned us forward. I was surprised when Struan got out of the car, too. "Are you going to the meeting?" I asked him.

"I'll not be sending you off with the likes of that one." He ground out.

I laughed. "I think I'll be well enough chaperoned with one of the Praying Sisters along."

The driver looked skeptical at the idea that it required four of us to escort one granny, but the bus was far from full, so he let us on.

Faye was practically bouncing on her seat beside me. I worried, knowing her elation would make her ultimate disappointment all the worse.

The sun was dipping low when the bus turned off the tarmacked road onto a dirt track that led around a long, narrow sea loch. "Where are we going?" I leaned forward to talk to Calum in the seat in front of me. "The church was back there." I had seen it just before we turned, a long, tan, harled building with no bell in its small tower over the door.

"Cottage meeting tonight." He pointed to a large lime-washed house sitting on high ground on the other side of the loch.

Halfway around the loch we passed a sign pointing south that read "Tursachan Chalanais" Callanish Standing Stones. I shivered recalling our aborted visit there what now seemed like ages ago. Then all thoughts of past adventures went out of my head as the bus gave an almighty shudder and came to a dead halt in the middle of the road.

The driver ground on the starter with disappointing results, each attempt eliciting a weaker moan from the engine. With a shake of his head, he pulled a spanner from a toolbox under his seat and left the bus. Through the front windscreen we saw him raise the bonnet but couldn't see any of his probings at the Leyland engine that had been built before the war. It made little difference what he attempted because he was soon back inside. "I'm that sorry, folks, but she's stone deid. Nothing we can do but wait for help."

Murmurs of disappointment—and some alarm—filled the bus. It was heart-breaking. We were within sight of our destination. Faye and I and our escorts could have walked the distance, no matter that the meeting would likely be more than half over by the time we arrived. But there was no possibility of such a feat for the elderly passengers.

"Nae fear." The driver held up a hand. "I'll walk to the town. There'll be help." He was making a good effort to sound brave. Town simply meant a somewhat denser collection of houses, barns and outbuildings scattered along the road. The likelihood of finding a mechanic seemed a forlorn hope. A crofter experienced in keeping his own prewar equipment running might be possible. With luck.

We had been sitting, somewhat glumly, for several minutes when Calum, sitting closest to the window, pointed to a small hut on the shore of the loch. He turned to me. "If ye'll look out for Aunt Ida, I'll just nip across this field and see if there's any aid to be had over there."

Unlikely as it seemed, what harm could it do?

A few minutes later he was back, a big grin on his face. "Success! There's a boat. We can be across that loch in twenty minutes." He glanced out the window at the large, black gneiss boulders poking through the turf. "Well, if ye don't object to walking across the field. What do you think, Auntie Ida, do ye fancy a wee row?"

She gave a surprisingly young laugh. "What a fine thing for ye bairns. Off ye go and row the lassies to their meeting. I'll stay right here and wait for aid."

Calum's conflict was apparent, torn between duty to his aunt and his desire for an evening with folks his own age. He hesitated.

But Ida was insistent. "Away wi' ye now before ye miss the singing. Ye can find a body to drive ye home after. I'm right comfortable as I am, and I can pray better nice and snug here than in a wee rowboat in the middle of a loch."

Calum spotted a friend of his auntie's sitting a few rows back who readily moved up to sit with her, so he could leave with a clear conscience.

It was a fine evening—crisp, but not as cold as it had been recently. Just enough breeze to ripple the surface of the water. The low-hanging sun would soon disappear behind a bank of pink clouds that reflected on the loch. The small shed was little more than a shelter, not even a door on it. It was a matter of seconds for the men to untie the boat and slip the oars in their locks. Calum handed Faye into the prow, and Struan helped me to the seat in the back. Each man, sitting side-by-side in the middle, facing the rear, wielded an oar. For all the apparent competition and animosity between the two, they teamed together surprisingly well as oarsmen. Perhaps it was their rivalry that spurred the energy behind their strokes. I doubted that it was just worry over arriving late at the meeting.

We were nearing the middle of the loch when the sun disappeared. Gradually the clouds dimmed to a narrow rim of color. Even though there was still light in the sky the water darkened and it felt suddenly colder. I shivered and pulled my coat tighter around me, wishing I'd worn a warmer hat. There was no talking in the boat as the men focused their energies on the rowing. The rhythmic dip, splash, dip, splash sound of the oars repeated over and over and the soft plash of water washing the side of the boat was almost soporific until a snipe, flying low over the water from the marshy bank, added his haunting whoosh, whoosh winnowing sound.

The peace was broken when Faye gave a startled cry as Calum's oar hit the water beside her with increased energy and drops of cold water showered her. I leaned away, thinking the stroke would emerge with equal vigor, bringing spray with it. Instead, Calum gave a grunt and strained to bring his oar to the surface.

I was first to see when it came up. Calum's oar had caught in a rope securing a long, dark bundle that must have been floating just below the surface. "Do you have your torch, Struan?" I extended my arm as I was closest to the object, but he ignored me, riveted as he was on the dark, dripping bag.

"Whit on earth?" His face filled with consternation. "Shake it off, man! Ye've hooked a passel of rubbish."

Faye pulled a torch from her bag and aimed the beam at the end of Calum's oar. I saw another rope tying the end of the bundle that floated near me. I grasped it with both hands and pulled, letting out a loud "Ooomph!" at the surprising weight. The parcel draped itself over the gunwale, causing the boat to tip dangerously.

"Throw it back, man! Ye'll sink us." Struan sounded genuinely alarmed.

Instead of throwing my end overboard, however, Calum seized my rope and pulled the remainder of the bundle into the boat, sliding to the center of the bench himself to make room. The rowboat righted. "What is it?" Faye's voice was barely above a whisper and even in the dim light I could see how white her face had gone.

Calum pulled a pocketknife from his jacket and slit the rope at my feet. My unease grew as I observed the size and shape of the roll that extended most of the length of the boat. I didn't want to see what was inside. And yet I reached down and gave a firm yank to the dark green duck tape sealing the edge of the rubberized tarpaulin.

"Let me." Calum took the tape from my icy fingers. "Get back," he ordered. Another rip at the tape and the corner of the tarp fell open.

"Aaaagh!" I covered my mouth and nose as the sickly-sweet odor of rotting flesh assailed me in a wave. My eyes watered and my stomach churned.

Calum, whose head had been bending close to mine, pulled back, gagging, as the acrid reek of sulphur followed.

"Cover it up!" Struan yelled through his raised hand attempting to block the foul stench.

But Faye, sitting upwind, leaned forward, aiming her torch at the head peering out of the rubber shroud. She let out a single cry, then crumpled to the bottom of the boat.

Her dropped torch extinguished, but I had seen. In spite of the pale, bloated skin, the sunken eyes and gaping mouth, I knew.

We had found Euan.

Chapter Seventeen

Felicity put the notebook down. Reading of finding a body—even one so long ago, made her shiver. It seemed to bring her own discovery on Iona even closer to her. What had happened there in that beautiful, peaceful spot? Would the mystery ever be solved? Even as drowsiness overtook her, unanswered questions swirled in her head. Behind the veil of sleep she grasped at possible answers but they were as insubstantial as fog.

Oddly, she slept soundly and awoke the next morning feeling more refreshed than she had for days. A glance out the window told her the world was refreshed, too. Sunshine, blue skies with fluffy white clouds, just enough breeze to keep the midges at bay—she hoped. Another surprise greeted her when the door sprang open, and Teddy marched into the room. She hadn't even realized he wasn't still in his bed on the other side of the room. "Where have you been? How did you get out of the room without waking me?" She sat up and swung her feet to the floor.

He shrugged. "I was quiet. I wanted to show Tyr to Anna."

"Who?"

He held up his chessman. "We named him Tyr. It was Anna's idea. Because he's from Norway and Tyr was a god. He was really, really brave. He killed a terrible wolf and he carries a sword like my knight. Anna said he's the god of courage and justice—that's good, isn't it?"

Was this the right time to explain about mythological gods? Felicity considered for a moment, then merely hugged her son and said, "That's great. Hello, Tyr of courage and justice." She got out of bed. "I'm starved. How about you? Have you had breakfast yet?"

"No, the porridge is ready, but Anna's frying bacon, so I said I'd wait."

"Very wise." She talked as she selected clothes for both of them. "And guess what—I don't have to work today, so I can spend the whole day with you, and we can go for a picnic and whatever you'd like to do."

The air was filled with the sound and smell of sizzling bacon and eggs. Anna looked up with a smile as Felicity and Teddy settled around the big, comfortable table. "And what are you two going to do today?"

Teddy didn't need to be asked twice. "We're going on a picnic! Just me and mummy." He paused and his brow wrinkled. "Should we invite Isla? She might feel bad if we don't."

"She might be glad of some free time. How about I ask her what she wants to do?"

Teddy gave a satisfied nod and bit into his bacon.

Anna placed several slices of bread in her enormous toaster. "Where are you going for your picnic?"

"I hadn't thought. What would you suggest?"

Anna considered. "Well, Dalbeg Beach is beautiful and only about half an hour away. Luskentyre Beach is amazing—white sands, turquoise waters—but it's clear down on Harris. Have you been to the Callanish Stones? They're fascinating." She set a rack of toast on the table. "But really, shouldn't you take Tyr to Uig Beach? I think he'd like to see the place his ancestors landed."

The decision was made by unanimous consent. "Great, I'll pack a hamper for you," Anna said.

"Oh, you don't need to do that," Felicity protested.

"Ach, it's no trouble. I can make bacon butties with the leftovers here. And I think I can even lay my hand on a Viking helmet my wee'uns used to play dress-up."

Isla was out when Felicity rang, but Cameron gave her hearty assurances that she couldn't do better than a picnic on Uig beach and Isla would not be bothered that they went on without her.

So, a short time later, with picnic hamper duly stowed in the boot and Teddy strapped into his high-backed booster seat, Felicity was driving across the island with a feeling of lightness she hadn't experienced since she set out on this adventure. She delighted in the sense of accomplishment she had in having completed her research and found what she needed to prepare for her big event with her spiritual directors' group. She had worked her way through all but three of Aileana's slim notebooks and had even tucked one in her bag today in the probably vain hope of having a few moments to read while Teddy played. It all combined to produce the blissful joy of knowing she could return to mainland Scotland—and more importantly, to Antony—the day after tomorrow, conscious of having successfully accomplished her task.

She also enjoyed a buoyant sense of freedom. As much as she had appreciated Isla's indispensable help, being out with her son for a you-and-me holiday was a moment to relish. Lately she had been all too aware of how quickly the time was passing and how alarmingly fast he was growing.

A third pleasure was the beauty of the day, with intense blue skies broken only by a few pristine clouds. Like most journeys on this island, one had to drive about twice the distance it would be were one not required to circumvent numerous lochs and inlets. Today, however, that didn't frustrate her in the least. There were no time limits on them, she had no appointments, she was free to enjoy the scenery—something the exceedingly sparse traffic allowed her to do.

She started an audio book of *Ten Little Dinosaurs* for Teddy and joined him in the exuberant "Rawrr!" that followed each count.

Once they had crossed the peat-covered, green plateau that formed the center of the island, they detoured around Loch Ceann Hulavig and crossed a meandering water marked Abhainn Dhubh, Black River—which was much nearer to a stream than a river in Felicity's estimation, and today shone a clear blue reflecting fluffy clouds. From her earlier study of the map, Felicity knew they were near the Callanish stone circle, so kept a careful watch but caught no glimpse of the location of the mighty dance of stones. Even so, she couldn't repress a small shudder when she recalled Aileana and Faye's experience crossing the loch she knew was just beyond the green horizon to her right.

"Mummy, I'm hungry."

Felicity smiled. They had gone through several books of the popular counting rhymes and were on *Ten Little Monsters* with appropriate Boos, Clanks, and Caws. Of course, her little monster would be hungry, too. She pulled into a layby and handed a packet of crisps across the seat. "Do you still have water in your cup?"

He did, so they continued. The terrain became more rugged for a while with impressive outcroppings of dark stone. Then back to green turf winding around lochs and streams. And *Ten Little Pirates*. Finally, the single-lane track with grass growing down the center took them to the tiny car park where she unsnapped Teddy from his seat and gathered their picnic supplies.

"Can we race?" Teddy started out before she answered.

"Wait! Certainly not, young man. You will help me carry all this. Here." She handed him the plaid rug supplied by Anna and he skipped ahead of her down the path. When they topped the slight rise in the path and saw the vast curve of white sand with the aquamarine sea lapping its shore, Teddy gave a whoop, dropped his bundle and set out at a run. Felicity smiled, retrieved the blanket, and followed more slowly.

As on their previous visit, they chose a somewhat sheltered spot to the south side of the crescent and devoured the contents of the hamper. Then it was time to perform the rite they had come for. Teddy drew Tyr from his pocket and held him out to view the beach where his original had been found. Next came the reenacting. Teddy wearing the Viking helmet supplied by Anna, ran to the edge of the water, then strode up the beach carrying his prize.

"What do you think happened next, Mummy?"

"Hmm. Maybe the Viking played a game with his crewmates?"

"We can't play chess with just one piece."

"That's true. And Tyr does seem a little lonesome. Since there were a lot of pieces found, why don't you gather some stones and shells to represent the others, then you can discover the whole hoard?"

The suggestion gave Felicity a brief space of quiet to relish the moment: the sound of waves washing the shore, seabirds calling, breeze rustling the grasses on the bank behind her, laughter from the few, scattered fellow holidayers enjoying the beach. When Teddy returned with his hands full of imaginary chessmen the play-acting began. First with Teddy burying Tyr up to his stubby neck in the sand with his companion bits around him. Then solemnly removing his horned helmet and undertaking the scene of discovery, playing the part of the crofter who made his remarkable find. Next Felicity was directed to play the part.

"Can we do it again?" Teddy reached for his helmet.

"Well, one account I read claims that Malcolm MacLeod, the crofter, stumbled on a sandbank uncovered by the storm. Underneath the sand was a stone chamber holding the chess pieces. That sounds like it might have been above the beach a bit."

The idea appealed, so Teddy set about selecting a spot on the higher ground rimming the beach. He found a sandy spot among the rocks and turf that formed a ridge extending into the sea.

"That's good." Felicity produced an empty baggie from the hamper. "I think they said the chessmen were in a pouch. Will this do?"

Indeed, it did, and the play-acting continued with Felicity taking pictures of Teddy in alternating Viking and crofter mode, sending each one to Antony somewhat in the manner of a stop-action video. She was beginning to wonder how much longer this would go on when Teddy pointed out to sea with a shout. "It's that boat."

Felicity watched as *Selkie*—or what must have been her twin sister—sped across their view, streaking down the island. It was a beautiful sight, the sleek ship cutting through the blue, sun-dappled water, trailing her long, white wake behind. So why did it give her a chill?

She just finished sending her picture of the yacht to Antony when Teddy asked, "Can I paddle now?"

"Sure. But let's take our supplies to the car first." Teddy put Tyr in his pocket and the other bits in the hamper. In a few minutes they were back on the beach where Teddy pulled off his shoes and socks and ran to the water's edge. It took little encouragement from her son for Felicity to do likewise. The tide was ebbing, so they were able to edge further and further down the beach and still get their rolled-up jeans only barely damp.

Then Teddy spotted the newly bared strip of sand leading around the tip of the ridge to the next beach. "Look, Mummy, it goes on. Can we explore? Please?"

Felicity recalled how appealing the neighboring cove had appeared when they viewed it from above on their previous visit. They donned trainers and socks, then Felicity was once more following her energetic son. Around the rocky end of the promontory, which had been lapped by waves on their earlier visit, they discovered a small, immaculate beach. Teddy stopped, drew in his breath, and flung out his arms. "It's all ours."

Uig Beach had been near enough to unoccupied, but this was entirely untouched. "Do you think anyone else knows about it?" Teddy's eyes were big.

"Oh, I'm sure it's on all the maps." She struggled to recall the name she had seen when studying their route. Carnish, maybe? "I don't suppose many people come here. I think you can only get here during low tide. Or maybe by boat." She observed the steep walls of the low cliffs surrounding the small crescent. Not a place one would want to be stranded by a rising surf.

"Look, Mummy. Can we go in?" Teddy pointed to the opening of a cave across the sand.

Felicity well understood the appeal of caves to small boys, but her mothering instincts made her pause and consider. She recalled Aileana writing about the caves in her journal. As children they had played pirates and smugglers and all sorts of things in the caves. The entire coast of the island had been sculpted over eons by powerful forces of wind and water. Surely, they could stand invasion by one small boy. "We can look in, but don't go too far."

Teddy set off at a run, his usual gait of choice, and Felicity followed, feeling the sun warm on her head. At the mouth of the cave, they stopped and peered into the blackness. Felicity pulled her mobile out of her pocket and shone the bright beam from the flashlight onto the walls. The shine on the lower parts of the walls told her how high the tide had been. Six feet? No, more than that, even. She wasn't a good judge of distance, but it was high enough to tell her she needed to keep an eye on the tide. A glance behind her, though, reassured her that the ribbon of sand by which they had rounded the point was widening, not narrowing, so she could continue to indulge her son's desire to explore.

And sure enough, he was off with all the wonderful freedom and energy of childhood, around yet another narrow cape. "Not too far, Teddy," She called above the sound of the surf. "This is the last one—then we need to go back."

She hoped his whoop indicated he had heard her. This beach was equally unspoiled, but much larger, without the cozy, secret feeling of the tiny half-moon behind them. Here the stony wall surrounding the sands was higher, steeper, more forbidding in its rugged, black formations. "Teddy, I think we should go back."

But he was too far across the beach to hear her, heading for the far cliff wall which offered an array of gaping black caves like open, toothless mouths all screaming. "Teddy!" she yelled and set out at a lope across the sand. "Stop!"

Fortunately, for all his liveliness, Teddy was obedient. He stopped just inside the entrance of the smallest cave. "It's just as tall as I am."

In spite of her breathlessness, Felicity smiled when she saw that Teddy's head almost brushed the top of the tiny cave. "I'll take your picture. It looks like you're holding the cave up."

She didn't have the heart to spoil his fun, so acquiesced to his desire to look in each cavern. After all, there were only five or six. "Okay, but then we go straight back. Agreed?"

"Okay, Mummy." And he was into the entrance of the next cave.

The largest of the caves didn't reveal itself until they were almost to the edge of the waves. It was set apart and partially hidden by boulders set at angles that nearly covered the entrance. "Take my picture in this one, Mummy."

"All right, but then we go."

Teddy nodded and stepped into the cave. And disappeared.

"Teddy! Where are you?"

"I'm here. Come see."

The slight echo to his words told her he had gone deeper in than she would have approved. "Stop! Don't go any further!" She yelled, desperate that he hear her.

She turned on her flashlight and hurried into the cave. "I'm here. See, Mummy."

Felicity froze at the sight. "Teddy! Come! Now!"

"Take a picture."

It was quicker than arguing. "Now, out."

He obeyed. Before leaving, though, she turned back and took one last photo. Those barrels would be evidence. Antony could send the picture to the police. It must all be part of whatever was going on.

Teddy was obediently waiting for her at the mouth of the cave, gazing out to sea. "It was here again."

"What?"

"That boat."

She grabbed his hand and didn't let go until they were safely back on Uig Sands with its comforting sprinkling of holidayers.

"Can I paddle once more, just before we go? Please, Mummy?"

"Five minutes. No more. We need to get back." She struggled to keep her voice calm. She knew the near-panic she felt was irrational. She was certain she had stumbled onto an important clue in what must be a smuggling operation, but all she needed to do was get her photo to the police. She needn't be involved. No one knew that she knew, so there was no real danger. Although it was impossible to convince the prickle that chilled her skin.

Teddy was happily wading at the water's edge within her line of vision. She pulled out her phone and sent her photo of the barrels to Antony with a brief explanation of where they were and her belief that they had something to do with the dodgy diesel operation. *Send to police.* She clicked send, pocketed her phone and called "Time to go!" all in one motion.

"Teddy, did you hear me?" She started toward the small figure splashing in the foam. "We need to..."

The words died on her lips. The child was not Teddy. "A little boy—About your age—He was right here..." She had to restrain herself from grabbing the strange child by the shoulders. Why wasn't he Teddy?

"He went with the man."

Felicity fought for control. Hysteria would only waste precious time.

"What man? Where did they go?"

"Dunno. That way, I think." The child pointed toward the promontory where they had played finding-the-chessman.

"Peter!" A man called the child.

Felicity ran to him. "My little boy. He was paddling here. Two minutes ago. Did you see him? Your son said a man..." She stifled a sob at the horror of her own words.

"Is that richt?" He asked the child.

The boy nodded, but further questioning from his father didn't gain any more information.

Then Felicity saw Teddy's red and blue sneakers and socks piled in the sand at the edge of the water. He had been grabbed and carried off barefoot. How could it have happened so fast? He wasn't really out of her sight. Ever. Why didn't Teddy scream? "Did the man cover his mouth?" She tried not to yell at Peter. But he only shook his head in a bewildered fashion.

She ran to retrieve the precious shoes. She was in motion to hug them to her chest when she saw the note inside: "Drop it or we drop him."

Chapter Eighteen

Afterward Felicity could never remember how she managed to get back to her car and drive across the island. Nor did she know what instinct took her to Isla's home. When she looked back at the horror of the time it was all a black void. She recalled gripping the steering wheel so hard her hands were numb. She remembered Catriona wrapping a blanket around her and shoving a mug of hot, sweet tea into her hands. She remembered insisting to Cameron that they couldn't call the police. She tried to explain George but she knew she wasn't making sense.

Her mind came into something like focus when she called Antony. She tried to give him a rational explanation, but the words just kept tangling and sobs kept breaking through. She recalled Cameron—or maybe it was Catriona—taking her phone from her and doing their best to explain the situation to Antony.

There must have been a sedative in the tea Catriona gave her because the whole night was a blur. She remembered calm hands putting her to bed. And Isla's soft voice reading to her. Did the girl really sit by her bed all night? It somehow seemed so because every time Felicity floated to consciousness, she heard the soothing voice reading to her from Aileana's journal which Isla must have pulled from her bag.

My instinct, as usual, was to throw my arms around my sister who had been helped to an upright position by Struan. I wanted to shield her. To comfort her. But I didn't dare move. The added weight made the boat sit lower in the water and the wind had stiffened. Faye nodded that she was steady enough to sit alone, clenching the edge of the plank forming her seat. Calum and Struan wordlessly gripped their oars. They turned us around and began rowing back the way we came. Faye sat as if she had been turned to stone. Shock. We all felt it, but I couldn't imagine how much worse it must be for my sister.

By the time we reached the shore the driver had, indeed, found a local farmer accustomed to working with prewar Leyland engines. Struan pulled his warrant card from his pocket and issued orders to the driver before we boarded. The men had no more than stowed the body in the luggage compartment under the bus than the driver managed to start the motor. The elderly passengers gave cries of relief and thanksgivings, thinking they were now on the way to their meeting.

At the turnout onto the main road, however, the driver stopped. "Ah'm richt sorry, folks, but this fine jantleman here's with the polis," he gestured to Struan. "Seems they picked up a bothersome bundle in the loch that needs to get delivered richt speedy." There were muttered protests and questions, but he turned the bus northward, back towards Barvas.

I held a trembling, but still silent Faye in my arms all the way up the island. She was desperately in need of a warm blanket and a beaker of strong, sweet tea. We all were. But even such mundane comforts were unavailable. Instead, I simply held on, trying not to focus on the dripping black nightmare stowed just a few inches beneath my feet. There was no use trying to erase the grisly vision or the foul odor from my mind.

Somehow, we got home. The next morning, I had impressions of being in the back of Calum's car. Still holding Faye. Of boiling the kettle. I must have made tea because I remember the feel of scalding on my tongue. And I remember drawing a hot bath for the limply unresisting Faye. I longed for the same for myself, but her need was greater, and I didn't want to take my hand off her for fear she would simply dissolve into her despair. Flannel nightgowns for both of us. And thick woolen socks. I took her into my bed and put a pottery pig filled with hot water at her feet. Then held her in my arms all night.

I must have slept because the sun hitting my eyes came as a surprise. Faye! I sat up with a jolt. I was alone in my bed. Dear God, where was she? Don't let her have done anything stupid. The realization that I had actually uttered a prayer shook me to action. I threw back my covers and bolted into the hallway. Our parents' door was still shut. I ran down the stairs.

In the kitchen I was greeted with the soft whistle of the kettle boiling. Could anything so commonplace still exist? Faye came from the next room to tend to it. She was pale and her motions were slow and jerky, like those of an automaton, but she was functioning. Even if she wasn't speaking yet.

"I'll make toast." I pulled a loaf out of the breadbox and reached for a knife. A dish of butter and the marmalade pot were already on the table, as usual.

A few minutes later the sound of biting into crisp toast crunched alarmingly loud in the silent kitchen. At first, I didn't realize Faye had spoken. I washed down my bite of toast with a swallow of sweet, milky tea. "Sorry, Darling, I didn't hear you."

"My flowers. Started this morning." She repeated.

I blinked. Then realized. "Oh." Her monthly visitor. "Oh! That's good." Relief washed over me. Faye had been spared disgrace. We had all been spared. Shame, reproach, ostracism—I couldn't imagine what the results might have been to our lives.

A single tear trickled down her wan cheek.

"It is good—Isn't it?" I insisted. This didn't seem like the time to explain the practicalities of the situation to her.

"I don't know. With Euan dead, I suppose so." There, she had said the words I feared to voice. "We had plans…"

This was not the moment to point out the unlikelihood of any such pipe dreams coming to a happy ending. Or the fact that she was desperately young. Life would offer lots more opportunities for dreaming. And for fulfilling. Eventually.

Nor would I question her as to how sure she was that she had even been in the family way. That could wait. For now, I just walked around the table and took her in my arms again.

I was looking out the window late that afternoon when Struan's little blue car marked Poileis came bumping up the lane to our house. He got out, tugged at the hem of his jacket, straightened his helmet, and even adjusted the chin strap. It was unusual for Struan, who often didn't even bother wearing his helmet at all. This must be an official visit.

I hoped it wouldn't be necessary to involve the rest of the family. I had privately told Mam the bare outlines of the night's events. Enough to keep her from questioning Faye. And Faye had finally agreed to lay down with a hot water bottle. I didn't want to upset the fragile balance. Thankfully, Da was at work. He wouldn't have been so easily put off.

I met Struan at the door and showed him into the front parlor before anyone else knew he was there.

He unbuttoned his breast pocket and pulled out a small notebook. All very official. "Right." His pencil was poised. "I need a statement."

I stared at him in silence.

"About last night. What you saw. Who did what," he prompted.

I frowned. "Why? You were there."

"I need your version."

As much as I didn't want to think about it—I had spent

most of my hours since then trying to forget—the details sprang readily to my tongue. As I began recounting everything as accurately as I could I realized it was a relief. Insisting the memories go away had only enlarged them. Getting them out into the light of day seemed to release them. I went through it all. Struan wrote.

At last, I sighed. "That's all I remember."

"Good." He seemed satisfied. Almost as relieved as I felt. "That's as I recall it. Good," he repeated and tucked his notebook away.

"I have been wondering, though..."

"What?" Struan's voice was sharp, with something like a warning note in it. Apparently, he was the only one allowed to ask questions.

"It's probably a silly question." I hesitated. I'd always been useless at science. Still, I'd lived around water all my life. "Euan's been missing for ages. I didn't think bodies would float after that long." I was unable to suppress a small shudder at the renewed image of the sodden bundle beside my feet in the bottom of that rowboat.

"Ah." He cleared his throat and squared his shoulders. I should have known he would be glad of a chance to show off his knowledge. "Several factors to consider here." He ticked them off on his fingers. "Temperature. Cold water slows the processes. Tob na Faodhail is a sea loch—glacial cold this time of year. Water density—saltwater is denser than freshwater. Waterlogging prevention—airtight bag prevented water from entering and saturating the body—a primary reason why bodies eventually sink. By keeping water out, the overall density of the body remained lower than the water, aiding in flotation." He sounded like Mr. Morrison, my third-year science teacher.

By the time he held up his fourth finger I was ready to clap my hands over my ears. But I had asked. "Presence of gasses—decomposition gases that typically cause the body to bloat and eventually escape were contained within the bag."

"So, whoever did it wanted the body to be found?"

Struan shrugged. "More likely a numpty without the brains to put rocks in too." He sounded disgusted. "Probably took that rubber tarp from the same shieling where we found the boat. The duck tape would have been a gift." He shrugged. "Why it would have been in the hut is anybody's guess, but it must have been—unless the whole thing was premeditated, which I doubt."

"Lucky for us, I suppose. I mean, awful as it is, we needed to know." Then I thought. "Janet. And his mam. Do they know?"

He gave an abrupt nod. "Sent a woman polis constable from Stornoway, they did." Wounded local pride showed in his voice. "Couldn't leave it to locals who've known the family all their life. Bigwigs from Stornoway taking over. I should be grateful they let me interview you. Even called in some ministry high muckety-muck in Stornoway—whatever he has to do with the situation..." He grimaced, then patted the notebook in his pocket as if for comfort. "May need to talk to Faye later. That'll do for now." Interview ended. He stood.

I saw him to the door and turned with a sigh. What now? I suddenly felt as limp as Faye had been last night. I sank onto the brown plush sofa that filled one wall of the front room. Where did I go from here? Ever since my precipitous return to Lewis I had been consumed by Faye's desperation to find her missing fiancé and the ludicrous plan that we should attend meetings to search for him.

I was still shaking my head at the absurdity of it all when it struck me—Faye had been right. We did find Euan. On the way to a meeting.

Preposterous as it had all been, it had worked. And now I was free from having to endure the endless round of religious harangues. But that relief was part of the problem. I was completely clueless about what to do with myself now. I supposed I should look for some sort of a job. But what? The main jobs on Lewis were farming and fishing. Unthinkable. Besides, women taking up jobs that should be left for returning servicemen was heartily frowned on.

I toyed with the thought of going back to Glasgow. Would Moira have me back? The box of my belongings she sent on from her flat had been a complete clear-out. Could I really take up the fragments of my life there? Did I even have the energy to try again?

I was no closer to an answer when there was a knock on the door. I waited, hoping Mam or Faye would appear to deal with it, but they didn't, so I pulled myself out of the burrow I had sunk into.

"Oh hi, Kirsty Ann." I swung the door open and stepped back. "Faye's taking a nap. I'll see if she's awake."

"I just heard. About Euan. That's so awful. Is she all right?"

I shook my head and turned to the stairway. Was anybody all right? Would we ever be all right? What did all right even mean?

Faye met me halfway on the stairs. She was still pale, and her hair was tousled, but her cheeks showed spots of color, and she somehow seemed as if a bit of life had been breathed into her. "Oh, Kirsty Ann." Faye spotted her friend over my shoulder. Faye went down to greet her visitor, but I continued my upward motion to our room.

The hot water bottle in Faye's jumbled bed had cooled but was still comforting to hold. I crumpled into the covers...

"I'm going to the meeting in Shawbost with Kirsty Ann. Do you want to come along?" Faye gently shook my shoulder.

It was easier to pretend I was asleep than to answer. I heard her pull her coat and hat out of the wardrobe and the door click shut.

I tried the same charade some time later when Mam came

in, but she was more insistent. "Aileana, I want you up and out of that bed. Your Da and I are going to the meeting at Carloway. You can come with us."

"I think I've got flu, Ma."

She put her hand on my forehead. "Hmm." Her soft snort sounded skeptical, but she didn't insist.

Maybe I hadn't told such a lie after all because when I woke up late the next morning, after the first really sound sleep I'd had in ages, I did feel better. Actually able to face a bowl of Mam's porridge instead of just tea and toast.

Faye and Mam sat at the table, their large, crockery bowls pushed aside empty, crumbs of granary toast and smears of marmalade on their side plates. The Brown Betty teapot wearing its knitted cozy sat comfortingly in the middle of the table. Mam, facing the doorway, saw me first.

"Sit you down, Aileana. Faye has a grand tale." She nodded. "Tell it again, Faye."

I turned to the pan keeping warm on the stove and scooped porridge into a bowl, then pulled a mug from the shelf before I sat at the end of the table. That was when I saw Faye's face and gasped. I knew I wouldn't be able to eat after all.

Faye was incandescent. "Oh, Aileana, you should have come. It was brilliant. You should have been there. Just to see it all—the sunset, it glowed—set the windows afire. It was packed. People everywhere—even sitting on the steps to the pulpit. And everyone overflowing with happiness.

"'They are so full. I am so empty,' I thought. Then they started singing. Oh, you'd have loved it. You'd have outsung everybody. I'm certain Gaelic hymns are sweeter than anything else this side of heaven." She closed her eyes and sang softly, "'Set ye open unto me ye gates of righteousness. Then I will enter into them...'

"That was it! That was the cry of my heart, put into words. Tears were streaming down my cheeks, dripping onto my jumper." She pantomimed with her fingers tracing down both sides of her face and onto her chest. "I didn't have a snooter. Kirsty Anne's father passed me his big, white hankie and I sat there, just crying into it.

"Duncan Campbell preached on the Song of Solomon, 'The Voice of my Beloved! behold, he cometh, leaping upon the mountains, skipping upon the hills...' I saw how shoddy my life was—selfish, useless. Then I understood. The pleasures I had been seeking would never fill the emptiness I felt."

She paused as if searching for words, even though she had apparently just told it all to Mam. "I opened my heart to Love. That was all. Real love. Lasting. Not what I thought it was before." She took a big gulp of tea that must have been stone cold by now, but she didn't seem to notice. She was lost in her fairy tale. That was what it had to be. Such feelings as she described didn't exist.

"It was like a—I don't know—a, a time of singing of birds. It was like heaven on earth. The whole church just seemed to be full of song. The singing of birds and the harp setting me free. They sang, they prayed, and I was just in heaven. It was the singing. I've never heard anything like it before—soft, beautiful, angelic. Oh, Aileana, I wish you could have been there. You'd have felt it too, I know you would have."

I was certain I would not have felt anything like it. Not last night. Not ever. Somewhere in the middle of the night I had figured it out. I wasn't among the chosen. Nothing I could do about it. That was that. Closed door.

Mam looked in silent disapproval at the congealing contents of my bowl. "Yer parritch's gone cold." She pushed her chair back and went to the counter where her string bag containing the morning shopping still lay. I couldn't believe my eyes when she pulled two perfectly round, almost flame-colored oranges from the bag with the flourish of a conjurer.

Such showmanship in my ever-pragmatic mother told, more than any words could have, the miracle of the moment. I hadn't seen a fresh orange since before the war. "Mam! Yer a marvel!"

She nodded smugly. She set one aside for Da and placed the other on the table. Faye fell on it with a squeal of delight. In a few minutes juice was dripping from her fingers as she parceled segments out between the three of us.

"All this and Heaven too," Faye mused, sucking each finger noisily.

But my mind was on things more earthly. Thoughts of shortages, rationing and coupons jarred my memory. Events had been so all-consuming that, ever since I set foot on the pier off the ferry, the incident on the train with the fat man and his dropped coupon book had gone completely from my mind. I should have turned that in long ago. I had to think where I had even put it.

I was halfway up the stairs before I realized I hadn't even thanked Mam for the orange.

Back in my room I scrabbled through my handbag with no results. Side pocket, zippered pouch. I hadn't cleaned it out for weeks. The past few months passed before my eyes as I drew out each item: coins, lipstick, compact, hankie, train ticket stub, ferry ticket—my racing journey flashed through my mind. But no book of postdated petrol coupons. What could I have done with it? I left the theatre without a suitcase. All I had were the clothes I stood up in.

That was it! I rushed to the wardrobe and thrust aside the practical garments hanging there until I came to the glamorous white gown I had worn on that ephemeral concert night in Glasgow. My only proof that the entire thing hadn't been a figment of my imagination. And, sure enough, there it was. Right where I thrust it and forgot about it. Faye must have overlooked it when she sponged and pressed my sole garment for the ceilidh.

I found Mam and Faye in the washin' room at the back of the house engaged in doing the weekly laundry. Mam, standing at the big round copper, pulled one of Da's work shirts from the tub where it had soaked overnight, gave it a brisk rub on the washboard, and handed it to Faye who ran it through the wringer with a few vigorous turns of the handle, then stepped to the clothesline and attached the shoulders with wooden pegs. The stiff breeze billowed the shirt, raising it to the sun. The laundry would be dry in a short time. Long before the threatening rain clouds on the distant horizon reached us.

"I'm going into Barvas. Maybe even Stornoway. I need to find a job," I announced and stalked off before I could be offered an argument. Or before awkward questions could uncover the fact that I was headed to the police station to turn in what was likely contraband.

It was fortunate that I ran most of the way to the bus stop because the bus was just arriving as I reached it. I waved wildly for the driver to stop, but he was already applying the brake. The door opened before me. I leapt to the step.

And crashed full body into Calum who was coming down. "What are you doing here?" We asked in tandem, then pulled apart and just looked at each other.

"Are ye getting on or off?" the driver asked.

"On," I said. "To Barvas. Return." And held out my coins.

Calum nodded and handed the driver his return ticket.

The bus was no more than half full. We found a seat to ourselves in the back. "Lucky I caught you. I'd have hated to have a wasted journey," Calum said, then turned his full attention on me. Obviously waiting for me to tell him what I was about. When I was slow responding he cocked one quizzical brow.

So, I told him. All about the man in the train carriage, the strange coupon book, my forgetting it... "Just hanging there in the back of the wardrobe all this time. Until Mam got oranges at the greengrocers' this morning and got me thinking about rationing. Can you believe it? Oranges—two of them—big, bright, sweet, juicy. I didn't even remember what they tasted like. Do you?"

I paused for breath, but Calum didn't answer my question. Instead, he held out his hand. "May I see it?"

"Silly, of course not. We ate it!" Then I realized he meant the coupon book. "Oh." I dug in my bag and handed it to him.

He looked carefully, turning it over, then back to the front. I read over his shoulder, not really having bothered to scrutinize it before:

Motor Fuel Ration Book
For the six months
March, 1950 to August, 1950
Private Motor Car
This book is the property of
His Majesty's Government

There followed a warning about improper use of the book leading to prosecution. The square for recording the registered number of the vehicle was blank, but under it the square for the date and office of issue was already stamped as if it had been issued in March—over a month from now.

Calum turned the cover page to the thin booklet of individual coupons.

Issued under the authority
of the
Ministry of Fuel and Power
Two "N" Units

*This coupon is valid for the month of
March, 1950*

"You found this the end of November?" It wasn't a question. He knew exactly when I was on that train.

I nodded. "Like I said—I'm taking it to the police. I know I should have long ago, but I forgot."

Calum frowned. "Don't do that, Aileana. Not in Barvas."

I snatched the coupon out of his hand, secured it in the side pocket of my bag, snapped it shut, and folded both arms over it as if I were in danger of having my precious cache wrenched from me. I glowered at him. I knew what was behind his reaction. His jealousy of Struan had been evident from their first meeting. "Whyever not?" Not that I expected him to admit his motive to me.

"Please, Aileana. Don't misunderstand me, but I don't trust Struan."

I gasped. I couldn't believe he admitted it. I almost laughed. "You're off your head. I've known Struan all my life. What could possibly make you say that?"

He sighed. "I'm not sure. Something I sense. It's his reactions. Somehow, they don't feel right. He's…" He paused. "Well, underhanded. Slippery…"

"You are so wrong. Struan Macaulay is generous and caring and… Look how he's given every evening to taking Faye and me to meetings and…"

The bus pulled up at the Barvas stop. Most of the passengers were getting off so my desired grand, flouncing exit was spoiled by having to wait for the aisle to clear, but I held my head high, shoulders squared, not looking back—all to make the best effect I could. I continued storming all the way up the road to the police station. Possessive men! As bad as rutting stags.

I strode into the station, then stopped. Instead of Struan's tall, uniformed figure, a young trainee stood behind the counter. "Where's Struan? Er—Officer Macaulay?" I stuttered as the wind went out of my sails.

The lad shrugged. "I'd not be knowing, miss. He just told me to mind the desk and left."

"Do you expect him back soon?"

He looked as blank as I felt. I walked out and let the door slam shut behind me. Then just stood there. It would be ages before the bus returned from Stornoway on its circuit up the island. My fictitious job search plan held no more enticement for me than when I had concocted it. There was a bench in front of the police station. I sat. At least it was sunny, and I was out of the wind.

I sat there in my funk for several minutes before I realized I was hearing singing. Where was it coming from? I stood up and looked around. A group was walking up the road from the loch, singing in Gaelic. Psalm 23, the first one I learned as a child. The soothing lilt took me back to my childhood. I walked towards them—maybe a dozen young people. I blinked when I spotted the girl in the green tweed jacket near the back of the group. Janet MacLeod? So soon after the discovery of her brother's body? I didn't know whether to be glad for her or to disapprove. Either way, I ran across the street to her.

"Janet, I'm that sorry about your brother." I hugged her.

We pulled away from the group. She nodded. "I know. We are, too. It's hardest for Mam. She never gave up hope." She sighed. "I suppose mothers don't. I think I knew—in a sort-of way. I knew he was gone at odd hours, had mysterious friends, too much money for someone who never worked..."

We just stood there and looked at each other until the young woman at the back of the group turned around. "Are you coming Janet? It's a long walk and we'll be late. I'm sorry, but..." She turned back to the group and continued singing.

Janet grabbed my arm and tugged as she took a step forwards. "Come with us, Aileana. It's just a cottage meeting up the road, but I feel like I have to do something. You can always pray, can't you?"

I wasn't about to answer that, but I didn't have anything else to do.

Chapter Nineteen

Felicity woke the next morning with her cheeks wet and a heavy, inexplicable weight in her chest. She was conscious of resisting waking up, facing the day. Her heart ached. Her brain ached. But most of all her arms ached. She reached out as if to enfold her son's lovely, five-year-old body...

Then it all returned with a crash. "Teddy!" She sat up with a sob.

She scrambled out of bed, tearing at the covers. Then just stood there. What was she to do? She spotted Teddy's trainers—his precious shoes left abandoned on the beach as a receptacle for that soul-piercing message. She staggered back and sat down heavily on the bed. The unreality of it all was like a thick, immobilizing fog. Somehow, she had to work through it. She had to get a grip, she told herself over and over. But there was nothing to grip onto.

She was still sitting there when her door opened a fraction. She caught her breath, expecting Teddy to burst in and fling himself into her arms. "Te—" The word ended in a gulp when Catriona came into the room.

She sat on the bed beside Felicity and took her into her arms. "I'm sae sorry, darlin'. I'm thankful you slept. Cameron's been on the phone since dawn. Got all sorts out of bed."

That jarred Felicity into focus. "No! No police. One of the officers is... I saw him..." She took a breath. She had to make sense.

"One of the police. I think he's the kidnapper. I don't know..."

"Nae, not polis, just friends. Friends with skills..." She didn't explain. Instead, Catriona stood to her feet, pulling Felicity after her. "Now. Wash. Dress. Tea. In that order. Do you need help?"

Felicity nodded. "No. I mean, I can do it. I will." Her movements were still leaden, but at least she was moving. A hot washcloth on her face did feel good. Catriona had laid out a new toothbrush. In a few minutes she appeared in the kitchen just as her hostess placed a fresh pot of tea on the table. "Toast in a minute. I don't expect you fancy anything more?"

Felicity shook her head and sat. She took a few obedient, mechanical sips from the filled mug in front of her. She was still sitting there with a half-full mug of tea and a half-eaten piece of toast when the door opened again.

She blinked three times before she dared cry out. "Antony!"

And then she was in his arms. Nothing in the world had ever felt better. She gasped and cried and tried to talk, but nothing really worked. At last Antony pulled away and guided her back to her chair. He took the one beside her with his hand still on her arm.

"How—?" Felicity began.

"It's good to have friends. Roger brought me. He knew I was desperate enough to get to you to try swimming."

"On *Selkie*?" With Antony beside her Felicity was beginning to feel like she could focus.

Antony nodded. "Just docked at Iona last night. Wasn't sure we'd make it. His captain didn't show up and then his first mate reported that the glitch in the engine the repair was supposed to have fixed was still there..."

"Never mind that. You're here—that's all that matters. Oh, Antony, what are we going to do? We can't call the police, and I don't know... We have to do something. I'll go crazy."

Before Antony could reply Cameron entered the room. The two men clasped hands and exchanged a few words. Then Cameron took his place at the head of the table as if he had called a meeting. "We should have some useful information soon. I sent in that note you found to check for fingerprints."

"No!" Felicity flung out her hands as if to stop him, barely missing her mug of tea. "No, no—not the police. That man who was following us—he's a policeman. I saw him—" Cameron's confused expression told her she wasn't making any sense. She took a deep breath and reminded herself of the need for calm reason.

But Antony was ahead of her. "What she's trying to say is she saw an officer at the Stornoway police station who looked like the man who has turned up in suspicious circumstances on Iona and here."

Cameron's silence indicated he wanted to hear more. Antony, with a few helpful prompts from Felicity, told him about the hiker on Iona. "Near the gully with the dodgy diesel," Felicity inserted. Antony nodded and continued about the same man showing up in a picture of Teddy at the Truishal stone. Felicity pulled out her phone and showed Cameron the picture. "His name is George—at least, that's what the female officer he was trying to chat up called him."

"May I?" Cameron held out this phone ready to air drop the photo to himself. Felicity nodded.

"You see why we can't go to the police—I'm sure this George is in on it—whatever it is. And the awful thing is that he knows everything I know—at least, everything I suspect." She told Cameron about reporting to the Stornoway police then seeing George in uniform behind the counter when she left.

"Right. No need to bring the police into this."

"But how—?" Felicity began.

"I can keep it all internal. Our industry operates in a complex, high-risk environment. Security is a major issue. So, we have our own department. Comprehensive background checks of all our employees, including fingerprinting, is a necessity. The police could take hours—days even—to get the results we can get in minutes—even seconds. We have the latest AFIS technology at our fingertips, so to speak." He cleared his throat as if he realized this was no time for levity. "Er, that's automated fingerprint identification systems. If there are prints on that sheet of paper we'll soon know who it is if they have any kind of record at all.

"Now, tell me about your day before Teddy was taken. Where were you? What did you do? Who did you see?"

Felicity took a deep breath. Replaying their lovely day through her head, hearing Teddy's sweet, high voice and carefree laughter, watching his freedom and delight as he ran with the wind, splashed in the waves… She gulped. "It was a perfect day. Until…" Another deep breath. Antony took her hand under the table, squeezed it and continued to hold it tightly. "We had a picnic. On Uig. We played finding the chessmen, ate lunch. Just us. There were a few other groups, but we didn't really see anyone close up. Not until later. Teddy wanted to paddle, then he saw the tide was out and we could walk to the next cove. It was a magical place—tiny, pristine, almost hidden…"

"Yes. Carnish." Cameron nodded.

The day was beginning to blur to Felicity. She remembered the activities, just not the order they did them in. "We explored Uig Beach, then the next one, went in caves…" Then she remembered. "Oh, I saw barrels!" She grabbed her phone again and showed Cameron the pictures she took.

"And this was at Carnish?"

"Um, yes, I think that was the name. A small beach just below Uig—past the sand with sheer rock walls above our heads. You could never walk there at high tide. Teddy wanted to go on, since the tide was out, but I was afraid it might turn, and we would get cut off.

Cameron returned to examining the pictures. Felicity nodded when he asked to air drop them. "Oh, and we saw *Selkie* again—or that boat that looks like her…"

That led to a whole new line of questions. Antony began explaining about his student's swish yacht, the one that brought him to Lewis, and Felicity picked up the thread to tell about their sightings when it was supposedly in Southampton.

Cameron made notes. "That should be easy enough to check." He turned to a fresh page in his notebook. "Now, any thoughts on what that message meant? Getting dropped?"

Felicity shook her head. "I've tried to think. This whole island is surrounded by cliffs—the sea—Lews Castle tower? Whatever…? I only know it means they'll hurt him. Bad." She covered her face with her hands. "I keep thinking how frightened he must be. Do you think they fed him? Will he be tied up?" She turned to her husband and grabbed his arm. "Oh, Antony, what if they've—" She stopped, the words were too terrible to utter.

Cameron's calm authoritative voice cut short her rising hysteria. "Never mind. We've got enough to be going on with. Let's wait until we get some answers from my security department." His gaze settled directly on Felicity. For the first time she became aware of her rumpled clothes and tousled hair. "Go back to your B&B. Shower, clean clothes, eat something."

Antony started to help Felicity to her feet, but she jumped up ahead of him. "No. I'm all right. I have to be for Teddy's sake."

She even drove back to the B&B. "Anna, this is Antony. He'll tell you what's happened. I need to shower," she explained in response to Anna's shocked expression at seeing her disheveled guest and a strange man at her door.

Cameron was so right. This was exactly what Felicity needed. She stood ages in the shower, just letting the hot water pour onto her head and streak down her body. She was back in her room, pulling on clean socks when she glanced up at the small desk in the corner and saw Teddy's drinking cup model of the Butt of Lewis Lighthouse. And she knew. "That's it!"

Antony must have heard her exclamation because he burst

into the room. "I've got it," she cried. "I know where Teddy is!" She pointed at the paper model.

Antony looked blank. "What is it?"

She explained about their visit to the lighthouse and Teddy later doing the craft project at the castle museum. "He loved it at the lighthouse. He wanted to go to the top, but it's all shut up." Her elation turned to horror, recalling how high the structure was.

"But don't people live there?" Antony objected.

"No. No. There's some kind of a radio station operated from some of the buildings, but the light has been automated for decades. Fog signals, everything, all monitored remotely." She headed to the door, still talking. "We've got to tell Cameron. We can get Teddy—we'll just look like tourists and find a way to sneak into the tower—"

Cameron opened the door on Felicity's first knock and listened intently to her excited explanation and rather muddled plan. "I'm sure that's where he is. So, if we drive up in a car they won't recognize—can we borrow yours? They might know the one I have. Or—"

Cameron held up his hand. "Wait. Come. Sit down."

Felicity realized they were still standing in the front hall. She followed their host into the living room. "Now," he said. "Let's think this through."

"It's high. It's uninhabited. And we saw *Selkie* near there. If the smugglers were using her—" Felicity ticked the items off on her fingers. "It makes sense."

Cameron turned to Antony. "So, your theory is that your friend's yacht is being used to smuggle petrol into the Hebrides? I'm not sure I'm connecting the dots here." Felicity opened her mouth to explain again, but he continued. "You explained about seeing her—or thinking you might have—at various locations around Lewis when she was supposed to be in for a repair. But I don't see what all that proves. Could have been out for test run."

Antony added the information about the first mate saying the engine problem hadn't been repaired and added that the captain seemed to be inexplicably missing. "Not proof, I know. But something definitely appears to be wrong there."

"So, you think your friend is part of this smuggling scheme, or whatever it is?"

Antony shook his head. "I don't see how he could be. He was with me pretty constantly this past week. He seems so genuine in his mission work and all that. I don't know what to think…"

A ring on Cameron's mobile interrupted the conversation. He pulled it from his pocket. "I have to take this."

Felicity and Antony were left in a vacuum of silence. He leaned over to put his mouth near her ear in a comforting closeness. "Pray."

At Antony's single word Felicity felt the tension drop from her shoulders. In a way, that was all she had done, but she wasn't certain her internal screaming at God counted for much of a prayer. Maybe now, with Antony beside her and laying it all out to someone in authority, she could manage some coherence.

Cameron was back soon. "Well, that's two mysteries solved. They found my missing crewman." He shook his head. "Washed ashore on the Isle of Mull."

"Missing crewman?" Antony asked.

"Kenny Shea." Cameron shook his head and explained about his newly hired assistant that took off on shore leave. "And nae bothered to come back. He had brilliant references—they just failed to tell me he was a barmpot."

But Felicity wasn't thinking about work references. The horror in her mind was the possibility of a small body washing up on a white sand beach…

No, she wouldn't go there, not for even a moment could she let such an image cross her mind. She wrenched her thoughts away, only to be flooded with pictures of flies buzzing around a swollen, extended leg on the edge of a deep gully on Iona. "Wait! That can't be right. You said Mull?"

"Aye. Fidden Beach, southeast of Fionphort, if that means anything to ye."

Felicity struggled to get a picture of a map of the Hebrides in her mind. It was hazy, but she knew Fionphort was near Iona. Southwest of that would be across from the Old Quarry—and its neighboring gully, wouldn't it? "It might mean something." She told Cameron about the body she was sure she saw, "but then it disappeared without a trace."

Cameron questioned her about the timing of all that, then thought for a moment. "Aye, that'd be about richt. Currents hereabouts tend to flow from northeast to southwest. The high seas of a few days ago could certainly have propelled a body ashore. Even washed one from a beach." He went on a bit about prevailing winds, tides, currents.

But Felicity was still reliving the scene on Iona—that was the first time they saw George. And George saw Teddy.

"You said two mysteries," Antony prompted.

"Fingerprints on the note. I told ye we'd get a result. Easy enough to locate a match. Seems it was yon dodgy policeman."

It was all too horrible to take in. Felicity's head felt light, but she refused to faint. Still, she swayed.

"Felicity!" Antony grabbed her. "This is too much for you. You lay down. We'll get Teddy back. Cameron and I will make a plan." He led her down the hall and guided her to the bed. "Try to sleep. You can't help Teddy like this."

She knew he was right. She closed her eyes obediently.

A few minutes later, though, she realized she was squeezing her eyes shut and every muscle in her body was tense. Maybe a distraction? She looked around and spotted a lone, thin notebook still on her nightstand. She picked it up.

Chapter Twenty

I didn't bother asking where we were going. It didn't matter. I just put one foot in front of the other like everyone else was doing. Only I felt like I was trudging. The others seemed to be almost skating. I had heard talk about how people all over the island thought nothing of walking miles and miles to a meeting. And no one got blisters or ever seemed tired. Even when they went on to cottage meetings after a church service. No one ever seemed to be the least bit weary. Show up at work on time, all bright-eyed, they did.

Well, none of that applied to me. I had slept. And I was still exhausted. It felt like we had been walking for ages. "How far is this?" I asked Janet under the haunting tune floating above my head. I, whose whole life had been spent singing, could barely manage to hum along.

"Och, it's only three miles." She went back to her singing. "Mo Dhia, mo Dhia, c'ar son a thrèig thu mi? C'ar son a tha thu cho fad o chòmhnadh a dheanamh dhomh, agus o bhriathran mo bhùireadh ?..."

"My God, my God, why hast thou forsaken me? Why art thou so far from helping me, and from the words of my roaring?" My mind translated. The cries of our ancestors were in that melody: Longings, struggles, hopes—mostly unfulfilled; the rolling of the sea, clouds gathering over the machair, lonely shepherds calling their flocks at sundown, smoke rolling from peat fires darkening the ancient blackhouses...

"Ach na bi-sa fada uam, a Thighearna : O mo neart, greas a chum mo chuideachadh..."

"But be not thou far from me, O Lord: O my strength, haste thee to help me..." *I realized I was mouthing the Gaelic, even as my mind found the English meaning. And each step seemed less of a trudging slog. I wasn't gliding like the others seemed to be, but at least my steps were less labored.*

"Iadsan uile a theid sios do'n duslach cromaidh iad 'na lathair : agus cha'n urrainn neach 'anam fein a chumail beo."

"All they that go down to the dust shall bow before him: and none can keep alive his own soul."

I almost bumped into the person in front of me before I realized the group had stopped walking and was turning onto a beaten dirt path that led to a tan harled cottage beside the road. I hung back. Walking with Janet and a clutch of meeting goers, even singing with them, was one thing. Attending a prayer meeting was altogether another matter. What a hypocrite I would be. And what would I do? Just sit there like a bump on a log? With one foot on the threshold, Janet looked back at me. I just shook my head. She went in and shut the door.

Now what? I stood in the middle of the path, gazing blankly at the closed door. I didn't much fancy walking home alone. I didn't even know where I was. Why hadn't I been paying attention? We had turned off the Port of Ness road a little ways back. I looked around. The mid-afternoon sun was moving to my left, so that must be west. Then I saw it, rising out of the turf, just a few hundred feet on up the road—Clach an Truishal, *the standing stone.*

My heart sank. It would take me more than four hours to walk home from here. And, unlike the holy meeting-goers, I would get blisters. The only option was to make my way to the nearest bus stop back on the main road. I groaned. Goid kent when the next bus was due. Still, what choice did I have?

I turned towards the road, but pulled back when a small, dark car trundled past. A tourist going to gawk at an old stane in the middle of a field. What a thing to spend a petrol coupon on. I started to shake my head, then thought. I only noted one person in the car. The energy boost I felt while walking with the group had departed and left me flatter than before. I would be very glad of a lift to the nearest bus stop—even if it meant an extended wait. Or a tourist might be going up the island to see the lighthouse after they gawked at the stane. What luck that would be. I hurried after the car, although there was no need to rush. The road ended just beyond the stone, so I wouldn't miss him.

The lone figure was halfway across the field to the monolith when I went through the gap in the stone wall that blocked it off from the road. Perhaps he heard me or at least sensed someone following him because he turned. I started forwards. "I beg your pardon, sir, but I wondered—" My words and my feet came to an abrupt halt. I took a step back.

It was the man from the train. He was even carrying the same briefcase.

Instinctively I clutched my handbag to my chest and turned to flee. My first step brought me crashing into a solid figure clad in a blue serge uniform with silver buttons. "Struan. What—"

I tried to pull away, but he grabbed my arm and jerked me back around so hard my bag flew from my grasp and crashed against the stone wall, spewing the contents over the turf. Struan and I both dived for it. He reached my scattered belongings first, the coupon book virtually at his feet. With a single snatch he held it aloft in one hand and grasped me with the other, pulling me further away to a corner of the field. "Struan, stop. You're hurting me."

He stopped and gave me a one-handed shake that made my head snap. "What do you think ye're doing?" His words were no less threatening for being kept to a level that wouldn't reach the other man. "Where did you get this?" He shook the coupon book in my face as if he would hit me with it.

"From him." I tried to gesture with my head to the man I assumed was still standing by the stone. "He dropped it on the train. I was bringing it to you at the station, but you weren't there."

That pacified him enough that he eased his grip on my arm, but he was still angry. "Ye've ruined everything. I've worked for months on this."

"Worked? With a—a black-marketer?" My heart sank. Calum was right. Struan—my oldest friend—the man I considered so much more than a friend—a criminal. No better than Euan. I had been as blind as Faye.

"Well, of course I have. We've known about this ring for donkeys' years. How else do you think I was going to get evidence?"

I heard the words. I wanted to believe. Struan had thrown me a lifeline. A logical explanation. I was still on firm ground. So why wasn't I relieved? I just stood there, staring at him. Willing my mind to work, but the world was frozen.

Struan gave me a firm shove towards the wall. "Sit there. And don't move. I've got an arrest to make." He turned and strode towards the stone.

My belongings still lay strewn across the rough ground a few feet along the wall. Not wanting to call attention to my movements I crawled the distance and began gathering keys, coins, lipstick… I wasn't sure what all I had been carrying, but this was most of it. I snapped the clasp of my bag shut and leaned back against the wall, too tired and confused to think, or even to pay attention to what Struan and the man were doing.

Then I heard the singing. From the meeting down the road.

They must have opened their windows or moved outdoors. The melody seemed to swirl above my head, then move onward. Upward. I relaxed just enough to breathe. A long, shuddering breath that sent oxygen to my brain. With that I realized I had been holding my breath, but now I could think.

What was going on here? I looked at the two figures, dwarfed by the massive monolith standing behind them. It didn't seem right. If Struan was making an arrest, why did he seem to be in a deep discussion with the man? Now the harsh sounds of an angry argument from the pantomime before me jarred through the floating melody from behind. I wanted to know what they were saying. Needed to know.

The two men were so engrossed in their altercation they wouldn't notice me. Whether my shiver was from fear or a chill from the darkening clouds and rising wind, I wasn't sure, but somehow, I found the courage to get to my feet and creep forwards.

"Careless... Stupid..." I was close enough for random words to reach me before the wind snatched the rest of the sentence away. I didn't dare move closer without attracting attention. "Floating..." It was odd that Struan's voice reached me in spite of his back being to me, when the other man—who seemed to be pleading and protesting—was intelligible.

And then I got a full sentence, barked in Struan's most commanding officer tone. "Put the case down and move away, Dougal." Unbelievably, Struan had pulled a gun on the man he called Dougal. Could it be? Scottish policemen didn't carry guns. The sky was darkening by the moment, but there was plenty of light to see that.

Dougal did as he was told.

"Alright, Aileana. You can pick up the evidence."

I gasped. Struan had been aware of my creeping movements all along. I moved on stiff legs to the tattered brown bag abandoned on the turf.

"Now bring it to me." Struan's command was clear, although he didn't take his eyes off the man he called Dougal.

I took one step forwards.

"Don't do that, Aileana." It was as if the Truishal stone had spoken.

I was so startled to hear Calum's voice from the gloom I screamed. He stepped from behind the menhir. Was I hallucinating? "What—"

"Bad advice, Calum. You don't want me telling her about your little scheme, do ye?"

"Don't listen to him, Aileana. He's in league with these neds."

"Give me the case." Struan's voice was more commanding. Urgent.

My arm was beginning to ache with the weight of the heavy bag. I looked from one man to the other.

Struan's voice softened. "Why don't you ask yer lad about his Glasgow contacts? You don't think he made his money promoting half-baked singers, do ye?"

He shifted to point his gun at Calum and his voice became scornful. "Is that why ye came to the island, Calum? To take care of Euan for yer Glasgow bosses?" Struan aimed at Calum with more precision. "Well, pleasant as this is, it's getting too dark and cold out here for an extended chat. Aileana, my dearie, just bring the coupons along. Calum, Dougal, ye're under arrest—both of ye."

"Aileana," Calum held out his hands.

I had to choose. And I had to get it right. I knew too much to get it wrong. I could feel the black waters of the loch closing over my head. A seabird called as the last tiny streaks of red died in the west.

"Now!" Struan barked.

I looked at Calum. And heard the singing. My mind translated the Gaelic "Make me know Your ways, Lord…" The words cleared

my confusion, even as the rising melody strengthened my arm.
With all my strength I lobbed the case of counterfeit ration books at Struan's head.

My aim was wide. I knocked the gun from his hand, but he launched himself at Calum. Out of the corner of my eye I saw Dougal snatch the case. A moment later I heard the sound of an engine roar away, but all my attention was on the struggling men in front of me. I held my breath. Calum seemed to be getting the better of the contest.

Then Struan tripped him. Calum fell heavily, hitting his head against the stone wall. He didn't move.

"No!" I shrieked. In pure, wild terror I ducked behind the stone just as the first spatters of rain hit.

A roll of thunder crashed over my head so close it felt like it shook the stone.

"Don't be daft, lass." Struan's voice was silken. "Ye canna get away. I'll explain it all to ye. There's nae need for anyone else to get hurt."

He was right. This was daft. There was no way I could escape. I couldn't outrun Struan. I couldn't overpower him. It was cold and wet and getting darker. And what did it matter anyway? I realized I didn't want to live in a world without Calum. Let Struan do what he wanted.

I stepped out from behind the stone. "You win, Struan. But why did you do it?" His laughter echoed off the stone above the sound of the rain. "For the money, of course. What else is there? Do you think I want to be stuck for the rest of my life in a nothing job in this nothing, God-forsaken place?"

A strain of Gaelic hymn-singing reached me above the sound of the storm. People leaving the meeting. Walking over the fields singing the lilting melodies that since the beginning of the Awakening could be heard all over the island from one village to another. The same aura of peaceful knowing I sensed at the meetings flooded over me. Faye's words to Mam rang in my ears as clearly as if she had just spoken them beside me. "I opened my heart to Love. That was all. Real love."

And that was it. The most desperate place I had ever been in my life, and I was flooded with peace.

"No, Struan, you're wrong there. This place is definitely not God forsaken."

He shoved me back against the stone. "Nice that you've had your God experience. That way ye'll feel right at home in Heaven."

I had no words, even for prayer. But I was determined I wouldn't give Struan the satisfaction of thinking he had triumphed. Even when he stepped aside and picked up his gun. Even when I looked at Calum lying lifeless at the foot of the wall, I refused to cry.

"Right over here, my dear. That should be just the right distance." Struan thrust me a few inches further, nearer the edge of the stone.

I felt the rough surface behind my back, I almost caressed it with the palms of my hands. Never taking his eyes off me, Struan backed towards the wall where Calum's crumpled form lay. I saw then what Struan planned to do. Shoot me, then place the gun in Calum's hand. Claim Calum had shot me, then tripped and hit his head on the wall, maybe?

My mind raced. Could I calculate it right? Duck around the stone fast enough just before he fired? What then? Attempt to outrun him and his gun in the dark? Could I possibly get to the cottage? What could they do against an armed gunman if I did? Could...

The world exploded. Pain pierced my forehead. I hit the ground in blackness.

Chapter Twenty-One

"We're going to the lighthouse."

Felicity dropped the notebook and jerked her head toward the door where Antony stood. "What?"

Antony sat beside her on the bed and took both her hands in his. "Your idea of where Teddy is being held seems right. So, we'll go there. But not as tourists. As conspirators. Cameron agrees with your theories about *Selkie* being used for whatever's going on. So, if the kidnappers see the boat, they'll think we're part of the gang. Maybe even bring Teddy down to us—certainly open the door for us. There's no way a mere tourist could get inside even if they got close enough to try."

Felicity started to protest. Surely there were a million things that could go wrong. Things that would put their son's life in danger. And yet, she couldn't think of anything better. And Antony seemed convinced. "How do we get *Selkie*?"

Antony held out his phone. "I've already called Roger. He's still in Stornoway harbor. He'll meet us in a dinghy on the pier."

Felicity nodded, feeling like she should salute. It seemed it was all worked out. Apparently, all she had to do was to put one foot obediently in front of the other. And pray. Unlike her normally independent self as it was, she had to admit that in the present circumstance she was thankful she wasn't in control. Antony and

Cameron seemed to have everything well in hand. She just hoped God did, too.

Roger Wellman was waiting on the north pier for the three of them as promised. Smaller craft were docked alongside the quay, many of them sailboats, their bare masts creating the impression of a leafless copse, but larger ships, like *Selkie*, were anchored out in the harbor. A few minutes' bouncing across the bay in Roger's small runabout brought them alongside the sleek white yacht Felicity had admired from a distance. A shiny, steel boarding ladder was already in place. Roger and Antony gripped Felicity's arms on each side and offered to steady her, but she shook them off and scurried up the ladder. A crew member met her at the top and helped her over the gunwale.

Once they were all aboard, the crewman pulled the ladder up while other crew members saw to the dingy.

Roger introduced his first mate as Owen, then explained what they wanted to do.

Owen did not look happy. He shook his head. "Good luck to that. You're talking about notorious waters. The Butt of Lewis is considered more dangerous than rounding Cape Wrath. Without a fair, moderate wind in the right direction and the tide going right we'll need to give the point a berth of at least five miles."

Undeterred, Roger slapped his officer on the back, "Well then, your job should be easy. We'll pray for fair winds and good tides. All you have to do is steer."

Owen still did not look happy, but he saluted and turned toward the stairway to the cockpit. Felicity followed him up. She was amazed that the luxury of the yacht extended to the pilot's compartment as well. The wrap-around windows offered a panoramic view. Below the windows was a bank of display screens. It struck her as offering as much technology as the cockpit of a jetliner. She sank into one of the plush, pale leather chairs.

"Drinks in the fridge. Help yourself." Owen nodded at the side table that apparently concealed a tiny refrigerator, then took his seat in a high-backed leather chair at the helm. It seemed he had fitted easily into the captain's role.

Felicity felt slightly guilty in such comfortable surroundings as her mind filled with the stark contrast to the danger and deprivation her five-year-old son was undergoing. She took Antony's advice and spent some time fervently beseeching the Almighty for Teddy's protection and the success of their endeavor as *Selkie* got underway.

Once around the extended head that protected Stornoway harbor they headed what Felicity assumed was straight north. Her attention was glued out the left windows as she mentally urged the ship onward, faster and faster, to reach Teddy before it was too late. Before he had to suffer one more moment of fear. The coastline was an almost solid wall of dark gneiss cliffs with jagged rocks at their feet—all washed by foaming white waves. The scene was broken occasionally by a sea stack, tiny island, or a small white beach.

They had been sailing maybe ten minutes when Owen pointed to a promontory jutting out into the water. "Tolsta Head." He said, then returned his hand to the wheel. The turf atop the bluff appeared to be dotted with a few scattered grey, harled homes, but the sight that caught Felicity's attention was a long, silvery sand beach that brought an ache to her heart as she recalled Teddy's delight in visiting beaches on the other side of the island. Was that only yesterday? It seemed like a lifetime ago. It had certainly encompassed a lifetime of fear and pain. She squeezed her eyes shut in an attempt to clear her internal vision of her son running carefree, his arms outspread, his laughter floating behind him across similar white sand.

Then the scene beyond her window returned to forbidding stone walls and crashing waves, bringing new terrors to her imagination. "Here you are." She jumped at Antony's voice. He sat in the chair next to her and reached for her hand. Roger and Cameron, who had come up with him, took seats near the helm.

They sat in wordless silence until Owen pointed again. "Port of Ness." Felicity tried to concentrate. Yes, the beach, seawall, quiet cove with a few small boats... she tried to recall what she had read about it in Aileana's journal. It seemed like months ago that she was there with Isla and Teddy.

Past Port of Ness they turned eastward, and Felicity felt the heavy swells of the sea as the wind increased. And the fury of the waves beating cliffs that were even more precipitous than those she had seen before. How could they ever dock there? Surely, they would be dashed on the rocks if they even tried. This had been a fool's errand. Why didn't they call in the coast guard, Royal Marines, Lifeboat society? Shouldn't Cameron have known better than to attempt this on their own? Panic rose in her chest.

Antony must have felt her tension because he rose and pulled her to her feet. "Come with me."

He led her to the small landing beyond the cockpit out of the pilot's hearing. "We explored the hold."

"And?"

"No obvious proof we could see, but Roger thinks there's plenty for a forensic team to examine—fresh scars on the floor, stains, ropes he can't explain, even a faint smell of petrol. It's his theory that Rog Junior commandeered *Selkie* in his father's absence and got rid of the captain. Figures his son is working with the ring because he's short of money. Now Roger is blaming himself for cutting off Rog's allowance."

But Felicity was thinking in another direction. "Wait a minute. If the captain was gone—who ran *Selkie*? Does that mean Owen is in league with the smugglers, too?"

"Not sure, but that's why I brought you out here—so he wouldn't hear. And that's why Roger is keeping an eye on his first mate. Doesn't want him communicating with the kidnappers to warn them."

Felicity started to ask another question, then cried out at sight of the lighthouse. "There it is!" She looked at the surf crashing against the rocks at the foot of the point. They would never be able to land there. Even if the sea were calm, there was no beach. The motion of even a gentle wave would throw the yacht against rocks more sharply serrated than any knife.

Apparently, the pilot agreed with her because she felt the ship turn and head out to sea. "Oh, Antony, he's giving up. We're leaving." She felt her heart tug as if Teddy were being physically torn from her.

A few moments later, however, they seemed to swerve back toward the Butt and the lighthouse came into view again. They made another pass in front of the lighthouse, this one closer to shore than before, but with no more success. Felicity held her breath, then let it out in a gasp when they turned out to sea once more. She bit her lip against the urge to cry. That would help nothing.

"What on earth is he doing?" she cried when they turned once more toward the shore.

"Let's ask." Antony turned toward the door.

Roger looked up when they entered the cockpit. Felicity was amazed to see him grinning. Owen was intently studying his navigation instruments, looking none too pleased.

"What's going on?" Antony asked.

"My scheme worked a treat. I was sure our antics out here would get their attention." He nodded toward the lighthouse. "They radioed to ask what we were doing. Fortunately, my son and I sound enough alike they thought they were talking to him. Gave us the helpful information that there's a tiny cove around to the west." Roger managed to stop just short of preening when he continued. "I said I wanted to quiz the kid. Told them to bring him out."

"And they agreed?" Felicity couldn't believe her ears.

"Didn't disagree. But they sure sounded impressed that I knew what they were up to. Maybe Rog wasn't in on this part of the operation. Still, I hope they throw the book at him—might bring him to his senses."

Owen looked up from his chart. "Tiny doesn't begin to describe that beach," he grumbled. "At least the tide is favorable. There're life jackets under the benches in the main cabin. I suggest you put them on."

Roger nodded. "You three go on. I'll stay here with my pilot. In case he needs my help."

Felicity translated that to mean *to see he doesn't try any tricks*. Apparently, Roger's presence was sufficient because by the time Felicity, Antony, and Cameron had donned their life vests crew members had the boarding ladder attached to *Selkie's* side and the younger of the two deck hands was getting the dinghy in position. Felicity gulped when she felt the wind and saw the white waves washing the beach. But nothing was going to deter her from getting to Teddy.

Afterwards, it was all a blur: the relief of reaching the shore and pulling her vest off, the feel of the sand slipping under her feet as she lunged across the beach, and the roughness of the rock she clung to as she followed Cameron up the steep, narrow trail winding up the side of the bluff.

At the top Cameron turned back and extended his hand to her to help her onto the turf, Instead, she grasped a nearer stone and heaved herself up to propel her spring onto the machair. Antony was beside her in a moment.

Now what? Run to the lighthouse and pound on the door? Stand at the base and yell upward? But there was no need to decide. Before she even realized it Felicity was racing across the grass, her arms spread wide, tears streaming down her face.

"Teddy!" She scooped him into her arms as he leapt toward her. Her sobs came out in gasps.

"Mummy, Mummy!" He snuggled his face into the crook of her neck. She thought she could never let go.

At his cry of "Daddy!" though, she knew she had to share. She loosened her grip to let Antony share the joy. Even as she felt the wind replace the warmth of her son's sweet body, she registered that she saw no obvious marks of abuse, and the smear of jam beside his mouth indicated that he had been fed.

And then Teddy was back in her arms and Antony's arm around her shoulder. They were complete.

Then she froze. George stood less than six feet in front of her, leveling a gun with both hands. Across the lawn, at the edge of the car park, she saw a police car. Apparently, even in plain clothes, he was keeping up the pretense of being an officer. "Sorry to interrupt, ma'am, but I need to talk to the lad."

Before Felicity could respond Cameron stepped forward. "I think not. We know all about your crooked ways. Just what is the penalty for corrupt police officers who engage in kidnap? You won't get away with this." He reached out as if to take Teddy from her.

Felicity felt Teddy jerk in her arms, his whole body tense. Then he burrowed his face in her chest and clung to her with ferocity.

George stepped closer, holding his gun pointed at Cameron. "Just step over here, ma'am. The lad will be safer."

"Are you out of your mind? Are you really bent enough to shoot all of us?" Cameron demanded.

Still, Felicity hesitated. George sounded so plausible.

"Come with me, Felicity. You know this imposter's been following you. His fingerprints were on the note," Cameron urged.

The pressure of Teddys arms increased.

"Officer George Taggart, HM Revenue and Customs. My ID is in my pocket." He indicated the left breast pocket of his sport jacket. "Come get it."

"Don't move, Felicity," Antony said in her ear. He stepped in front of his wife and child as a protective shield.

Felicity thought furiously. She had to make a choice. And all their lives depended on it. Would the ID be fake? Or had Cameron lied about the fingerprint report? Was George working undercover with the Stornoway police? Or was Cameron investigating for his oil company? *Help me*, her mind cried heavenward.

An image of Ailena forced into a similar decision sprang into Felicity's mind. Aileana had made the right choice by following her heart. Felicity's heart was not involved with these men. But Teddy's was. And his reaction to Cameron's voice had spoken volumes.

She stepped from behind Antony and, still clutching Teddy, walked to George.

"It'll be fake," Cameron sneered.

But before she could do more than spot the official stamp of HMR&C with its encircled Tudor crown, two uniformed officers appeared behind them. "Suspects in custody, sir." Felicity recognized the voice of the young policeman who had taken her statement in Stornoway.

"Cuff him." George indicated Cameron.

Hours later Teddy was finally sleeping peacefully in his bed at Anna's B&B. Careful, but seemingly casual, questioning by his parents and Senior Investigator George Taggart had elicited assurances that after being carried from the beach by "Isla's Daddy" he had been well treated.

"He said you'd gone on up to the car and he was taking me to you—but he didn't." Teddy seemed confused.

"No, darling, I'm sorry I was so slow getting to you." Once again, she felt herself tearing up. "But you did enjoy getting to go up in the lighthouse?"

"Yes. But I would rather have gone with you. I didn't like Jim. Ian was okay. He made me jam sandwiches." He thought for a minute. "They kept asking me about barrels in the cave and stuff like that." He shook his head. "Ian played Snakes and Ladders with me, but Jim just smoked stinky cigarettes. And we played lighthouse keeper." He smiled. "And then you came."

"Yes, darling. I'm so sorry it took me so long." Another intense hug.

Teddy considered for a moment. "That's okay. I 'spect you had to wait for Daddy." He suddenly sat up straighter, pulling slightly away from his mother. "I was brave like Tyr." He pulled the treasured chessman from his pocket. "And I got to sleep there all night—just like a real keeper. Only they don't do that anymore. And the bed was hard."

"Well, Anna's is nice and soft, and Daddy has a super bedtime story for you, young man." Antony intervened and carried his son off.

Felicity patted the seat beside her on the sofa when Antony returned to the sitting room. It felt so good to have him there beside her. "George was just telling me about the body on Iona. It was one of his investigators, Kenny Shea. He was working undercover as Cameron's assistant. And then he disappeared."

Antony looked at George. "And you were following up on his disappearance?" He sounded skeptical. "Then why did you move the body?"

Felicity jumped in. "He didn't. You'll never believe—it was that efficient volunteer fire leader—Lachlan."

George nodded. "We suspected for some time the ring had a contact on Iona. The abandoned equipment in the Old Quarry was a perfect convenience for bringing barrels ashore. When Kenny failed to report in, I went looking for him. I found him alright but couldn't move him myself. Before I could get back with help he was gone. We're not sure yet, but we think Lachlan delayed calling his crew. It wouldn't have been hard to roll the body on down the gully and get it into the sea before the others arrived. Then that storm washed it ashore on mull."

"But what about the fingerprints on the kidnapper's note?"

George shook his head. "Cameron stuck it in his desk drawer.

It never made its way through any official enquiry lines that we can trace. The oil company's investigation lab deny any knowledge. Saying the prints were mine was probably unplanned—just taking advantage of the moment."

Felicity sighed. "Poor Catriona and Isla. I'm so sorry for them. I keep thinking how awful they'll feel." She shook her head. "How did you get on to Cameron?"

"We knew all along there had to be a mastermind. It was a big operation, there had to be someone at the top who knew the industry from the inside. There are always a lot of small fry in an enterprise like this—Lachlan, Rog Wellman, Jim and Ian at the lighthouse, Owen on the *Selkie*... They get paid for their bit, but we wanted the man at the top."

Mention of the first mate reminded Felicity. "Oh, what about Roger's captain? I hope they didn't push him overboard or something."

"Cade? No, he's alive and well in Glasgow. He strode into Atlantic Square, our headquarters in Scotland, with invaluable information about a week ago. He had stumbled across what Owen and Rog were up to and he was afraid for his life. I'm sure Roger senior will be happy to have him back. Especially now that he's without a first mate. Hopefully he'll give the man a well-earned raise."

It was still so hard to take it all in. Practically impossible to believe when they were all sitting in this cozy room. "I still don't understand. Why did Cameron help us? Why did he wait until the last minute to show his colors?"

"I suspect he was hoping to pull it off still appearing to be on the side of the angels. The truth only came out when there was no other option. By then he realized the small fry in the operation would rat on him. Matter of fact, Ian has already proven very helpful."

"A plea bargain?" Felicity asked.

George smiled. "Been watching American shows on the telly? That's not done here. He'll have to plead guilty, but we might be able to enter a lesser charge, or he could be hoping for a lighter sentence."

Felicity hoped so—after all, he had kept the experience from being traumatic for Teddy. But she couldn't think about that now. The anguish and upheavals of the day were catching up with her. The serenity of the room, the comfort of the sofa with Antony so close beside her… But she had to know one more thing. "How did you manage to show up at just the right time at the lighthouse?"

"Cameron's daughter called police."

"Isla? She *knew*?"

"Clever girl. She made a shrewd guess. She found the kidnap note and a drawing Teddy made of the lighthouse. She put two and two together."

Officer Taggart looked severely at Felicity. "It could have saved a lot of time if you'd come straight to us, you know."

"But I thought you were one of them. You'd been following us."

"I was following leads—" he began.

"You were on Iona, you were at the Truishal stone, you were at the police station. I thought—"

Antony interrupted her growing flow with his favorite technique. At the end of the kiss, he grinned at George. "It works every time." He turned back to Felicity. "Bed. Then home tomorrow."

Chapter Twenty-Two

"And don't let him out of your sight." Felicity instructed Antony the next morning when he volunteered to take Teddy to the loo.

"Felicity, relax. We're on an aeroplane."

She nodded and merely blew her husband a kiss. She knew he understood. In two and a half hours they would be in Manchester. Plenty of time for reading Aileana's last journal entry. And basking in being safe with her family.

The first thing I heard was the angels singing. I was warm and comfortable. Held by strong, loving arms. Through my half-opened eyes, I could see spots of light moving around. A candlelight procession? Did angels carry candles? Why was it dark in heaven?

"Aileana. Aileana, my darlin', wake up."

"Calum? Are you in heaven, too?"

He laughed and clasped me to him in the grandest hug I could ever imagine. "Oh, don't let me go. Let's just stay like this for all eternity."

He laughed again and released me. "Aye, my love, it's a fine sentiment, but we aren't in eternity yet."

"Where are we?"

"Cottage hospital. Ye've been well out for a good two hours, lassie. Now you're awake they should let us go soon."

I struggled to sit up. "I thought..."

"Aye. That was a sharp blow you had to your head. I managed to grab that de'il's ankle enough to shift his aim, but he still hit the stane and a big enough chunk hit you to give you a right goose egg." He leaned over and kissed the exquisitely sore lump on my forehead.

"But I thought you were dead."

He rubbed the back of his head gingerly. "A good enough bump, that. I saw more stars than there are in God's heaven. When I could think straight again it seemed best to let Struan think I was done for, too. Thank God I came to in time." He tightened his arm around my shoulder. "My bonnie wee lassie..."

I smiled at his endearment, but I had to know what happened. "Struan. Where is he?"

Calum must have heard the fear in my voice. "Nae worrit. Artair took him firmly in custody, then stopped at the phone box to call for help to apprehend Dougal."

"Artair?" I had a vague memory of Faye saying she'd seen him and Calum at a meeting she had gone to with Kirsty, but I couldn't see...

"Aye. I'm brave enough as matters go, but I'm nae foolhardy. You don't think I'd hare out here on my own do you? I met Artair when he interviewed several of my Gorbals mates back in Glasgow. When I saw him again at that meeting, he gave me a pretty good idea what he was doing on Lewis. Then you told me about that fellow on the train and showed me that ration book. I put it together, but you flounced off before I could explain it to you."

"Oh. Sorry." I did realize that was a pretty pale apology for actions that led to both of us nearly getting killed. "So, you found

Artair?"

"I found the nearest phone box and rang the police station in Stornoway. Thank heavens, they told me he was already in Barvas—turns out he'd been following Dougal since he got off the ferry yesterday. Figured he would lead him to the big yin on the island."

"Struan?"

"Aye. Just a cog in the wheel, really, but important because it's so remote."

"Wait. Were you following Dougal or me?"

"I was following you, ye daft girl, I saw you head up the road with Janet and the others. Then a bit later, I saw Dougal head off the same way. After all, there's only one road up the island, so I kent Dougal was likely to see you. And I knew that could be bad news. Then there was Artair, following Dougal. He wasn't best pleased to have me tag along, but I think he saw my anxiety. And determination."

Several hours later, Calum and I were finally alone, sitting by the glowing peat fire in our parlor, both our heads swathed in professional white bandages. We had given formal statements to the Chief Inspector summoned from Stornoway. Struan had been formally charged with conspiracy to defraud, and the Stornoway police had apprehended Dougal and charged him with the murder of Euan McLeod.

In spite of it all, I was relieved to know that Struan hadn't killed his old acquaintance. "The blood we saw at Callanish?" I asked.

Calum nodded. "Human, certainly. Euan's, we think. That's Struan's best defense that he wasn't involved in the murder. He wouldn't have sent that bit of turf in for analysis if he'd known what it was." Calum thought for a moment. "Still, the fact that he didn't try to launch a major investigation when the forensic lab in Glasgow declared it to be human blood won't help him any. My guess is that he suspected the connection to his own shenanigans."

It was all too much. I just snuggled closer to Calum and basked in the silence—at last. The final hurdle had been fielding the barrage of questions from my family. But now it was just the two of us in a rosy glow as the first streaks of dawn reflected on the walls.

Side by side on the faded brown sofa, sinking ever more comfortably into the cushions with our fingers linked and my head on his shoulder. I finally thought I understood how it had all come about. At least enough for now. But the marvel of realizing that Calum loved me would take a lifetime of getting used to.

Finally, he spoke. "And do you want to continue singing, lass? Or should we just stay right here and make bairns?"

I wanted to laugh until I cried, but the shock completely took my breath away. "Calum Finlay Alexander, ye're indecent." But his question deserved an answer. "Since you have the effrontery to ask, though, can't I sing and have bairns both?"

"And ye're a brazen hussy, Aileana Rossalyn Mackay. Of course we'll do both." He kissed me soundly on the lips.

When I had caught my breath, I turned and put my free hand on his chest before giving him a long, serious look. "One thing, though, I'll have to insist on it with my brilliant manager."

"Anything, woman. You ken ye can ask for the moon."

"And what would I be wanting with the moon? It's heaven I'm thinking of. What we've experienced here. I want to share whatever of it I can. Whatever the program, I want to include hymns—Gaelic and English—in every performance. I want to take some of this with me always. Wherever I go." I held my breath. This was important to me, but Calum and I hadn't talked about such things. We had been engulfed with religion and prayers and meetings, but we hadn't talked about it. It was all

so new to me... what if...?
He gave me a long, slow smile that made my toes tingle. "Aye. I've been thinking about that, too. We've had no time to talk. But The Aunties have had plenty of time. Talk and pray—that's what they do. And powerfully, too. I've given plenty of mind to what Aunt Ida said to you that night in Tarbert."

I nodded. So had I.

"What she can't see around her, she makes up for with what she sees beyond. It's her idea that Duncan Campbell will be needing help with his Faith Mission in Edinburgh. How would you feel about singing in Edinburgh, my lass?"

I grinned. "It sounds a wee bit tame after the back room at the Lochnagar, but I suppose I could adjust." Then I got serious. "But we'll always come back to the island."

He nodded. "Aye, if that's what you want."

I sighed. Like Mam always says, "We island people are home-birds."

Chapter Twenty-Three

Felicity took a deep breath and looked around the familiar space of the largest lecture hall the College of the Transfiguration had to offer. She had been appalled when she was informed that her opening talk to the spiritual directors' conference was to be held in a room that accommodated nearly a hundred people. There was no way that many SpiDir members would come to hear her. Why couldn't they put her in a small classroom so it would be less embarrassing?

To her amazement, however, the room was almost full with her coworkers coming from all corners of the United Kingdom. She had been told that many from Scotland had made a special effort to attend when they learned what she would be talking about.

And now she realized, she needn't have worried. The room would have felt full to her anyway. She looked at Antony on the front row in his familiar black cassock. He had given the opening prayer and introduced Father Oswin from the community of monks who ran the college to welcome their visitors. And farther back, near the door, Teddy wiggled on his seat. One of Antony's students who served as a frequent babysitter sat beside him with orders to take him out to play as soon as he had seen Mummy. Felicity's world was in order, so she could concentrate on the job at hand.

She took a deep breath and plunged. "One of the major lessons I have learned from studying and living here at the College of the Transfiguration—especially since I happen to live with their resident historian, is how strong the impact of history can be on the present.

"Just a month ago I journeyed to the furthest point in the Outer Hebrides where I had a remarkable encounter with an event few have heard about today, even though it occurred during the lifetime of our parents or grandparents. Learning about the Hebrides Awakening, and the events I underwent in that single week, will stay with me for the rest of my life. I want to share that experience with you in the hope that the things I learned can be of use to all of us in helping others on their spiritual journey.

"I went to the Hebrides looking for information. For answers.

"I found despair, fervor; grief, joy; greed, and love. In other words, I found life. And instead of answers, I found questions. And I learned the importance of asking the right question."

Even as she talked and clicked to show the next slide on the screen behind her, her mind raced with its own images of the marvelous experience. "I found myself following in the footsteps of a young woman only a few years younger than myself who experienced it all and kept a remarkable record of the events. Life-changing events that take a different form for each generation, and yet, remain the same at the core for every generation through all time. Basic truths that are unchanging."

She shared the insights she had gained from studying—she could almost say experiencing—the Awakening: the importance of Community, Prayer, Obedience and Openness. Important for each director and important for each person they sought to guide. Important for our world.

Then she shared some of the individual stories she encountered and the lessons of confidence, patience and unity she had drawn from them. And the ultimate lesson that there were no one-size-fits-all answers.

"Ultimately, in this experience and in my own momentous experiences encountering history during the last fifteen years—" even as she said it, she gulped; had she and Antony really been married that long? "—the things I've learned are that, number one: God really does know more than we do, and letting Him take charge is truly the best policy. Number two: No matter how dark times seem, they have been worse before, and the Light has always won. As it will always win. Number three: God can use anything to work His will. Our job is twofold—don't get in the way, and say 'Thank you.'"

She resumed her seat by Antony to a thorough round of appreciative applause. But all she heard was Antony's whispered, "Well done, you." And then Teddy broke free from his minder, rushed up, and threw his arms around her.

Her world was complete.

Historical Note

I have portrayed the story of the Hebrides Awakening as accurately as I could, although even eyewitness accounts differ and I had to choose whose narrative to follow. Aileana's story is based on that of Mary Morrison, who did, indeed, walk away from a singing career in Glasgow, even without performing the first part of her concert.

Mary has written of being in Glasgow, developing a budding singing career, when the Awakening visited Lewis. Mary's goal was to be free. And she was experiencing that freedom in Glasgow. Sort of. "It was not easy to get away from the influence of home, for at heart we islanders are 'home birds,'" she admitted later. Her first reaction, though, to news of the revival was anger. "Why should God intrude and spoil our enjoyment, just when everything was going so well for us!" She was booked to sing at a concert and had bright prospects for the future.

Then came the phone call. "Mary, you must come home. Your parents are ill. Please hurry. They need you." Mary was unhappy, but she was obedient.

She was even angrier, however, when she arrived home and found that her parents weren't nearly as desperately ill as she had thought. And then there was this air of religious expectancy everywhere.

Although her parents weren't converted, they attended the meetings. Mary was furious. She refused to attend with them. Why, oh, why had she ever left Glasgow? In Mary's own words: "I seemed to be hemmed in, like a bird in a cage, and longed to be set free.

"My parents finally prevailed upon me to attend the meetings, in order to see and hear for myself." Finally, Mary went, much against her will. And continued so to do, in spite of her deep annoyance with the entire situation. Then her mother became converted, an event which shook Mary deeply. "Still, the truths I was hearing kept repeating themselves in my mind."

One morning after a cottage meeting Mary stood, feeling "like a fish out of water," listening to a group of young people singing, when "it dawned upon me that here were people who had something I didn't possess." She continued to search for almost four months until the Truth brought a "healing balm to my soul." At two o'clock in the morning, while the village slept, Mary and her friends walked along the shore singing.

A few years later Mary married Colin Peckham who became principal of the Faith Mission in Edinburgh, second after Duncan Campbell. In looking back on the Lewis Awakening, she said, "The central facts of the revival were the awareness of the presence of God and the preaching of the Word. The preaching was a powerful revelation of Christ—alive and challenging."

Faye and Kirsty Ann are based on friends of Mary—young women who have left accounts of their experiences at the time. The often-told story of the dance abandoned by the pipers is based on Faye's account, as is her conversion. A few years after the revival Faye went to Central Thailand as the wife of a missionary doctor.

The Praying Sisters—Peggy (in some accounts called Ida), 84 and blind; and Christine, bent almost double with arthritis—are historical, as is, of course, Duncan Campbell.

I had the privilege of visiting with Donald John Smith at his home in Ballantrushal on the Isle of Lewis in 2001, having taken one of the first planes to leave Boise after 9/11. My journal reads:

> Seventy-seven-year-old Donald John Smith is looking out for us as my friend Evelyn and I pull into the drive of his bungalow overlooking the wild western coast of the island. He welcomes us into his sitting room and shoos out the golden cat. He has the wonderful clear, glowing complexion everyone on Lewis seems to have, and his eyes are as blue as his jumper—worn properly over a white shirt and tie. I begin asking questions and he hands me a pad with his handwritten testimony. "It saves me a lot of talking," he explains. It seems that here, in this remote falling-off place—next stop Iceland—the world beats a path to his door to hear his story. Even as we talked, he was expecting six South Africans, he had had 12 intercessors from Glasgow last Friday, people from Colorado Springs, six from a Lanark (southern Scotland) prayer group...
>
> His testimony was worth traveling almost 4,500 miles to read. Donald John Smith is a poet. "I saw the beauty of God's creation in a different way. The singing of the birds was different. The grass was greener and the sea was a different blue. I saw people and my heart was full of love for them—the love of Christ and the warmth of the Gospel.
>
> "We heard of religion in other places, but we saw it in floods. Waves of spiritual blessing—we saw it everywhere. The spirit of prayer poured down like rain. Daily living was fragrant.
>
> "On the road, by a cottage, beside a peat stack, behind cairns of stone—everywhere there were loud prayers. Everyone could hear them. Even singing could be heard from village to village as if it was floating on the air. After the house meetings, which followed the meetings in the church, people walked home—three or four linked arms together and walked home singing. It could be heard in the next village.
>
> "It was 'Every home a sanctuary, every shop a pulpit, every barn

an altar." People's faces radiated beauty, their daily living was fragrant. It was a wonderful thing, but there is a price to pay for revival: Prayer. There is prayer—prayer and tears. We still have prayer meetings every week. People still enter into joy every week."

I told him that I had heard that it was a very quiet revival, that there was simply an overwhelming sense of the Holy. "Yes, that's right," he said. "'Be still and know that I am God.' That is all we did—just humble ourselves."

I ask what effects are still felt today, some 55 years later, on the island. "We still bear the hallmarks. I can tell in the singing—there was something in the singing. And there are more people going to church and wanting to know the Lord now. It starts in the home. And we still have good religious education in the schools here."

In many cases I have assigned the experiences of various people to different characters, or condensed time and events for the sake of my story. Euan and the nefarious doings of his friends are a fictionalized account of actual black-market activities in the Hebrides in 1949, although the murder is my own invention. I take full responsibility.

DFC

About the Author

Donna Fletcher Crow, Novelist of British History, is an intrepid traveler and an indefatigable researcher. She is also an award-winning author who has published some 50 books in a career spanning more than 40 years. Her best-known work is *Glastonbury, The Novel of Christian England*, a grail search epic depicting 1500 years of British history. The Celtic Cross is a 10-book series covering the history of Scotland and Ireland from the 6th to the 20th century.

Crow writes three mystery series: The Monastery Murders, contemporary clerical mysteries with clues hidden deep in the past; Lord Danvers Investigates, Victorian true-crime stories within a fictional setting; and The Elizabeth and Richard literary suspense series, featuring various literary figures. Where There is Love is a 6-book biographical novel series of leaders of the early Evangelical Anglican movement. The Daughters of Courage is a semi-autobiographical trilogy, about a family of Idaho pioneers.

Reviewers routinely praise the quality of her writing and the depth of her research. Crow says she tries never to write about a place she hasn't visited and one of her goals in writing is to give her readers a you-are-there experience.

Donna and her husband of 60 years live in Boise, Idaho. They have 4 children and 15 grandchildren, and she is an avid gardener. You can see pictures of her garden, subscribe to her newsletter, and learn more about her and her books at: https://www.donnafletchercrow.com/

All books are available at: https://www.amazon.com/stores/Donna-Fletcher-Crow/author/B000APWGI4

Books by Donna Fletcher Crow

Glastonbury, The Novel of Christian England
An Arthurian Grail search from the birth of Christ
through the Reformation

The Monastery Murders, Clerical Mysteries
A Very Private Grave
Legendary buried treasure, a brutal murder and lurking danger—
an itinerary of terror across a holy terrain
A Darkly Hidden Truth
Ancient puzzles, modern murder and breathless chase scenes
through a remote, waterlogged landscape
An Unholy Communion
An idyllic pilgrimage through Wales becomes a deadly struggle
between good and evil
A Newly Crimsoned Reliquary
Murder stalks the shadows of Oxford's hallowed shrines
An All-Consuming Fire
A Christmas wedding in a monastery—
if the bride can defeat the murderer prowling the Yorkshire moors
Against All Fierce Hostility
Is Felicity and Antony's spectacular train journey across Canada
carrying them away from murder—or toward it?
A Wind in the Hebrides
Anguish and ecstasy in the midst of a spiritual outpouring on the
Isle of Lewis
Watch for:
Father Antony's Book of Saints
Coming soon

The Celtic Cross Series
Part I, Scotland: The Struggle for a Nation

The Keeper of the Stone,
Of Saints and Chieftains: Saint Columba brings Christianity to Scotland

The Forger of a Nation,
Of Kings and Kingdoms: Kenneth MacAlpin unites the Picts and the Scots

The Refiner of the Realm,
Of Queens and Clerics: Queen Margaret reforms the court

The Vanquishers of Tyranny,
Of Priests and Patriots: William Wallace and Robert the Bruce triumph over tyranny

Part II: Ireland: The Pursuit of Peace

The Planting of Ulster,
Of Visionaries and Builders: The Scottish settle the Plantations

The Hammering of the Inhabitancy,
Of Brothers and Strangers: Cromwell conquers Ireland

The Strife of Ascendancy,
Of People and Rulers: The English establish rule over the land and the church

The Shaping of the Union,
Of Plots and Parliaments: Ireland is united with England and Scotland

The Famishment of the People,
Of Hunger and Fulfillment: The story of the potato famine

The Dawning of Peace,
Of Dreamers and Designers: The birth of Northern Ireland

A WIND IN THE HEBRIDES

The Elizabeth & Richard Literary Suspense Mysteries

The Flame Ignites
Elizabeth and Richard's strife-filled first meeting in a New England autumn

The Shadow of Reality
Elizabeth and Richard at a Dorothy L Sayers mystery week high in the Rocky Mountains

A Midsummer Eve's Nightmare
Elizabeth and Richard honeymoon at a Shakespeare Festival in Ashland, Oregon

A Jane Austen Encounter
A second honeymoon visit to Jane Austen's homes turns deadly

A Most Singular Venture
Murder in Jane Austen's London

Lord Danvers Investigates, Victorian True-Crime Mysteries

A Most Inconvenient Death
The brutal Stanfield Hall murders shatter a quiet Norwich community and pull Danvers from deep personal grief into a dangerous investigation.

Grave Matters
Lord and Lady Danvers' honeymoon in Scotland is interrupted by the ghosts of Burke and Hare-style grave robbers.

To Dust You Shall Return
Catherine Bacon is murdered in the very shadow of Canterbury Cathedral but Charles and Antonia are overwhelmed with their own problems.

A Tincture of Murder
William Dove is on trial in York for poisoning his wife while Lord and Lady Danvers struggle to assist in a refuge home where fallen women continue to die mysteriously.

A Lethal Spectre
A glittering London season set against the horrors of an Indian mutiny

Where There is Love Historical Romance

Where Love Begins
Can Catherine Peronnet find God's purpose for her life when her beloved Charles Wesley marries another?

Where Love Illumines
Mary Tudway must choose: a life of pleasure amidst London's high society or a life of faith and service with the devout Rowland Hill?

Where Love Triumphs
Charming, brilliant and lame, Sir Brandley Hilliard believes he can do very well without love of any kind in his life—until he meets Elinor Silbert—and then Charles Simeon.

Where Love Restores
Granville Ryder must struggle to find his place in his illustrious family, in God's work and in Georgiana Somerset's heart

Where Love Shines
Blinded in the Charge of the Light Brigade, Richard, inspired by the Earl of Shaftesbury, gropes through physical and spiritual blindness to the light of Jennifer's love

Where Love Calls
Kynaston Studd is on fire to carry the love of God to the ends of the earth with Hudson Taylor;
Hilda Beauchamp adds fuel to another kind of fire.

The Daughters of Courage Family Saga

Kathryn, Days of Struggle and Triumph
The unique story of Idaho's desert pioneers in the early days of the twentieth century.

Elizabeth, Days of Loss and Hope
Kathryn's daughter finds her way through the challenges of the Great Depression and World War II

Stephanie, Days of Turmoil and Victory
Strong family ties help Stephanie achieve success in the turbulent days of the 1970s

A WIND IN THE HEBRIDES

Short Story Collections

Going There, Tales from the Riviera and Beyond
A memoir of travel in troubled times with short stories
A Lighted Lamp, Scenes of Christmas Through Time
A collection of short stories for holiday reading

For other books
by Donna Fletcher Crow

To learn more, visit:
donnafcrow@aol.com

Made in the USA
Middletown, DE
14 December 2024